Candles in the Darkness

Candles in the Darkness

LEAH McMICHAEL

WestBow
PRESS
A DIVISION OF THOMAS NELSON

WestBow Press books may be ordered through booksellers or by contacting:

WestBow Press
A Division of Thomas Nelson
1663 Liberty Drive
Bloomington, IN 47403
www.westbowpress.com
1-(866) 928-1240

Scripture taken from the New King James Version. Copyright 1979, 1980, 1982 by Thomas Nelson, inc. Used by permission. All rights reserved.

ISBN: 978-1-4497-8350-1 (sc)
ISBN: 978-1-4497-8351-8 (hc)
ISBN: 978-1-4497-8349-5 (e)

Library of Congress Control Number: 2013901583

Printed in the United States of America
WestBow Press rev. date: 2/25/2013

To God, from whom all good things flow. I'd like to thank my family as well: parents, grandparents, and cousin Cheryl, as well as all the friends on that first email list (that's you, Roie), for sticking with me through the first draft and putting up with your weird writer friend. Lastly I want to thank Carol Park, who showed me what friendship is. You all know I'm not wise enough to do this—anything good I have to give comes from Him.

Contents

Treason

From the dark parking lot, the regional hospital in Villach was nothing more than rows of glowing windows. The walls of the buildings were scarcely distinguishable by the watery light. No stray glow found its way into the cab of the Gestapo van parked only meters from the main entrance.

Agent Karl Zehr stifled a yawn as his eyes swept the dark building for the hundredth time. Beside him, Chief Inspekteur Fredrik Schmidt seemed as unmoving as the walls of the hospital. A small wall, of course—slouched far in his seat, the diminutive Inspekteur barely reached Karl's broad shoulders. Karl drummed an imagined military march against the door of the auto and tried to remember why they were here. *Something about a pastor—it must be Gottlieb. None of the other clergy has been such a pain.* He frowned faintly at the thought. Coming from the street fights and gray bureaucracy of Berlin, he had somehow expected more resistance out of these rural churches. But the task of converting the Austrian clergy to the new religion of National Socialism had been almost embarrassingly easy.

Karl shook his head suddenly, surprised by his train of thought. Perhaps in the army it might have been different, but he was now a Gestapo agent—his only concern with subversives like Gottlieb was convincing them to abide by the law of the Reich. A variety of tactics were useful to that end, beginning with simple harassment and quickly progressing to harsher measures. With a flicker of unease, he realized Gottlieb's little hospital game had probably pushed him over that line.

1

Fredrik cleared his throat and turned with an abruptness that made Karl wonder if the Inspekteur had read his mind.

"Gottlieb is not in there," Fredrik stated coolly, as if he were remarking on the weather. "He came three hours ago. He is not there."

Karl sighed, frustrated by the long wait and Fredrik's confident pronouncement. "Why are we still here?"

In reply, Fredrik turned the ignition and shifted the car into gear. "Where would Gottlieb have gone?"

"His church. Home. I don't know!" Karl snapped, his hard Berliner accent growing sharper with the words.

"No. You don't. He did not want to be followed, so he led us to the hospital. You see?"

Karl grimaced and pressed his hand to his deaf ear. He suddenly wished he could shut out Fredrik's wheedling questions completely.

"So check the road. Maybe he saw us watching and decided to leave."

Fredrik scowled in response to Karl's sarcasm and accelerated toward the dark road.

The gothic steeples of St. Jakob and St. Nikolai glowed steadily above the dark road, twin beacons drawing Pastor Reinhardt Gottlieb to safety. He was less than a kilometer from town, but the pastor's thoughts lingered with the refugees he had sent off only an hour before. They were traveling by boat to Italy, to freedom. When the sun rose tomorrow, the Third Reich would be four people closer to solving its Jewish question—though perhaps not in the way the Nazis intended.

Reinhardt's auto topped a gentle rise, and another pair of headlights cut a swath through the night. The pastor drew a slow breath and fought the fear that rose in his throat. He had not expected to encounter anyone this late, but he clung stubbornly to the sense of peace that had flooded his heart at the river. The approaching car flicked its headlights on and off, signaling him to stop. Reluctantly, Reinhardt complied. *Yea, though I walk through the valley of the shadow of death, I shall fear no evil, for Thou art with me ...* Psalm 23:4

The unmarked car ground to a halt only meters in front of Reinhardt's vehicle. The headlights blazed directly into the cab of his auto, and Reinhardt had to squint to glimpse the two shapes that moved toward him. They were Gestapo, he guessed. Villach's ordinary police force did not enforce the new Nazi curfew.

Reinhardt swallowed hard as he recognized Fredrik Schmidt, the notorious head of Villach's Gestapo. The little rat-like man swaggered as he strode the remaining distance to the auto. He rapped on the window as if he would like to smash it. Reinhardt slowly rolled it down.

"Pastor Gottlieb? It is quite late. Are you not aware of the curfew?" The Inspekteur's voice was high, mocking.

Reinhardt set his jaw and stared straight ahead. "I am aware."

"Then surely the clergy are not above the law, *Pastor?*"

Reinhardt closed his eyes and resisted the urge to look back, toward the river. The faces of the two little girls and their parents seemed to burn in his mind. They had not had enough time! Their tiny boat would still be on Austria's—Germany's—side of the border. His fingers tightened on the steering wheel. The Gestapo could easily trace his route back from the river, and when they searched the river, they would find the craft and the precious lives it carried. *Unless …*

In that instant, Reinhardt made an impossible decision. "I am under a law higher than any edict of the Reich." *Forgive me, Eva,* his heart pleaded, even as his blue eyes flashed defiance.

The shadows in Fredrik's face seemed to deepen with anger. "Do not play games with us, Gottlieb," he warned. "You are hiding something, and I will have the truth!"

"The truth." Reinhardt smiled sadly, looking past Fredrik to the tall man who stood behind him. He thought he glimpsed a flicker of discomfort on the agent's proud features. "Truth has been with you for a long, long time. 'The light shines in the darkness, and the darkness did not comprehend it.' John 1:5 You have laid eyes on Truth in these cathedrals, and replaced Him with a swastika. You have held Truth in your hands, and you have cast Him into the flames. You have mocked the One Who is True; you have spit on Him; you have taken your stand against Him. The lies that you serve will not last, and when the fire burns out, do you know what will be left? Not the man you swore your soul to. Not the empire you strove to build. In the end, Truth is all that will remain, shining in the midst of shattered lives and your broken promises, calling men and women to Himself!"

"Treason!" Fredrik's eyes smoldered with rage as he pronounced the fatal word. "By order of the Gestapo, you are under arrest. Out of your car! Now!"

Reinhardt did not tremble as he opened the door and stood.

Fredrik shoved him down to his knees.

"So now this is the verdict: 'Light has come into the world, but men loved darkness rather than light, because their deeds were evil.'" Reinhardt continued in the same vein, still baiting the Inspekteur.

Fredrik swore and spun toward him again. "You! Remember whose power you are under!"

Reinhardt met Fredrik's eyes calmly through the play of light and shadow. "Not yours, I think."

Fredrik aimed a vicious kick at Reinhardt's stomach. The pastor doubled over, retching onto the ground.

"Does anyone see, Pastor? Can your God help you? The only power is the might of the Third Reich, and no one—*no one*—can defy it and live!"

Reinhardt dragged the back of his hand across his mouth and lifted his head slowly to face Fredrik. That same inexpressible peace rushed over him, through him, until he was no longer afraid. "I have hope of a life that will not end. Can you say the same?"

Fredrik shrieked something incoherent as he lashed out at Reinhardt. The force of the blow slammed Reinhardt's head against the smooth metal of the auto. Fredrik raised his fist to strike him again.

"Inspekteur, wait." Karl had been forgotten amid the tension of the pastor's arrest, and now his quiet voice caused Fredrik to whirl angrily.

"What?"

"I—should we not ... take him into Villach?" Karl glanced from Reinhardt to Fredrik and back again. "They will want him in the records. That is how it is done in Berlin, at least." He managed the last sentence with an air of superiority.

Reinhardt blinked and stared up at the agent in dazed gratitude.

Fredrik mumbled a grudging concession as Karl stepped between him and the pastor.

"Can you walk?" Karl asked.

Reinhardt nodded, and Karl dragged him unceremoniously to his feet. The pastor placed a hand on the hood of his auto to steady himself as he searched Karl's strong face. The shadow of pity he had seen there was gone.

"That was a foolish choice," the agent warned as he secured Reinhardt's hands behind his back.

The pastor bowed his head in silence. Had he been too rash? Too foolish? *The Gestapo have me. They will look no further tonight. The family will be safe.* These thoughts came automatically, without emotion. Reinhardt breathed deeply and closed his eyes. *I'm so sorry, Eva. So sorry.* Loneliness tightened at the base of his throat, and he stumbled forward obediently as Karl prodded him toward the Gestapo car.

Light of Day

If I knew how to knit, I would have a dozen scarves and sweaters made strictly by worry, Eva Gottlieb thought wryly as she clasped her graceful hands and willed them to be still. The first distant clanging of a church bell began to toll eleven o'clock. It was immediately joined by three others, until the faint individual rings were indistinguishable—indistinguishable and all ten minutes early. Eva smiled faintly and then yawned. She and Reinhardt had lived in Villach for nearly four years now, and in all that time, the bells had never once rung on the hour.

They always toll like this, as if they are hurrying on the hour about to slip away forever. Tonight that thought was oddly disturbing. Eva yawned again and looked down. Her fingers were moving again, keeping time with the final echoes of the bells. For a moment she considered the baby grand across from her, but she did not rise. She did not want to break the silence of the waiting.

Reinhardt will be home soon—eleven o'clock! He should be home already! Eva stood suddenly and hurried into the kitchen. A full pot of vegetable barley stew still sat on the cold stove. She had left it there in hopes of a late supper.

He has been gone this late—nearly this late—before. Surely it is nothing. A delay with the refugees. Nothing.

Reinhardt rarely spoke of his "special work," so what Eva knew was constructed mainly by his absences. *I cook extra food—refugees are somewhere here. Sometimes for two days, sometimes two weeks. Then there is a night like this, and when he comes back he whispers that a few more sheep are in safer pastures.* It had been like this for almost five months, since March 11, when Hitler had rolled into the welcome of the howling crowds of Vienna.

Eva's thoughts kept pace with her jerky motions as she ladled the soup into a smaller container. It was cold in the kitchen, cold despite the summer night. She put the soup away and returned to the familiar comfort of the living room.

He will be back, she promised herself as she wrapped herself in one of the blankets given at their wedding. She shook her long, coffee-colored hair free of its bun and drew her knees to her chest. *He has always come back. He will walk through the door, and I will tease him about missing too many meals, and we will be safe …*

Eva's thoughts wandered back to the afternoon, when Reinhardt had come home early to tell her he would be late.

Another delivery, he had mouthed as he set his Bible on a swirl of hand-carved flowers on the coffee table. "They want me to tell you that you are an excellent cook, and the girls would like more cookies if we have any."

Eva laughed. "Are the girls pretty?"

"Beautiful. Five, I think, and twins."

Silence for a moment, and then they both laughed. "I do have a few jam cookies left, yes. Anything else?" Eva was already moving to gather the food.

Reinhardt leaned against the doorframe, simply watching her. "No. A hug, perhaps, and—" He slipped his arm around her slender waist and gently turned her around.

"Be careful." She leaned her head against him and listened to the steady beat of his heart.

"Of course." He paused. "May the LORD bless you and keep you—"

Eva picked up the recitation: "The LORD make His face shine upon you and be gracious to you. The LORD lift up His countenance on you—" Numbers 6:24-26

"And give you peace." Reinhardt finished softly. He smiled down at her and then kissed her gently. "Wait for me tonight. And pray!"

Eva jumped as the solemn chimes of the grandfather clock began to toll. The hour was gone.

Karl craned his neck to watch the pastor's abandoned auto recede into the night. Reinhardt did not speak as Fredrik sped toward the city, and Karl wondered what he was thinking. The enormous bell tower of St. Jakob loomed ahead. Orange streetlamps flashed through the windows, flickering over Karl's hands like flames. *When the fire burns out, do you know what will remain?* He started and glanced uneasily at Reinhardt. Had the pastor spoken the words?

Fredrik accelerated as they passed the square towers of Christ Church—Gottlieb's church. Was that a faint smile on Reinhardt's face at the familiar sight? The Inspekteur turned left and braked at an imposing pink building catty-corner from the church.

"Frightened, Gottlieb?" Fredrik asked in a taunting voice. When there was no response, Fredrik opened his door and stalked toward the building. "Get him inside," he growled over his shoulder.

Karl nodded slowly as the Inspekteur disappeared indoors. Gottlieb's defiance would end tonight.

"Come, Pastor," he said at last, opening Reinhardt's door and urging him away from where the light of the steeple was still visible through the trees.

They passed silently through the empty lobby and down the stone staircase leading to the jail. Karl shivered as they entered the prison. A line of bare lightbulbs sent distorted shadows skittering across the walls, and the stale air was thick with the scent of fear. He raised a hand to his deaf ear unconsciously. An eerie quiet had settled in the corridor, and their footsteps seemed conspicuously loud.

Karl hesitated as they stopped in front of cell twenty-seven. At last he unlocked Reinhardt's handcuffs, and ushered the pastor into the cell. The door swung shut at his touch, slamming with a hollow clang. He flinched at the sound. It echoed like a thunderclap through the underground prison. Had Reinhardt even noticed? He was leaning against the rear wall of the cell, watching Karl intently. Karl met his gaze for an instant and glanced away.

"Why, Pastor?" he blurted suddenly. *Why indeed? You might not have been arrested! If Fredrik had thought you were afraid, he would not have touched you! Why did you throw your life away like that?*

"Karl, look at me," Reinhart commanded softly.

Reluctantly, he raised his head. The pastor seemed taller than he had a moment ago—unafraid, but with an air of gentleness that seemed entirely out of place in the prison. Clear blue eyes shined out from a battered face.

"I wish—how I wish you could know! But my Savior has always been faithful to me. I cannot turn away from Him."

"It has never gone well for those who defy the Gestapo," Karl said, staring past Reinhardt as if this grim future was written on the wall behind the pastor. "They will not stop with you. Your church—your wife ... the Gestapo will come."

A thousand other things echoed, unspoken, behind the ominous words. For a moment the prison corridor seemed to ring with the steady tramp of storm troopers' boots, and the air trembled with the cries of the helpless.

Karl risked another glance at the pastor. He had closed his eyes, trying to shut out the vision Karl already saw.

"Is your God worth that?" he pressed cruelly.

Long minutes passed in anguished silence before Reinhardt answered. "Yes."

Karl looked up in surprise. "I hope you are right." He shrugged and gripped one of the bars of the cell. "And I wish I was not. But you will die tonight, Pastor. And then ... then what will happen?"

"My life is safe, though I lose it." Reinhardt was calm—joyful, almost. Then his countenance dimmed. "But ... can I ask of you a favor?"

"I will not be able to grant it."

"All the same, you know the law of family guilt. My wife, Eva, will be counted guilty with me."

He locked eyes with Karl, pleading. For the first time the Gestapo agent heard desperation in his voice.

"Is there anything—any way—to protect her?"

Karl hesitated for a moment before he nodded. "Possibly."

"Please—" Reinhardt faltered, then fell silent. His hands dropped limply to his side, and he bowed his head.

Karl cleared his throat. Something in Reinhardt's sudden surrender was compelling, wakening him to decision. He looked again at the pastor and nodded abruptly. "I—your wife will not be harmed. You have my word."

Reinhardt whispered something that might have been a prayer. There was a strange look of peace behind the strain on his face. "Thank you," he said simply.

Karl nodded. What else was there to say after that? He left Reinhardt with pen and paper, and the promise that Eva would receive his letter.

Hours later, Reinhardt rose from his knees as footsteps sounded in the hallway. He was ready.

Karl and Fredrik halted outside the cell.

"Prisoner Gottlieb?" Fredrik wheedled, smiling hideously. "I am quite sorry for the delay. There is so much paperwork for an execution …"

Reinhardt made no reply except to move toward the door.

Karl unlocked it and stepped inside. As he fastened the pastor's handcuffs, he caught sight of the letter, tucked halfway beneath the bench. He would have to come back for it. After …

"Tonight, Karl!"

With a gentle nudge the letter disappeared completely. As Karl turned, he read the pastor's unspoken thanks. He shrugged slightly in reply, suddenly wishing he had time to ask Reinhardt the questions that flooded his mind. *Aren't you afraid? Do you know you would be home by now tonight if you had not said so much on the road? What on earth were you doing, and why …?*

The Inspekteur impatiently cleared his throat, and Karl opened the door. Reinhardt closed his eyes for a moment, straightened, and followed Fredrik down the long corridor. Karl lagged behind. He could find the little execution-courtyard with his eyes closed, and for a moment he was tempted to do just that. Maybe tonight he could get through it without watching, accomplish his task without seeing what it was he was actually doing.

Fredrik slammed open the door of the courtyard, and he and Reinhardt disappeared into the blackness. Karl heard him order the pastor to his knees, and then a quick series of thuds and cries echoed in the bright hallway. Reluctantly, Karl stepped outside. The pastor lay unmoving on the cold stone. Karl scowled blackly at Fredrik as the Inspekteur offered him his pistol. "You do it."

With a cheerful shrug, the Inspekteur cocked the gun and squatted beside Reinhardt. "Up!" he bellowed, jabbing the barrel into his side.

Reinhardt stirred, struggled to his knees—calmly, somehow, as if there were nothing now left to fear. Dawn was melting the darkness above him. As Fredrik fingered the trigger, a thin shaft of light pierced the shadows to illuminate Reinhardt's upturned face.

A single shot rang out in the courtyard. Karl turned away as the pastor collapsed. *So it is done.*

Alone

Eva woke suddenly from a fitful sleep. Last night's despairing uncertainty came rushing back, seeming all the more grim and terrible with the first gray light of day. The somber chimes of the old grandfather clock confirmed her fears. Four, five … six times they echoed, hollow and haunting in the empty house. Reinhardt had not returned.

Maybe he stayed out by the river all night. Maybe he stopped to call on someone from the congregation. Maybe … The list of desperate possibilities went on, with each less likely than the one before. At last she raised her eyes to the window. Dark and flat against the deep blue of the coming dawn, the silhouettes of the Karawanken Alps towered over her. *I will lift up my eyes to the hills—from whence comes my help? My help comes from the LORD, who made heaven and earth.* Psalm 121:1-2

Was it only yesterday morning that Reinhardt had said the same thing? The memory was so vivid that for a moment she could almost see him, black hair still untouched by brush or comb, eyes sparkling with boyish delight. Eva blinked, and she was alone again. *Alone!* There was something terrifying in that word. Shaking, she stood and staggered to the phone. It took the last of her control to still the tremor in her voice.

"Hello, operator?"

The groggy response on the other end suggested that her call would be better appreciated at a more sensible hour.

"Please connect me to the house of Fraulein Donsky."

A fumbling noise, muttered curses from the operator, and then the phone was ringing. Silently Eva willed her friend to pick up.

At last, Katrina's sleepy voice came through the line. "Hello?"

"It's me, Eva. You see, I—well Reinhardt has been—he's gone, Trina!"

Eva knew she wasn't making any sense, but she couldn't get the words out.

"Eva, can you hear me? I'm coming over right away."

Gray sky. Gray countertop. Gray light … Katrina's gaze swept the room before she looked again at Eva. Eva's eyes were also gray, she realized. She had always believed them to be blue, but today the color seemed to fade as the silent hours ticked by.

"Can I turn a light on, Eva?" she suddenly asked, desperate to break the terrible quiet.

Eva shook her head.

Katrina jumped as a cannonade of hail rattled the windows. A low roll of thunder rumbled an answer to the clattering ice, and she rose from the table. "I'm going to make tea. Would you like some?"

Eva nodded absently.

Katrina filled the kettle and set it on the stove before she turned to watch her friend. Eva's gentle face was a mask of fine control—so fine that Katrina expected it to shatter to pieces at any moment. *Where is Pastor Gottlieb?* For the hundredth time she asked herself the question, and for the hundredth time she tried to imagine that worst had not come to worst.

"Aren't you missing work?" Eva asked. The words came haltingly, but Katrina was encouraged by the spark of interest in Eva's eyes.

She shrugged. "I called in sick to the hospital. They will not miss one nurse today." Behind her, the kettle shrieked, and Katrina reached for two cups.

"Where is he, Trina?"

Eva's plaintive question froze Katrina mid-motion. She slowly set the cups on the counter and sat beside Eva again. "I … I don't know," she replied, desperately wishing she had some answer for her friend.

Eva rested her head in her slender hands; seemingly exhausted by the agony of this terrible *waiting*. Katrina touched her arm gently.

"Refugees," Eva whispered at last. "He was taking them to the river ... to Italy." She looked sharply up at Katrina, the fear in her wide eyes making her look more like a child than ever. She tugged a strand of hair loose from her bun and twirled it distractedly.

Katrina bit her lip, suddenly terrified for Eva. *Refugees, of all things! If he has been arrested ...* "We must keep praying," she said simply.

Eva did not reply. Her strong fingers danced across an imaginary keyboard, playing a melody of desperate hope on the silent table.

Thunder rumbled sullenly from a dirty gray sky, and the wind wailed and keened with ragged force in the valley. Karl leaned into it, wishing he had dared take a Gestapo car on this illegal errand. He could have been asleep in his little apartment by now if he had not decided to walk. A white-hot burst of lightning suddenly tore the sky between two of the peaks that surrounded the city. For a wild instant, Karl wished fire from the heavens would strike him where he stood. Such a dramatic end did not seem entirely out of character with what he had seen today.

The image of his father's sneer intruded in his thoughts, mocking him. *Do-gooders. Playing make-believe because they're too feeble-minded for anything else ...*

The subject of his derision that day had been a young, round-faced pastor going door-to-door, visiting the boys in the neighborhood's confirmation class. *What was his name? Something-hoeffer. Perhaps Bonhoeffer?* It mattered little. That class had grown to include nearly all the unruly boys in the neighborhood of Wedding, but Karl had not been among them. *Waste your time with that nonsense? Over my dead body!* So Karl had prowled the streets with the older boys of the Hitler Youth. He had whooped and hooted and cheered for Hitler with the rest of that crowd on election day—the same day, incidentally, as the confirmation.

That had been 1932. Adolph Hitler had come in second in the presidential election, only to be appointed chancellor the following year. *I was fourteen.* Karl rechecked the address he had taken from the Gestapo file as he passed the city limit. Now, six years later, the choices of that day seemed almost prophetic.

Karl nervously patted the pocket of his light gray jacket as the first fat raindrops splashed around him. He was certain he was breaking some law in delivering the pastor's letter; it would not do to have the ink run as well. The Gottlieb house—more accurately a cottage—appeared through the trees in front of him. The storm exploded in earnest behind him as he dashed toward the steps. He stopped just within the shelter of the roof, struck by the thought that he had somehow usurped the pastor's place. Gottlieb should have walked up these stairs last night, not Karl.

The large curtained windows regarded him balefully. For a moment, he considered simply depositing the letter in the black wrought-iron mailbox. The pastor's death would be in the papers soon enough, and at some point the letter was sure to be discovered. He removed the folded paper hesitantly. It seemed an important thing, maybe even a precious one. He frowned, suddenly aware that if he had become a soldier, he would not be playing mailman to the widow of a man he'd arrested the night before. Such ironies were left to the Gestapo, to the eavesdroppers and spies and half-deaf men unfit for anything else.

With that in mind, he raised his fist to pound the heavy wooden door.

Beneath the steady drumming of ice and rain, the knock at the door was nearly lost. A moment passed before it came again, firmer and more insistent, shattering the illusion of peace that had settled between the two women. Eva was on her feet in an instant, eyes wide and full lips pressed to a bloodless line at the long-awaited sound.

"Eva?" Katrina followed her through the parlor to the door.

Eva flung the door open and froze. The man who stood in the entryway was a stranger.

Water dripped from his blond hair and ran down the strong lines of his guarded face. For a moment, the only sound was the roaring of the rain.

Then he spoke. "You are Eva Gottlieb?" The words were reluctant, amplifying the discomfort in his light-blue eyes. When she nodded, he extended the letter. "Your husband ... Reinhardt—he was executed by the Gestapo this morning."

The words hung in the air, suspended on shock and disbelief. "The letter, Frau Gottlieb." The messenger cleared his throat and searched the doorway behind her. Seeing Katrina, he held the paper out further. "From Pastor Gottlieb ..."

Katrina positioned herself directly behind her silent friend. "Who are you?"

"Gestapo."

The word shattered the numb pause. Eva recoiled, frightened, and Katrina reached out to take the letter. "Please leave us. Now."

The man nodded curtly, closing the door behind him.

Katrina bolted it and then turned slowly to her friend.

"Eva? I'm afraid—it is true. He's gone. Pastor Gottlieb ... is gone. I'm so sorry."

Reprisal

Several days later, the clouds still lingered low and heavy on the mountains. Fredrik stared pensively out the window of the small café. A perimeter of vacant tables ringed him like the scab on an old sore. Even now, in September, five months after the *Anschluss*, many were still edgy about the new Nazi government. And as the head of the local Gestapo, Fredrik Schmidt received the brunt of their suspicion.

Another man might have been troubled by the loneliness of the position, but Fredrik did not mind. He rather enjoyed not being bothered by the trifling issues that plagued ordinary people. After all, he had more important things to deal with. *Such as a certain church that refuses to be intimidated.* Fredrik glared into his now-cold cup of coffee as if the murky liquid contained the faces of the foolish congregation. So intent was his focus on the mug that he missed the theatrical entrance of Oskar Kraus, the town's mayor.

"Heil Hitler, Herr Schmidt?" Startled, Fredrik stumbled to his feet to face the portly mayor.

"Heil Hitler, Herr Kraus. I did not see you come in."

"No matter. Your cup was quite intriguing?"

"I did not mean—"

"Never mind, Inspekteur. Now, about Gottlieb. You dealt with him quickly. If only politics moved that fast, no?"

The man chuckled at his own joke, but Fredrik's scowl remained locked in place. He did not trust Oskar Kraus. The mayor had been born into an influential family in Villach—his position was practically inherited! Not like Fredrik, who had begun his career at the lowest rung of the then-illegal Nazi Party in Austria. Not like Fredrik, who had risen through his own skill and ruthless determination. Not like Fredrik, whose prestige and power had come from his unflinching loyalty to the Nazi cause.

No, Herr Kraus was not like Fredrik. Not to be trusted with such matters as breaking a church. Fredrik's frown deepened further at the thought, giving his narrow face an almost comical appearance.

"What is wrong? The resurrection has not come to Villach, has it?" The mayor arched his eyebrows sarcastically.

"No. Gottlieb is dead."

"And are you certain that was the wisest move, Herr Schmidt?"

"What?" Anger colored the confusion in Fredrik's voice.

"You have long held a grudge against Pastor Gottlieb, have you not? Will this silence his congregation? Or will it harden their foolishness into something dangerous? Such things ought to be considered *before* you pull the trigger, you know." Mayor Kraus smiled thinly.

"The man was *dangerous!*" Fredrik slammed a bony fist on the table. "An enemy in every sense! He opposed our cause from the beginning! Mocked us! He—"

"Made a fool of you?" A placid expression settled on the mayor's doughy face, and Fredrik sputtered angrily. "Really, Inspekteur, have you not seen such men before? They preach a religion of weakness, yet they fear no one. An odd sort." Kraus squinted thoughtfully. "Five hundred years ago, we might have made him a saint."

"You … treason … I—"

"Yes. That should not happen. You must see that it does not." The mayor nodded his large head agreeably.

"What should not happen?"

"They must not make him into a saint, of course. Nor a martyr. If they do, your little grudge may cost the Reich much more through the stubborn resistance of this congregation."

"He was dangerous, I tell you! A voice that would not be silenced—"

"You hated the man because he did not fear you," Kraus stated matter-of-factly. "And now he is silent. Keep him that way. Keep his congregation that way."

Fredrik huffed angrily. "Why? Are you afraid of a memory?"

Kraus shifted his ponderous bulk and inclined his head as if instructing a slow student. The gesture was not lost on Fredrik. "People draw strength from stories. Martyrs. Heroes. Call them what you will—have you ever been to Mass, Herr Schmidt?"

"No."

"I went as a child. Full of stories. All the saints. All the suffering. A grim picture, if you ask me. But these fanatics draw their strength from it. Surely you've seen the crucified Christ? Broken. Bloody. Martyr." He cleared his throat, as though the name of Christ had stuck there. "You are beginning to see what harm is done?"

Fredrik nodded slowly, reluctant to agree with the mayor on even one point.

"Good. So, your pastor." Kraus paused for a moment. "What accusation has the Fuehrer used to incite hatred against the Jewish swine?"

The answer came readily to Fredrik. "He declares them to be Bolsheviks. Blames the Great War on them and stirs up fear."

"Precisely. Your answer."

"You want me to announce that Reinhardt Gottlieb was a Communist?"

Kraus seemed amused by Fredrik's incredulity. "Yes. I admit it is a bit unlikely. Gottlieb did not strike me as a politician. Too good a man for that." He smiled wryly. "But I have faith in your abilities, Inspekteur. Speak, and the people will listen. Provide papers. Evidence. Witnesses, if you like. The Gestapo are experts in such matters, are they not? Whatever it takes. We will tarnish his martyr's crown, yes?"

Fredrik did not understand the mayor's last quip, but the instruction was clear. Simple, even. Never mind that the idea had come from Oskar Kraus. This would prove to be a satisfying job. "It will be done, Herr Kraus."

The Villach Gestapo headquarters was a blur of activity. While the city had held a parade in March to welcome Karl and the other three agents from Berlin, comparatively few people were willing to divulge any useful information to the Gestapo. Many simply didn't want the Nazis in Austria, and those who did support the National Socialist Party feared those who did not. For months now, this balance had held up in favor of the hunted. But Reinhardt Gottlieb's execution had tipped the scales. Former patriots betrayed neighbors in a rush, hoping to avoid arrest themselves. Backstabbing and double-crossing flourished with the fervor of a religious revival. Much of the information proved fruitful—this latest string of arrests was testament to that. Teachers, doctors, husbands, wives—it made no difference to this strange new form of justice. Arrests were accomplished efficiently and with only the slightest provocation. The once-silent halls of the underground prison now rang with the resigned clamor of the condemned.

Karl stared at the arrest warrant without seeing it. The flickering profile of a face interposed itself on the printed words. It could have been anyone … everyone. He gripped the pen tighter, unwilling to connect the pink slip of paper to the actual life it would destroy. It was better that words remain words and people remain forgotten. Still, as he pressed the tip of the pen to the paper and watched ink flow as thick as blood, he saw Reinhardt Gottlieb collapse to the cold stone of the Gestapo courtyard.

No. Karl closed his eyes, dully resisting the repetition of the scene that had haunted him in the past days. He knew he had done more than he should in helping the pastor. What was it to him if the Inspekteur beat someone to death for a curfew violation and a sermon? The arrest he was authorizing was based on less. It had been foolish of him to get involved. Protecting the pastor, delivering his letter—such actions were dangerous, Karl knew. He practically shared Gottlieb's guilt!

His guilt. Yes. What was that, exactly? He'd made Fredrik angry? Preached something rejected by the Nazi Party? Karl shook his head. Fool though he might be, the events of the past week disgusted him. It was common knowledge that Fredrik hated Pastor Gottlieb. Long before the pastor's execution, Fredrik had railed against Reinhardt. He hated the man's courage, hated his integrity—and he especially despised the respect Gottlieb received from his congregation. Reinhardt had been well-known and well-loved long before the Anschluss. When Fredrik Schmidt was still scraping together a living as a bank clerk, Reinhardt had held influence. Held power. And in Fredrik's eyes, such an offense was unforgivable.

Thoughts like that made Karl angry again. The Inspekteur's personal vendetta should not have involved the Gestapo. If Fredrik had taken care of the pastor on his own, Karl could have easily looked the other way. Such things had happened at least a dozen times during the year and a half he'd worked at the headquarters in Berlin. The power of the Gestapo settled old grudges with frightening ease—the law of nature, after all. The strong were meant to dominate the weak. Victory was its own justification; mercy was a weak and silly product of Christianity.

Such lessons had been obvious to a boy raised in the gritty poverty of North Berlin. They had only become clearer as he progressed through the Gestapo training, learning not only how to follow and file but also to kill. He was strong—the fate of those weaker ones did not concern him. But there had been something about that pastor ...

Karl shoved the authorized warrant across the table and moved on to the next one.

"Have you seen the paper today? They're talking about that pastor who was executed four days ago. You know, the one you helped arrest. Gotthart or something." The voice of the agent beside him was cheerful.

"Gottlieb," Karl corrected.

"Yes, exactly! Congratulations, by the way. They say he wasn't really a pastor. That the church was just a disguise and Gottlieb was really a Communist and a danger to all of Villach and—"

Karl snatched the paper away from the agent beside him and scanned the article. *"Comrade" Gottlieb spread dissent and rebellion throughout the Fatherland. It is suspected that his "church" exploited many Aryan families in his depraved lust for power. The heroic and daring Gestapo arrested this untermensch and showed him once and for all the power of the Reich. Heil Hitler!*

Karl grimaced at the last lines. So the Inspekteur's hatred extended even past death. He shook his throbbing head and winced. Slander was becoming an increasingly popular tool among both the Gestapo and the Ministry of Propaganda—but this? It was like calling in a Panzer division to serve as a firing squad.

An apt comparison, he thought wryly. This was an execution of memory. If told and remembered, Reinhardt's story might cause people to question ...

things. It had certainly shaken him. The pastor had gone to his death with an air of triumph that Karl could not comprehend. It was as if the threats and beatings and fear the Gestapo commanded had not even touched him. Only by obliterating Reinhardt's memory could Fredrik hope to ease the sting of that defeat.

Yes, Karl understood the reasons behind the pastor's destruction—the principles of greed and revenge were not difficult to grasp. Still, he could not dispel the longing that things should be somehow different. *Courage and fear. A good man dead. And now how many will suffer?*

As if in answer, another prisoner was herded roughly through the doors. Dark eyes and hair contrasted against the pallor in the man's face. Karl could only wonder at what had brought him here. A malicious neighbor? A slip of the tongue? An unfortunate heritage? It mattered little. The man was prodded forward until the edge of the counter pressed against his stomach.

"You will sign this form," Pieter instructed dispassionately, giving him nothing but a cursory glance.

For a moment there was quiet as the man's eyes swept the document. Then he shook his head adamantly and attempted to step back. One of the guards shoved him forward, slamming him against the counter's edge.

"You will sign it," Pieter repeated as the prisoner sagged to the floor. When a sudden flurry of kicks and blows brought no further progress, Pieter shrugged, took the paper, and placed his own signature there.

"You see? You have already signed it. Not so hard a thing, is it?"

The prisoner groaned as the guards lifted him to his feet, but no one in the office turned to the sound. They had seen the same spectacle a dozen times this week. Only Karl remained frozen, staring at the place where the prisoner had fallen as if he were witnessing the brutality for the first time.

Pieter was maddeningly calm as he filed the paper that contained the prisoner's forged consent to imprisonment. He hummed a few measures from a Wagnerian opera as he settled back to continue with the paperwork. That single gesture was more than Karl could bear. Trembling with sudden anger, he stood and shoved the arrest warrants away.

"Karl! Wait! Where—"

That was as far as Pieter got before the door slammed shut.

"We have mail today," Linda Haider announced as she entered the kitchen. Tall and fair-skinned, she was gracious even at forty-five. "Mail," she said again, and the weight in that simple word drew quizzical looks from Ramond and his father.

"We have mail most every day, wife." Bernard Haider swirled his coffee.

In reply, she dropped an open envelope onto the table. Bernard removed the letter unhurriedly and tilted his chair into the sunlight to read aloud.

"To Herr Haider. I have heard of your work with valuable antiques. My wife and I have come across two items we believe might be of value. Due to the difficulty of transportation, however, it would be necessary for you to come to appraise them."

Bernard folded the paper and removed his glasses. "Ah. Children," he murmured, twirling the spectacles absently.

Linda pursed her lips and nodded. She had understood the code as well. "It is addressed from Sankt Michael. Not too far from us in Salzburg. Will you go?"

"I will." Ramond volunteered from the other side of the table.

Both parents turned toward their lanky, brown-haired son.

His cobalt eyes flashed excitement, but he talked slowly, anticipating their resistance. "I know the mountains well. 'Difficulty of transportation'— they probably don't have papers. They will need a guide. It's what I came back from university for, after all."

"But children, Ramond. Are you certain—"

"He is right, Linda," Bernard interjected, holding his spectacles up like an instructing finger. "A fine, strong boy we have. A man," he amended with a slight smile. "Ramond has been a guide as often as I have. And I may be missed here."

"I'm nineteen, Mama. Out for an adventure in the mountains. They'll never see me—and if they do, they won't catch me." Ramond grinned hopefully, but his mother only closed her eyes and turned away. His smile faded as he heard her whispered words.

"You ask so much, Lord …" For a moment, the sorrow in her voice seemed to turn her to stone. There was silence, except for her unsteady breathing. But then life returned. Love pushed back whatever unnamed dread that had surfaced at the mention of Ramond's leaving. Slowly, gingerly, she lowered herself into a chair beside her husband.

"*Ja*," she said softly. "Ramond, you will go. For these strangers that the Lord loves, you will go. But I will not stop praying until you come back."

Ramond reached out to touch her hand, uncomfortable with the emotion that brimmed in his mother's eyes. "I will leave in an hour. A short trip, you see? I will be back before you know it."

Karl walked for a long time. When he finally stopped, he found himself at one of the three bridges that spanned the Drau River. The milky, almost-blue water swirled around the pilings of the bridge, already carrying with it the first bright leaves of autumn.

Leaning over the railing, he let the rush of wind and water drown out the noise of the city behind him. *Who were you, Gottlieb?* Karl remembered the pastor's gentle courage. *And why do I need so much to know?* He pressed his palm against his deaf ear in an unconscious habit. Perhaps the answers lay on the other side of this silent wall.

"Who were you?" he whispered again to the indifferent wind.

The communist pastor you helped arrest, Karl! Pieter's words returned as a taunt. Karl frowned. A Communist Gottlieb was not; a pastor he had been—there was nothing so unusual in that. A handful of clergy had passed through the central headquarters while he was in Berlin. He had once been in charge of investigating an old choir director from some cathedral or another. The man hadn't really been guilty of anything, but he had babbled his way through the interrogation and in the end given Karl leads enough to make several arrests. That was the last he'd seen of any church, until Reinhardt. Until the *different*, joyful strength of the pastor's final hours sent a tremor of doubt through all the lessons Karl had learned so well and made him wonder if his not-chosen position at the Gestapo had been the right "choice" at all.

Karl flicked his deaf ear angrily. *It* was the reason he was on this bridge in southern Austria instead of training as a soldier in the Rhineland. He could not be blamed, he reminded himself, that the Gestapo was only too eager to snap up the army's rejects. And who would fault him for accepting? The promised glory of such a career might have been a consolation prize, but it was *something*—enough to stop his good ear to the screams that often echoed through the airy corridors of the central headquarters in Berlin, enough to make him forget the faces and the names and remember only words like *enemy* and *subversive* and *subhuman*.

After the Anschluss, when he was transferred to Villach, he had muffled the occasional twinge of conscience with the knowledge that his work was now almost entirely bureaucratic. He was seldom required to dirty his hands anymore. There were exceptions, of course. Weeks like this. Men like Reinhardt Gottlieb.

Karl exhaled slowly and closed his eyes. His thoughts had come full circle now. In his mind he saw himself and the pastor, and the two images were nothing alike. Why then did Reinhardt's memory make him ache for the parts of himself he had lost? For a shattered innocence and a hope long-forgotten? He shook his head and ran a hand through his close-cropped flaxen hair. The choices he had made could not be undone. It was as impossible to take a different path now as it was to bring Reinhardt back to life.

A bird trilled overhead, mocking him with the joy of its song. As Karl listened, the liquid notes became a chant, taunting him in his misery: *Too late! Too late!* And he knew it was.

Dangerous Games

KATRINA POUNDED EVA'S DOOR, anxiety mounting with every moment of passing silence. Her worried gaze swept around the side of the stone cottage, probing for some trace of activity. *Have they taken her too?* She craned her head to stare up at the steep grade of the roof. Designed to keep snow from accumulating during the long winters, the eaves plunged downward at an angle that made motion inevitable.

It is a good picture, Katrina thought. In the six and a half months since the Anschluss, the congregation of Christ Church had somehow balanced on the peak of a very steep slope. For nearly half a year they had clung to that precarious position ... but Pastor Gottlieb's death was the tremor that began the avalanche.

Katrina was suddenly gripped by the sensation of falling. They were all falling, she knew. Eva. Herself. Every friend she had among the congregation. The last illusions of security had been blasted away, and they were all tumbling toward an uncertain brink—here Katrina checked her thoughts. She forced herself to remember the message of hope Pastor Gottlieb had preached two weeks prior—had it only been that long? He had spoken of an eternal city and a living hope. *Did he guess ...?* Katrina sighed softly and lifted her chin. The brink was not so uncertain, after all. But she still feared for her best friend.

"Eva? Eva!"

She was a stranger to her own voice. What had the past two weeks done to her? *So many arrests. So many gone. As if Pastor Gottlieb really was the last barrier between us and … all this.* The madness that had gripped Vienna by the throat had finally exploded here as well. Evil graffiti blossomed like parasitic flowers across windows and walls throughout the city. Just today she had seen a man dragged from a park bench and beaten to the taunts of *Jew-pig* and *Christ-killer.*

Eva! Where are you?

The image of the solemn Gestapo agent who had come to this doorstep days ago reared up in her mind. The letter he had brought was genuine—she had seen Pastor Gottlieb's handwriting on the wrinkled paper. But why had he come? Any such kindness from the Gestapo was unheard of. Had it been some sort of elaborate trap? Was Eva now just one more face among the thousands in the living hell of Mauthausen?

"Eva!" she called again hoarsely.

The door opened abruptly as she raised her fist to knock, and Katrina nearly wept with relief.

"You're safe!" she blurted, feeling suddenly foolish. Katrina stepped into the cool interior of the house and shut the door.

Eva seemed to waver in the shadows. She was pale, almost luminous, against the dark backdrop. "What's wrong?" she asked softly.

Katrina said nothing as she led her friend to the settee. Tracing the red fabric with her finger, she wondered how to reply. "Eva, do you know what is happening now in Villach?"

Eva shook her head. Her world had vanished with Reinhardt.

"The Nazis … are taking full control. Hundreds have been arrested already. No reason. No warning. Just … gone." Katrina suddenly stopped, conscious that her words had hit too close. *Your husband, Reinhardt Gottlieb, was executed this morning …*

Eva nodded.

"There is chaos—deliberate chaos in the streets. No one knows what is coming next. People are terrified."

"Have you come to warn me then?" Eva interrupted quietly. Her eyes seemed empty as she watched Katrina.

"Yes, but there is more. The Reich Church"—her voice choked in anger—"the Reich Church has just now filed an official complaint against Christ Church."

Eva looked up sharply. "Now? They waited …" She did not finish her sentence. She was crying again, alone.

"Pastor Gottlieb fought them. Intimidated them. Clung so fiercely to the truth that they would have been ashamed, if they had hearts to feel. You know that. But now … now they have put us in the hands of the Gestapo." Katrina looked sadly at Eva. "They claim that we do not support the unity of the Reich, that we are allied with the Communists. That Pastor Gottlieb …" Katrina stopped again, uncertain if she should continue.

"That Reinhardt what?" Eva demanded.

"They speak nothing but lies, Eva. You know that. They cannot bear the thought of even one righteous man."

"What do they say?" Eva asked again. When Katrina hesitated, she leaned forward and spread her hands imploringly. Even in the dim light Katrina saw the glint of the delicate gold wedding band on Eva's finger. The sight filled her with fresh sorrow for her friend.

"They have set out to convince the world that Pastor was a Communist," she said quietly, reluctantly.

Anger hardened Eva's gentle features. "They are imbeciles! Fools to say such things! They do not know—" Her voice broke suddenly, and her rage fled with it. She hugged her knees to her chest and sat staring at nothing.

She looks so much like a lost child, Katrina thought. Out loud she replied, "Yes. They know nothing, Eva. They don't know what they do. They don't know Who they raise their hands to fight against when they persecute us. And … I am so sorry." Katrina reached out to brush the tears from Eva's cheek. "Forgive me. I have nothing but words to offer you. Nothing but words when your heart is breaking."

"My heart is already broken, Trina." Sad blue eyes sought Katrina's face, and Eva shrugged slightly. "You needn't say that. A thousand times I ask Him why, and there is no answer. What else could you do?"

"I'm so sorry," Katrina offered again, feeling small and helpless at the sight of Eva's grief.

"I miss him." Eva whispered. "So much. What will happen now? There is no mercy from the Gestapo. How much did he suffer at their hands? How much now must we?"

"I don't know, Eva. But we must trust in the Lord and stand firm."

"Trust? Stand?" Eva asked incredulously. "They're coming, Katrina. And we have nowhere to run."

The fear of the chase sounded in her words, and Katrina shuddered in spite of herself. Could it be true? There was no way to resist! No way to stand against the power of the Nazis! Would it not be better to simply end things now rather than live in constant terror …?

"No," Katrina said aloud, in answer to Eva's fears and her own. "Why was Pastor Gottlieb killed while evil men are exalted? I do not have the answers. But Eva, hear me! God has not forgotten us here. He knows what it is to suffer. He weeps with you. We do not know what tomorrow holds. We will either live or die. But in both, He is there."

Ramond was in high spirits when he stepped off the train in Tamsweg. This was exactly the sort of work he had imagined when he dropped out of the University of Vienna last March. He had studied law there for almost year before the Nazis marched in and turned that field into a twisted joke. Now he was pursuing a career in "antique appraisal." Ramond grinned. That was the official name for his game of frustrating the Germans and running circles around their absurd racial decrees.

He whistled as he passed the three wooden benches and lone ticket counter of the quaint station. His mother would probably urge him to be more careful, and he knew Father wished he would stop talking in terms of games and battle plans. Still, it was a fight, and a good one at that. Even Father had said that much.

Shrugging beneath the heavy hiking backpack, Ramond scrambled to present his identification to the Nazi at the door. The man gave the papers no more than a cursory glance before waving him through. "Next!"

The quiet town outside the terminal was bright with the promise of adventure. A single swastika flag spread a flickering, lazy shadow on the cobblestone street, and Ramond stepped over it defiantly. Sankt Michael was more than thirty kilometers away, but surely there would be someone traveling between the two towns. He could catch a ride and easily be there before nightfall.

✳

The posthumous trial of Reinhardt Gottlieb progressed quickly and without resistance. Like a skilled maestro, Chief Inspekteur Fredrik Schmidt directed all the proceedings from his cramped office at the headquarters.

Propaganda: visible evidence! Strong tone. Excellent! Perfect counterpoint to the newspaper reports. Now—witnesses! Louder, louder!

Of the witnesses there were four. Two had been bribed by Fredrik's Gestapo. One had been threatened. The last man, Geoff Krimmel, was a member of Christ Church, Reinhardt's congregation. Scrawny, with a head of thinning gray-blond hair and nervous green eyes, Krimmel somehow exuded the impression of a stray dog. Now, in the dingy room within the Gestapo headquarters, his behavior only served to strengthen the similarity.

"A Communist to the core. Yes. Yes," he whined in response to Fredrik's cue.

"How do you know?" Karl demanded, suddenly angry at the pointless vindictiveness of the trial. Fredrik shot an irritated glance at his unruly audience as Krimmel blanched and fidgeted in his seat. The witness had clearly not thought this far ahead.

"Ah—I—well—" Krimmel lost his place and stopped to compose himself. He risked a glance up at his conductor, who stared back in icy disapproval.

"He refused to recognize the authority of the German government in Austria. Said he had higher laws. He was a … a … anarchist!" *Amateur's work. An energetic child blowing tunelessly into a horn.* "He always carried his Bible! Did not want to be a part of the Reich Church! And he wore red! Had red tulips in his garden!"

The performance worsened, and Karl smirked behind his hand. Fredrik had certainly chosen a poor soloist for this part! Mercifully, the *Inspekteur* raised his arm, signaling an end to the recital. Fredrik then nodded slightly at the reporter, indicating that this testimony was not to be recorded.

"You may go." He dismissed the performer in a frustrated tone. Krimmel lingered a moment more—hopeful student seeking affirmation. Finding none, he turned, dejected, and slunk out of the room.

"Good job," Karl remarked as Krimmel left.

Fredrik shot him a withering glare, and the reporter turned to watch the confrontation with interest.

"A good thing we are above the civil courts." Karl smiled thinly. "With witnesses like that …"

Fredrik's eyes narrowed further, and the silent reported fidgeted his chair.

"Gottlieb was a traitor," Fredrik stated in a clipped voice.

This time, Karl caught the warning in the Inspekteur's mud-brown eyes and nodded. "Yes. A traitor. But why this? Surely the Gestapo has better things to do—"

"This *is* the work of the Gestapo." Fredrik's voice dropped almost to a whisper. "I'm sure you do not object?" Now it was his turn to smile patronizingly.

"Snarl" is a better word, Karl thought, as he caught a hint of his own danger written on the *Inspekteur's* ferret-like features. He slowly shook his head. "No, sir."

"Good." The half-human smile flashed again. "The Gestapo requires full loyalty from its employees. You have a promising career, Karl. You would be a fool to forfeit it over something like this. What is one man, more or less?"

Karl clenched his fist and met Fredrik's amused stare, willing the fear from his face.

"No. Not foolish, sir," he replied at last. *Not foolish for hating what you have done to a truly good man. Not foolish for wishing I was not part of it. No. Not foolish at all.* The anger from such thoughts lent him the nerve to return the Inspekteur's glare.

"Very good. You may go." Fredrik leaned back in his chair, the picture of indifference as Karl left. But Karl felt the mocking gaze pursue him through the cramped courtroom and into the dark corridor.

In the Arms of Strangers

RAMOND HAD MEMORIZED THE address before he left home, but still he glanced at the damp square of paper in his hand. He could probably talk his way out of trouble if he was stopped outside—that had happened once before—but it would make it almost impossible to get the refugees later. The house he hesitated in front of was identical to a hundred other homes in lower Austria. Narrow windows. White walls. A roof that sloped like an outlandish hat. Ramond turned around for a moment and pretended to peruse the assortment of breads in the little bakery.

In the glass he watched the reflection of the narrow cobblestone street. *Still empty.* He had certainly not been followed into Sankt Michael. Nodding with satisfaction, he crossed the road to rap on the heavy door. A pale face appeared almost immediately in the streaked window. It vanished with such speed that Ramond wondered if he had imagined it. But then the tarnished knob turned and the door groaned softly as it swung in on ancient hinges.

"*Bitte*, sir, I am Ramond Haider—"

The little man in the doorway gave a jerky nod and motioned him inside. His light-brown eyes searched Ramond's face, glanced away, scanned the street, and then came back again—moving; always moving. Ramond squinted in the sudden gloom as the door closed behind him. The room was dark and sparsely furnished. Two straight-backed chairs stood by a dusty fireplace, and a threadbare blue and yellow rug was the only splash of color.

"You are not Bernard Haider?" the man inquired timidly.

Ramond extended his hand. "His son. Apprenticed by him. In your letter you mentioned lamps to be appraised?"

The stranger relaxed as Ramond completed the code correctly.

"Yes. You are a friend, I see. I am Herr Dreher. We have been so nervous, my wife and I … every noise, and she is certain that the Gestapo have come to take us away!" The gray-haired man gestured broadly, as if to indicate the multitude of little sounds that had been masquerading as the secret police. "The children's father was a member of the Reichstag. Not an important member, but you know what they do to well-to-do Jews. Unthinkable." Herr Dreher grimaced. "Both parents are dead now. They would kill the children as well … but come. Away from the windows! You must be hungry from your journey."

Ramond smiled politely as he followed his anxious host into the kitchen. Frau Dreher, a woman of about fifty, rose to meet him. Her hair was pulled back into a tight bun, and her piercing gray eyes sought Ramond's face.

"Welcome, Herr Haider."

"Ramond." He smiled, stooping slightly to shake her hand.

"Ramond." She did return the smile. Her eyes were still fixed on him with uncomfortable intensity. "Did you leave Salzburg today?"

His nodded cautiously. "This morning."

The woman thrust an envelope at him. "This came around noon. My husband and I cannot understand it—perhaps it was meant for you?"

The envelope contained a telegram. Ramond quickly removed the yellow paper and unfolded it with fumbling hands. *PAPA DETAINED BY BUSINESS. STOP. DOES NOT INVOLVE FAMILY. STOP. COMPLETE TRANSACTION. STOP.* Slowly, he lowered the telegram to the table and sank into a chair beside it.

"It is bad?" Frau Dreher asked gently.

"My father—arrested." He faltered, not believing the words.

The old woman crossed herself and shook her head. "I am sorry." Fear tempered the sympathy in her voice.

"You are safe," Ramond muttered. "They did not take my mother. They will not find you. And I was not there …" He closed his eyes and leaned back, trying to silence the sudden flood of accusations. *You should have been there! If you had not run off after adventure, you* would *have been there! You might have fought them; stopped them*—Ramond exhaled slowly. The thought pounded behind his eyes with the conviction of a sledgehammer. *I should have been there …*

"I'm sorry," Frau Dreher murmured again.

He nodded dully and straightened. "Not your fault." He broke off abruptly as he sensed eyes on his back.

"These are the children," Herr Dreher declared, gesturing suddenly to the wide-eyed ghosts that hovered in the doorway behind him.

Ramond turned. A boy and a girl gazed back at him with solemn interest. *So young!* Both children looked underfed and pale from weeks spent indoors. Ramond studied them with concern. They had dark hair. Dark eyes. They were beautiful children—beautiful and unmistakably Jewish.

"These are Hirschel and Adina."

The quiet conference at the Dreher's kitchen table continued long into the night. There were so many preparations to be made, so many plans to be checked and rechecked.

What exactly did the children need?

They needed false passports that would enable them to travel outside the Reich.

Where would they get such documents?

"From a family in Tamsweg," came the ready reply.

At this Ramond shook his head in frustration. "I took the train from Salzburg to Tamsweg this morning! I could have easily picked them up!"

Herr Dreher waved an arm in frantic disapproval. "Unthinkable! How would we have told you this? Letters are not safe! Telegrams are not safe! Nothing—"

"Nothing is safe," Ramond finished wearily. "Still, I could go and get these papers for them. I can travel by car and have the passports back here by tomorrow night."

"The family will not trust you," Frau Dreher replied softly. "We know them. Unless Hirschel and Adina are with you, they will deny everything."

"Have you no way to contact them? You could not go and get them yourselves?"

Herr Dreher huffed at the outrageousness of such a suggestion. "We took the little waifs in! No one else cared to do that much! And now he wants us to travel with illegal documents, punishable by *death*? Unthinkable!"

Ramond raised his hands halfway. "No one ... no one is asking you to do anything, sir. Nothing more. I can take the children from Sankt Michael to Tamsweg by foot. I know a pass ..." Ramond's voice trailed off as he measured the distance in his mind. The drive from Tamsweg had taken more than an hour today. *Thirty kilometers by road ... it will be closer to forty if we go through the passes on foot. I can hike that in two, maybe three days. But with children it may take a week.* He lifted his mug of now-cold coffee and sipped thoughtfully.

"I think we can be in Tamsweg in a week's time." Ramond suddenly remembered the rotund Nazi official in the train station. Herr Dreher was correct about the death penalty—perhaps this arrangement was better after all. "Do you want me to send word when Hirschel and Adina are safe?"

Frau Dreher started to nod, but her husband interrupted loudly. "No! Unthinkable! We could still be arrested once they are gone, you know."

Ramond agreed silently, apologizing to Frau Dreher with his eyes. Briefly he wondered how this couple had ever found the courage to shelter the children in the first place. "I think that is all. It is late in the season to begin such a journey, but with warm clothing the children should be all right. They will need hats, mittens, coats ..."

"We have had children ourselves. I should be able to find these things in the attic," Frau Dreher murmured.

"Thank you. We will leave before dawn tomorrow morning." Ramond rose stiffly as he nodded to his hosts.

"I will have breakfast for you when you are ready to leave," she offered.

"Thank you. I appreciate it. And ... *Grüss Gott.*"

Ramond left the kitchen with a heavy heart. Tomorrow he would leave to take two children toward the promise of a future far from the evil that had destroyed their lives. Then he would catch another train from

Tamsweg to Salzburg—and then what? Would they arrest him also, when he returned?

He strained to see through the darkness in the parlor, as if the answers to such questions might be lying somewhere in the shadows. But there was nothing—no answer, no peace. Ramond slowly sat on the hard floor and kicked off his shoes. Had he ever *felt* the night like this before? The blackness was almost a presence, a viscous counterpoint to his paralyzing worry.

Should have been there. Should have been there. Should have been … He wondered about his father. *Detained by business…*It was a phrase Ramond had chosen months ago, as a euphemism for arrest. Then it had been part of the code, the challenge, the fight. Now, tonight, the reality behind the words threatened to overwhelm him. "Arrested" could mean any number of things, none good. Had they taken his father only as a warning to a stubborn family? Might he be released within days? Such things had happened before. Ramond exhaled slowly into the blackness, his assurances to his mother hollow in his ears. He had seen too much of the Nazi "justice" in Vienna to hold on to even that small hope. Petty criminals might be arrested and then released, but good men never were. The Reich had more to fear from political opponents and pastors than thieves or murderers. Any one of the latter might be made into an efficient Gestapo agent or a commandant in a place like Dachau, after all. But someone like his father … he was a threat on the highest level. In sheltering the persecuted and helping the helpless, Bernard Haider had obeyed the law of love.

Such actions were brutally punished by the Nazis, Ramond knew. The darkness hated any light that could be seen or touched or felt. Anything that challenged their monopoly of shadows … He tried to pray, but grief rose in his throat until he could find no words but that mocking refrain. *I should have been there.*

Fast asleep across the hall, neither Hirschel nor Adina heard the sound of Ramond's quiet weeping as the night faded into morning.

The first cold winds of autumn had begun to rust the verdant hills around Villach. In the city proper the trees blazed in brilliant red and yellow— bright before they crumbled to ash. On her hundredth aimless circuit of

Stadt Park, Eva thought the image fitting. The ancient pines behind her almost blocked the view of Christ Church. Beyond the fountain on her left was the shadow of the Gestapo headquarters. *So close!* Sometimes when the roads were quiet she could hear the screams.

Still she paced this narrow truce of land that divided the two buildings. How many afternoons had she come here *before*, waiting for Reinhardt? Maybe she was still waiting. It seemed impossible that he should not come hurrying around the side of the church at any moment, overflowing with apologies for being late and explanations about the wonderful text he had for the sermon next Sunday …

Her attention was suddenly diverted by a commotion outside the dreadful pink building. An agent seemed to be trying to drag someone from the van on the corner. The invisible prisoner was fighting hard, from what Eva could see. She drifted closer to the little drama. Two other agents came running from inside the headquarters. Laughing, they dragged the man out and threw him to the ground.

Eva turned back to the church as the beating began. The sky was still bright above the red and yellow bricks of the bell tower. The birds continued to sing as a passing car swallowed up the dead laughter and shouts. Why didn't the illusion vanish? Why did the light and trees and church not disappear with a roar and leave her alone in the night she walked?

She risked one more glance across the empty street, watching as they dragged their prisoner indoors. The door slammed; a merciful end to the spectacle. Eva remained standing at the edge of the park, daring the Gestapo to come and take her as well.

It had been an unusually slow day at the office. This morning Karl had been assigned the unpopular task of reading through the transcripts and confessions of last night's interrogations and comparing them with the denunciations that had brought the prisoners in. Often the two were more different than alike. Karl shook his head, remembering an old joke from Gestapo headquarters at Prinz-Albrecht-Strasse. *The prisoners may not know what they're guilty of—but we'll find out!*

It was only after lunch that he had been called from his position in the main office block and ordered to report to the Inspekteur's office *immediately.* Fredrik Schmidt was not there, however, so he had spent the last thirty minutes loitering in the hallway like a schoolboy waiting to see the headmaster. The break would not have been unwelcome if it hadn't called to mind the anticipation period regularly used to soften prisoners.

Karl scratched his deaf ear and leaned back against the wall. He had never been inside the Inspekteur's office. Dimly he imagined it decorated with human trophies of some sort. A skull on the desk, perhaps, and a head mounted on the wall ...

He straightened at the echo of footsteps in the stairwell. A moment later the door swung open and the Inspekteur appeared, an expression of something like cheerfulness stretched across his skinny face. Karl saluted as Fredrik brushed past him to unlock the door. The little man motioned him in, muttering about denunciations and tardiness and corrective measures as if he had been waiting on Karl all afternoon.

Karl cautiously took a seat in front of the neat mahogany desk. There were no skulls, he noted with relief, save the cap that bore the death's head insignia on the nearest corner of the desk. From here the Inspekteur commanded not only the Gestapo but the *Sicherheitsdienst,* or Security Service, as well. The latter organization conducted most of the information gathering, while the Gestapo carried out the executive work of the police state. *And the executions,* Karl added wryly.

"There have been further developments with Gottlieb's church," the Inspekteur stated suddenly. "The Reich Church of Villach has presented us with an official complaint. Naturally, we must act on it."

Karl nodded. Was this the reason behind Fredrik's strange cheerfulness?

"I am transferring you to B-2."

Karl leaned forward, confused by Fredrik's sudden shift of topic. "Sir?" He belatedly remembered what that division of the Gestapo oversaw. *Department B—sects and churches. Section 2 would be ... Protestants.*

"Yes," Fredrik continued as if he had read Karl's thoughts, "you are to be the eyes and ears of my Gestapo in the traitor's church."

Karl sank back in his chair as he took in the order. *So,* he thought grimly. *The Inspekteur does not trust me after all.* It was clearly a test. Fredrik had seen a glimmer of weakness in him, and now he would force Karl to prove exactly where his loyalties lay.

Fredrik waited until he had Karl's assent before he continued. "You may make your presence known. Half the city saw you and the other Berlin agents in the *parade* already. I want you in that church every Sunday. A Gestapo agent among them should get the informants talking. Do you understand?"

Karl nodded reluctantly. "Yes, sir. Heil Hitler."

Now, two days later, Karl sat near the back of the light-filled sanctuary. It was bigger than it had seemed from the outside. Stained-glass portals on both sides of the room depicted scenes of stories he had heard long ago. He ran a hand distractedly over the smooth, almost-satiny wood of the pew in front of him. Color from the windows splashed across the stark white walls as congregants filed solemnly in.

Karl was beginning to question the Inspekteur's wisdom in sending him here. He had already been identified as a stranger, an intruder—and he could sense the peoples' anger from where he sat. Behind him someone hissed the word *Gestapo*. Karl turned, smiled, and nodded curtly. Of course he was Gestapo. Perhaps he should stand up and announce that he had arrested their pastor, too. *Yes. If not for me, Reinhardt Gottlieb would probably be with you today. Furthermore, I am here to frighten some of you into betraying everyone else. Carry on.*

What else had Fredrik been expecting? Gottlieb's congregation was clearly aware of the peril their pastor had put them in. Karl's pew, along with the two behind and in front of him, was empty. *There is room to take a nap, at least.* Karl started to yawn and then caught himself. He could suddenly picture Reinhardt addressing these people with assurance and compassion: "In the end, Truth is all that will remain, shining in the midst of shattered lives and your broken promises, calling men and women to Himself!"

The pastor's memory seemed stronger here, in this place where colors broke and bled in glowing patchwork through the stained-glass windows. Karl grimaced as the image of Reinhardt's costly defiance presented itself again.

Dying, but still somehow full of life … But you had so much to live for, Gottlieb! Karl shook his head as Eva Gottlieb drifted past him. She was dressed entirely in black, but it was her frozen expression of grief and fear that made him drop his gaze.

Karl watched her lift her head toward the steps leading up to the empty pulpit and then look away as if she'd been stung. The gesture sent a surprising stab of regret through Karl. *I'm sorry,* he offered silently. *He should be here. It was the Inspekteur's personal revenge. I didn't know …*

A sudden clanging started Karl from his imagined apology. *Bells,* he realized belatedly as the solemn chimes resounded above him. The tolling continued for half a minute more, each note as deep and jarring as if the sky itself was cracking. Karl risked a glance up at the vaulted ceiling, half-expecting it to come crashing down with the weight of the noise above it. He had heard bells like this ring each week from a dozen different cathedrals since he was a child. But he had long since forgotten how *loud* they were from within!

The ringing slowed at last and faded to a merciful stop. Somewhere above and behind him the organist began to play, and the people all around Karl stood to sing. He ducked his head as he stumbled to his feet, feeling remarkably out of place.

The music swelled in somber richness as more and more voices joined in. There was sorrow here but also a hope Karl did not understand. At last the song faded and silence fell as a man ascended the pulpit with slow, heavy steps.

Karl forced himself to sweep the room again. Most bowed their heads reverently as the new pastor prayed. But Karl's sharp eye picked out a few who glanced uneasily away. Among these was Geoff Krimmel, the pathetic witness from Reinhardt's trial. The man was scribbling frantically in a little notebook as he scanned the faces in the room. Karl sighed quietly. Already he had an informant. The Inspekteur had been right after all.

By the end of the third day of traveling, Ramond judged them to be a little more than halfway to Tamsweg. They had followed the edge of hilly fields all day, and now Ramond urged the children back into the security of the tree line.

"We will find a good place to camp, and then we will eat supper. Are you hungry?"

Hirschel nodded and grabbed his hand. "Is this a good place?"

Ramond surveyed the little hollow of forest, carefully extricating himself from Hirschel's grip. "Good enough. Do you see the pine needles on the ground? I need you and Adina to scoop them into piles for beds. I'm going to find water, and then we will eat. Stay in this clearing until I come back."

Canteen in hand, Ramond struck off in the direction of the sound he'd heard. They could have gone farther tonight, but the children were tired and there was a stream somewhere nearby. He was in no real hurry to get to Tamsweg anyway. Once his charges were delivered, there would be nothing left to do but return to Salzburg and wait for news …

He stopped to listen again for the water, half-sick with fear for his father and the accusation that had repeated endlessly since he read the telegram. Of course he should have been there. What did he know about children, after all? If he hadn't insisted on answering this letter, Father would be safe in these woods telling stories to the children, and they would have taken Ramond instead.

He stooped mechanically to fill the canteen and then rose to jog back through the shadows to where he'd left the children. There was a new bite in the air tonight, though the sun hadn't fully set. Perhaps they should have pushed on farther.

Hirschel's thin voice greeted him as he returned to the clearing. "Herr Ramond, aren't you scared of the dark?"

"No."

"Why come?"

Ramond looked up from clearing the ground for a moment and shrugged. "It doesn't scare me." He struck a match and held it to the little pile of tinder he'd made. In the sudden glow he located Hirschel, perched atop a formidable heap of pine needles. "Does it scare you?"

The little boy nodded seriously. Ramond frowned for a moment and then motioned him closer.

"I have a surprise for you." He dragged the massive backpack to him, nearly running Adina over. "Sorry. There is a surprise for you too, Adina, if you want it."

Adina didn't answer. She was sleeping, or crying, or locked up in some private grief far from their campsite. Ramond sighed as he rummaged for the little paper-wrapped parcel he'd been saving. He felt like joining her in the dirt, but then Hirschel would be alone with no one to defend him from the dark ...

"Found it!" He held the little package aloft in the firelight. "Can you guess what's inside?"

Hirschel shook his head.

"Chocolate." Ramond unwrapped the brown paper carefully. "There's a piece for each of us. You can eat it now, or after supper, but what I like to do is make hot chocolate. I like it much better than coffee, which is good because we don't have any coffee. Although ..." On a sudden inspiration he plunged his hand back into the bag. A moment later he held two more packages. "I thought there might be more." Smiling carefully, he offered one to Hirschel.

"Did your mama pack it for you?" The voice was just above a whisper. When Ramond nodded, Hirschel reached out to take the chocolate with reverent hands. He stared at it for a long time, turning it over and over and finally pressing it to his cheek.

Ramond cleared his throat, humming the bright notes of some American jazz song. It sounded artificial in the still October night. "Three days until Tamsweg," he offered at last, but neither child replied.

"Eva, I want you to leave Villach." Katrina reached across her kitchen table to lay a hand on Eva's arm.

Eva lowered her cup with a *clank* and stared at Katrina. "What?"

"You should go. The law of family guilt—" Katrina's eyes swept over the stacks of books and potted geraniums on the countertop and scanned the framed prints on the wall beyond, searching for a reason Eva would heed. "It is not safe for you here," she finished lamely.

The autumn rain pattered in the silence. When Eva spoke at last, it was with a sad smile. "Where would I go, Trina? Is anywhere in Austria safe? We are all Germany now."

"Then leave Germany!" Katrina exclaimed with a fierceness that startled both of them. "I'm sorry, Eva. I didn't mean …" She sighed and stared at her hands. "I want you to be safe. You know I would do anything for you. But if they come …"

"I know. Would you like any more tea?" Eva rose quickly and gathered both cups. Katrina followed her to the sink.

"I'm not distracted."

Eva turned slowly. "And I can't leave, Trina. Reinhardt—" She faltered. "Reinhardt would have stayed. He said we would stay. Surely you remember that Sunday?"

Katrina nodded. Of course she remembered the Sunday Eva spoke of. Six months ago, on the day after the Anschluss, Pastor Gottlieb had stood before his congregation and warned them of the coming storm. He had addressed the Jewish members of his flock, urging them to leave the Reich by any means possible. "At one time, we believed we were safe in Austria. Now it is not so. What has already begun in Vienna will soon come here. My fear is not only for my Jewish brothers but for all who gather here today in the Name of Christ. I will think no less of anyone who decides to leave now. Some must leave and live to fight another day. But as long as even one of you remains, I will stay. My place is here."

"But he did not say *you* would stay," Katrina gently reminded Eva.

Eva shook her head quickly and looked away.

"Please. Sit down, will you?" Katrina led Eva back to the table. "At least consider it. Your parents are in Vienna, are they not? Perhaps they know someone who could get you a visa to somewhere. And maybe—"

"They don't. And how could I leave you, Katrina? My worrying friend?" Eva smiled, but the shadow did not leave her eyes. "I will think about it," she promised.

Eva did think about Katrina's words that night. They played again and again in her mind like a haunting refrain. *Germany … the law of family guilt … did not say you would stay …* She attempted to forget as she opened her Bible to read the cold and static verses, tried to hear a different song as she turned off the lights and retreated to her bedroom.

Yes, she knew well the law of family guilt. Of all the Nazi edicts, that single decree had made Reinhardt tremble and nearly turn back. "How could I forgive myself if my work brought harm to you, Eva? Will you promise me … promise that if anything ever happens to me, you will run?"

But Eva had not. She had looked him in the eyes and told him he was forgiven, but she had not promised to run.

My place is here also, she knew. *What is left of my heart is here. And so I must stay.* It was only a matter of time before the Gestapo came for her as well—she held no illusions about that. But she could not summon the energy to be afraid. They could not devise anything worse than the pain of living on, of living alone. It was ironic, she realized, that the law Reinhardt had feared was to be the single mercy the Nazis would show her.

She felt a brief pang of regret for Katrina, who wanted so badly for her to be safe. *But,* she reasoned, *I was right in what I said. My parents have no connections outside the Reich—they would like to get out of Vienna themselves. And if I left, Katrina would be all alone.*

So it was decided. Come what may, Eva would not leave Villach.

Strategy

"Herr Ramond, guess what?"

"What?" Ramond slowed his steps until Hirschel could keep pace with him.

"I've never, *ever* had so many days without a bath!"

"Is that a good thing?"

Hirschel nodded seriously. "Very good. I will not even take one when we get to where you are taking us."

"Really?" Ramond grinned through the brown stubble of his new beard. "And what does your sister think?"

"I don't know if she wants a bath. Except her braid came out yesterday and she wanted to know if you could fix it."

Ramond shook his head. "I'm afraid I don't know very much about braids." He glanced back at Adina, who was trailing silently behind them. She hadn't spoken to him since they'd left St. Michael.

"You never did one before?"

"What—no. No, I never did a braid before."

"Mama used to," Hirschel said softly. "She gave us a bath and then she braided Adina's hair before bed because she said it made it curly in the mornings. Except she can't do that no more because the bad men made her and Papa go away."

Ramond studied the long golden grass and dark-green firs that carpeted the slopes below. He counted the shadows on their path and glanced up at the snowy peaks behind them—anything to avoid the gaze of the sad little

45

boy as he replied. "They took my father—my papa, too. The day I left to get you and your sister ..."

But Hirschel was done talking. He drifted back toward his sister without another word, leaving Ramond very much alone at the front of their little band.

The Gottlieb house was just quiet enough to be unnerving. No human voices sounded, but a dozen little noises clamored in the stillness. Water dripped, the roof creaked, and the wind whined and brushed against the windows like a stray dog wanting to be let in.

Eva slowly placed the book she had been trying to read on the walnut table beside her. There was no one to see her pretending, after all. No one but her in front of the dark fireplace in the empty sitting room. Eva wondered why she had turned down Katrina's invitation to stay the night. Talking with her friend held back the quiet, even if it helped nothing else. *Help? What* could *help?* The black-and-white photo of her and Reinhardt's wedding taunted her from the mantle above the fireplace. They had had four years together. Or five, if she counted the months he had spent courting her. She could remember everything: the sound of his voice, clear and deep like the bells above the church; the laughter in his blue eyes; the strong warmth of his arms around her ... *everything!* Why could she not bring him back? Why did he have to go? *Why* ...?

Once more the unanswered questions grated through her like broken glass. She could guess what had happened on *that night.* They would have taken him on his way back from the river, when the family was already safe. They took him, and then—

Eva closed her eyes as the agony of his senseless death raked through her again. There was no purpose behind it! He had been in and out of the Gestapo headquarters for months, and nothing had ever happened! *Nothing ... but now he is gone, and there is nothing left.*

He would have been protecting the family. He must have been. With his own blood he had slaked the thirst of the Nazi wolves, and the sheep went unharmed.

Sacrifice! Had she ever before realized the depths of sorrow and love in that single word? Why had he chosen to freely give what so many now sold their souls to keep? *No greater love than this that a man would lay down his life for a friend.* But that family—the four who lived on because he died—they were strangers, not friends.

Why?

She held her breath, waiting, muffling even the sound of her own sorrow. But she heard nothing, and in the silence her questions ran together into the black sleep of grief.

"Are we there yet?"

The question that had not been asked once during the entire hike was repeated for at least the fourteenth time this morning.

"*Nein*, Hirschel, not yet, but by lunchtime we will see the town." Ramond did not bother to add that it would likely be a late lunch. Anticipation could drown out hunger for a few more miles—or so he hoped. At any rate, they were not far from Tamsweg. Already they had entered the valley, though Ramond kept them well within the tree line.

"When we get there will there be lots of food?"

"Certainly."

"And beds softer than pine needles, with real pillows for a pillow fight, and some—"

Ramond stopped abruptly, motioning Hirschel to silence. The voices on the road unnerved him.

"Is it bad men, Herr Ramond?"

"Stay here."

He set out at a jog, quickly leaving the children behind. The ground rose in a gentle wave, and he slowed, heart sinking, as the little town appeared below him. A hastily constructed barrier blocked the main road. Ramond stopped behind a tree as he considered it. It was not impossible to get the children around it, though it would certainly be more difficult. But why a checkpoint should spring up around this insignificant little town he did not know …

A shout ripped suddenly through the drowsy stillness of the forest, sending a cloud of pigeons swirling up over the road. Ramond was trying in vain to locate the commotion in the town when answering calls—dozens of them—roared out from behind the tree trunks through the dusty play of light and shadow. Newly fallen leaves crunched out a warning as the invisible army began to march, singing, toward some unseen objective.

> Wherever we are, we're always ahead,
> And the devil laughs along,
> Ha, ha, ha, ha, ha!
> We're fighting for Germany,
> Fighting for Hitler …

The words pounded in Ramond's blood as he whirled and sprinted back toward the children. The song of the Waffen-SS! Here, in these woods, *somewhere*—he skidded to a stop in front of his backpack. The children were gone.

"Hirschel! Adina!" The other voices seemed closer now. "Where are you?" He shouldered the bag and stood perfectly still, fighting the adrenaline that urged him to *run*. "It's me, Ramond. Please come out."

He waited for more than a minute before Adina appeared, dragging Hirschel behind her. "Are they finding us, Herr Ramond?"

The song was almost deafening. Ramond scooped up both children and ran, weaving through the trees in a wild attempt to escape the unseen pursuers. The singing stopped as suddenly as it had begun, though the crackling march urged Ramond forward long after he thought he could go no farther. When at last he did stop, safe in the silence, Tamsweg and all its promises were far, far behind.

The café Karl had chosen to meet Geoff Krimmel in was like a dozen others in Villach. Small circular tables occupied almost all the available space. A few lucky customers had already claimed the spots nearest the warmth and light of the window, so Karl retreated to a dim corner. The smells of tobacco and strong coffee mingled to make the air noticeably thicker, but he didn't mind. Growing up among the squalor of post-war Berlin had given him an appreciation for almost anything that did not reek of sewage or waste. Villach was almost a paradise for him, with its clean mountain air and local brewery.

Or at least it had been, until Reinhardt Gottlieb was killed. Until the terrible questions of right and wrong and meaning had come crashing into his existence, shattering his indifference and forcing him to face himself. Before all this, Villach had been a pleasant, easy place. Now it seemed almost haunted. Or perhaps he was the haunted one ...

He roused himself from gloomy thoughts in time to see Krimmel timidly enter the café. The sight reminded him of the purpose of this meeting. Karl raised his hand halfway and let it drop, and the motion brought Krimmel scurrying to his table.

"Heil Hitler, Herr Krimmel," Karl said without inflection.

Relief flooded the man's darting green eyes. "Heil Hitler! I was so relieved you called me here, Herr ..." The lack of a name did not dampen the informant's enthusiasm. "For weeks now I have been telling the Gestapo that they needed a representative in the church! Months now! You are an answer to—"

"Prayer?" Karl finished dryly.

Krimmel nodded automatically, and Karl couldn't help but wonder what god this man prayed to. Not the same one Gottlieb had served, certainly! Was Krimmel among those who saw the Fuehrer as a god, a messiah for Germany? For a moment Karl considered asking. Quickly he dismissed the idea and motioned for Geoff Krimmel to sit.

"You are correct, Herr Krimmel, in your *assumption*"—Karl let the word linger in the air—"that I am Gestapo." He smiled benignly as the informant turned to the nearest wall to study a clumsy copy of something by van Gogh. "And also in thinking I have been assigned to your church." He nodded at Krimmel, who now looked distinctly uncomfortable. "We are allies, you and I. And since you have been among the dissenters far longer than I have, I have come to you for help."

"I would be greatly pleased to offer my humble services to the wisdom of the Gestapo," he declared.

Is he joking? Karl wondered briefly. *Or does he always appear this foolish?* Remembering the trial a few weeks prior, Karl decided it was probably the latter. He replied, "Good. Now, there are a few questions I need to ask you. The first is this: Who was Reinhardt Gottlieb?"

"A Communist!"

Karl shook his head. The answer was reflexive, like a student who had over studied for an exam. "But what did he do?" Karl pressed. "Before we arrested him, when he was still your pastor—what sort of things did he say? What was he like?"

"Why do you want to know?" Krimmel asked curiously.

Karl stopped short, mentally kicking himself. He had made his questions too honest; too eager. His hand went to his deaf ear in nervous habit before he straightened with inspiration.

"Our investigations have hinted that he might have been part of more insidious plans. Perhaps even an assassination!" Krimmel's eyes bulged at the last word, and Karl smiled. This would work. "Of course we will thoroughly investigate such a threat. But that will take time and resources we can hardly afford to spare. That is why I wished to talk to you today. To determine what kind of man this pastor was, and if he would have been capable of plotting such things against the Reich."

Krimmel was silent for so long Karl thought he had lost him completely. Then the informant cleared his throat. "I do not claim to know the depths a man can sink to …"

With a focused effort, Karl kept the smirk from his face.

"But if it can help the discerning Gestapo in any way, I do not think Pastor Gottlieb could have planned such things. He was a Jew-lover and a dissenter but also a man of peace. Once he said it was better to be cheated than to cheat, and to be wronged rather than to do wrong." Krimmel paused, and Karl sensed he was answering honestly for the first time. "I myself was a little bit surprised when he was executed for treason. Of course, everyone had heard the rumors—"

"Rumors?" Karl repeated.

Krimmel nodded. "There were always rumors that he helped the Jews. No one ever knew for certain. And he was at the hospital quite often."

"He was ill?"

"No. He went to visit those who were sick. Even when there no one from the congregation was there."

Karl exhaled sharply, as if he had been punched in the stomach. Indeed, Krimmel's information triggered a memory so clear he felt like he had run straight in to it. *The hospital! We waited and waited, and he did not come out! We didn't know how long he had been gone when we caught him on the road. And this man says he went there often …*

He blinked hard and turned to Krimmel, who was watching him with interest. "You have helped me answer an important question," he said slowly. "Thank you. You may go."

There was no fire in the camp that night. Ramond had set a merciless pace all day, carrying the children when they could not keep up and making them walk only when his arms burned with weariness. There was probably enough distance between them and the army of unseen SS—probably. Still, a fire might draw attention to an illegal group of refugees going nowhere.

Nowhere. Ramond shivered and pulled his coat tighter around his chin. Tamsweg was walled off by a detachment of invisible SS—probably conducting drills, he reflected. It made little difference. He was certain the Drehers would not take the children back, and he had no way to get them as far away as Salzburg. *God, where will we go?*

"Where are you taking us, Herr Ramond?" Hirschel demanded suddenly, echoing his thoughts.

Ramond started to confess his ignorance but changed his mind. "Would you like to look at the map?"

Hirschel pressed himself closer against Ramond. Carefully, Ramond clicked on his little flashlight and pointed it down at the map already spread out across his legs. "We were supposed to go *there*," he explained, jabbing Tamsweg as if it were an insect to be squashed. "And now we are going … somewhere."

"Oh." Hirschel nodded once and closed his eyes.

Ramond continued his perusal of the map, glaring down at it until the towns and cities swam in the harsh beam of the flashlight. *Sinkt Veit. Feldkirchin. Klagenfurt. Villach. Villach?* The last city sounded vaguely familiar. Something he had heard, something about a pastor …

He clicked the light off suddenly as he remembered. "Gottlieb," he whispered hoarsely. With startling clarity he recalled the clandestine meetings he'd been so proud to be part of. They had been a place where adventures were conceived, where battle plans were drawn up against the darkness—and one week someone had mentioned a man named Reinhardt Gottlieb. He was a pastor, Ramond remembered, who offered freedom to anyone desperate enough to risk escape.

Or so it was said. Ramond's family had never directed anyone to the city that sat on the southern border of Austria. But now …

Ramond slowly nodded, acquiescing to his own wild plan. Villach was nearly a hundred kilometers away—more than twice the distance they had already come. *But we can avoid the towns if we travel through the mountains.* He folded the map, almost certain now. He and his father had once hiked a similar trek, and it had taken a week and a half. With the children it would probably be double that time. To attempt a hike like this in October … but Ramond could think of nowhere else to go. And so it was decided. They would make the desperate bid for Villach.

Karl couldn't sleep. Thoughts tumbled over and over in his brain like the dead leaves that scraped over the streets outside his window. He had told himself there would be time to ponder what he had learned in the morning, that everything would come together in the daylight. That had been four hours ago. Still sleepless, he was plagued be the sense that truth was tantalizingly near. Yet somehow a final conclusion lingered just out of his reach.

Finally he gave up on slumber. Stumbling out of bed, he groped blindly for the light switch only to squint and close his eyes against the sudden glare. He managed to locate a clean sheet of paper and a pen in the clutter that passed for a desk and stood for a moment in the middle of the room. At last he padded back to his narrow bed, silently cursing his restless curiosity.

Karl stared at the paper for a full minute before he began to write. Even then, the words did not make sense. He penned Reinhardt's name in the center of the page and circled it twice. Off to the side he wrote *hospital, cover,* and *arrest*. Rubbing his eyes, he resisted the urge to look at the clock. He knew it was well past three in the morning.

"Concentrate," he mumbled. The nearly blank paper glared back at him as he tried to recall exactly what Geoff Krimmel had said. "There were rumors. There were rumors that Pastor Gottlieb helped the Jews." Karl frowned as he scribbled *Jews* beneath *arrest*.

"But how would he help them? How?"

Karl did not ask *why*. During his days on Prinz-Albrecht-Strasse with the Berlin Gestapo, he had seen two pastors harassed and threatened for sympathizing with the Jews. Both times he had quietly pitied them, those two brave men whose only fault was their compassion. It seemed right to him that the weak-hearted Christians should care for the subhuman Jews. But for some reason he had not imagined Reinhardt doing such a thing. Karl gripped the sheet of paper tighter at that realization. He had not imagined Reinhardt doing anything at all that night!

But he was, Karl thought with growing excitement. *He led us to the hospital and then slipped away to do ... something. But what?*

He closed his eyes and tried to reconstruct the details of the night that had brought so much into question. *Reinhardt was returning to the city as we were leaving it. Fredrik stopped him and said something, accused him of breaking curfew. And then Reinhardt started talking. He spoke about truth. He claimed it alone would stand when all else crumbled, that through it—or was it Him?—men and women would be saved. What kind of truth is that? I wonder.*

"Concentrate, Karl," he muttered again. Returning his gaze to the paper, he wrote *truth* carefully above Reinhardt's name.

I have never seen Fredrik that angry, Karl mused as his thoughts returned to Gottlieb's arrest. Indeed, the white-faced rage that swept over the *Inspekteur* that night had frightened even him. *But it did not deter Reinhardt. If anything, he was encouraged by Fredrik's anger. But why—*

Karl sat up so quickly that the paper fell off his lap and drifted to the ground. "Because he was protecting someone!" he exclaimed in sudden answer to his own question. "Of course he was protecting someone," he repeated in a quieter voice, suddenly conscious of the thin walls of his apartment.

It made perfect sense. Gottlieb might have gone free if he had apologized and cowered before Fredrik. *Or the Inspekteur might have become suspicious and ordered an investigation. But Fredrik is like the rhinoceros from the zoo in*

Berlin—eager to smash and destroy but seldom able to see past his own nose. Gottlieb must have known that. And he gave himself up …

Karl closed his eyes and sighed, the sound echoing the unnamed longing in his heart. Knowing the *what* of Reinhardt's story did not make the *why* any easier to comprehend. *What kind of person simply gives his life away?* He remembered the pastor's words in the prison: "My life is safe, though I lose it." Geoff Krimmel's voice echoed Karl's own confusion: "Once he said it was better to be cheated than to cheat and to be wronged rather than to do wrong."

"What kind of person?" Karl whispered into the silence, desperately wishing he knew.

Broken Hopes

"Herr Ramond?"

Hoping it was not another question about the duration of the trip or a request for "just one more" story, Ramond answered with forced lightness. "What is it, Hirschel?

"Don't feel good."

Ramond stopped and squatted next to him, feeling the muscles in his legs shriek in protest. "You don't feel well?" He frowned, suddenly realizing how white the little face was. "What's wrong?"

"I hurt," Hirschel said vaguely, slurring the words.

Ramond stood quickly and looked around. *Trees. Mountains. Rocks.* They were far from any town, he knew. The loneliness was suddenly terrifying, but he forced himself to nod and gently ask Hirschel *where* he hurt.

"Everywhere."

"Up you go, then!" The words were light, as light as the thin little boy—but no one was smiling. Ramond eyed the small copse ahead. "We'll stop here tonight," he announced, motioning Adina to follow.

The grove of pines made an ideal camp, but Ramond was too distracted to appreciate it. The sun was still high above the swishing branches as he gathered firewood.

Hirschel dozed fitfully through most of the afternoon, often waking for a few minutes before drifting off again. Ramond hummed loudly as he worked. Imagined trumpets and saxophones kept the all-engulfing silence at bay. There was an orchestra of angels here, he explained to Adina, so they weren't really all alone. But Adina simply stared in silence—incredulous of angels that played American jazz, or maybe any angels at all.

By sunset Hirschel seemed somewhat better, and Ramond allowed himself to hope the boy was only exhausted. He smiled wanly in apology as he doled out rock-hard lumps of carefully rationed bread and sausage.

"I wish there was more, but this has to last. We'll be in Villach soon enough, and then what would you like to eat?"

"Everything!" was Hirschel's weakly enthusiastic reply.

Adina merely shrugged, flattening his attempts at conversation. Ramond volunteered to make his last cup of hot chocolate, but when that offer was refused, he fell silent as well. He could not help but remember the words Frau Dreher had whispered to him the night before he left. "Here in St. Michael it was two days before the Nazis came. Two days to plan and hope … but then they did come. They took the children's parents early that morning. The children were already hiding in the house of a churchman. Their father had been a politician, once … They killed both parents in the public square as an example. Adina was watching at a window, poor girl. She saw it happen …"

Ramond sighed deeply, anger and frustration and helplessness mingling in the impotent sound. What kind of evil would destroy the parents before a child's eyes? And then pursue the children as well, until they were forced to flee like criminals through the mountains at the start of winter? He was doing all he could, he quickly reminded himself. He was trying to undo what the Nazis had done, or at least keep the devastation from spreading any farther …

He leaned forward, urging Hirschel to finish his stale sandwich. The little boy shook his head and pushed the food away, and Ramond wondered how it could possibly be enough.

A child's rasping cough dragged Ramond from his nightmare to the cold shadows of their camp. He sat up quickly, squinting through the dull glow of the embers. *Alone alone alone alone alone*—the chant receded as the sleeping children came into focus. He suddenly realized it was Hirschel who was coughing like death.

"Hirschel!" Frightened and somehow awkward, Ramond crawled to his side and lifted him until the boy slumped upright against his chest. He felt him relax as the spasm subsided. The little body was hot in the cold air, as if Hirschel had somehow absorbed the heat of the dying fire.

"Hirschel? Can you hear me?"

The child blinked and gave a tiny nod.

"Good. Good. Don't be scared ..."

The words were a lie in Ramond's mouth, though they seemed to soothe the child. He raised his desperate gaze to the sky. Stars peered through the tree branches like the eyes of the jazz angels he had told Adina about— watching from afar, unable and unwilling to do anything at all. *O God, help us! Help us,* he cried silently.

A log popped among the embers, sending up a rain of sparks. Ramond hungrily drank in the glow. Was this to be his hope? The light faded, and he jabbed the coals fiercely with his free hand. Wary tongues of flame blossomed around a half-charred log, driving back shadows with wavering light.

Adina rolled over and scooted closer to the blaze. Ramond saw the terrible *knowing* flood her eyes as she came awake. "Hirschel—"

"Don't come any nearer," Ramond commanded urgently. "He's sick ... maybe contagious ... you must stay well ..." The faltering and useless explanation died away, and Ramond closed his eyes to the haunted expression on her face. "I'm sorry," he offered at last, knowing it made no difference at all.

Ramond stared wearily at the narrow trail winding up before them. The pass was familiar: common precipices, predictable switchbacks, and ordinary fatigue. But despite the climb ahead, he was hopeful. They couldn't be more than a week's hike from Villach once they made it through the pass. He shifted Hirschel's weight from one arm to the other, feeling the heat of the boy's fever against his chest. *That might not be soon enough ...*

Ramond addressed Hirschel quietly. "We are going to climb through the mountains now. It will be colder, and I need you to hold on to me, ja?"

Hirschel opened his eyes and nodded once. "Ja," he whispered, trying to snuggle deeper into Ramond's coat.

Ramond turned to face Adina. "Are you ready?" he asked gently.

She gave her tired assent, and the journey began in earnest. Soon the steep, streaked walls of rock rose to hem them in on either side, and granite clouds settled low in the stony corridor.

Minutes dragged into hours until Adina's voice broke the silence. "Herr Ra—"

Her cry ended in a gasp. Ramond whirled to see her skid backward in a shower of pebbles. She crashed against the boulders on her left and lay there, stunned.

"Adina!"

He clutched Hirschel tighter and slithered down to help her. She sat up slowly to regard him with wide eyes.

"Are you all right?" he demanded.

Adina nodded uncertainly, staring at something behind him. Ramond followed her shaken gaze to the edge of the world and the empty space beyond.

"You are a very brave girl, Adina. Can you keep going?"

He reached down to help her and then drew back, suddenly mindful of Hirschel's fever and the steady ache in his own body. Certainly it was only due to the long hike and the added weight of the little boy, but ... "I—I'm sorry," he stammered, leaning against the rough stone as she clambered to her feet. "But we must keep going." His voice was tight with helplessness. He shifted his coat to better shield Hirschel from the biting wind, and Adina followed silently behind him.

"Thomas. Good." Fredrik barely glanced up as the bulky man saluted. With dark, close-set eyes and a prominent nose, Thomas was hardly an embodiment of the Aryan ideal. But those features enabled him to move with greater ease among the enemies of the Nazis. What he lacked physically, he made up for in unflagging dedication to the Fatherland.

Thomas was a man after his own heart, Fredrik thought as he cleared his throat and continued. "There is a bit of unpleasantness that I need you to attend to." Despite the careful words, there was something chilling in his manner. "Karl Zehr. You know him?"

Thomas nodded. One of the Berlin agents, Karl had been mentioned frequently in the past two months in connection with Gottlieb's death.

"You will watch him and report his activities to me."

"Sir?"

Fredrik scowled as if Karl's treachery should be obvious. "Simply working with the Gestapo does not place one above suspicion!" he exclaimed, halfway rising from his seat.

Thomas took an involuntary step back from Fredrik's fury.

"He has failed to demonstrate the level of zeal necessary for an agent of the Gestapo. I have reasons to question his loyalty. But it would be a shame to lose one of our *Berliners.*" Fredrik shrugged. "Follow him and see if he is a good son of the Fatherland or not. But he is *not* to know of your duty. Is that clear?"

Thomas saluted, and Fredrik smiled at how easily such inconveniences were taken care of.

Ramond knew the wind-blasted ledge was a poor place to set up camp. There was no water, little shelter, and barely room enough for all three of them to lie down. Still, the fading winter day was fast disappearing. Adina had been lagging farther and farther behind for the past hour, and even he was tired. He glanced at Adina as he slid down the cold stone. She had not spoken since her fall the day before. *A boy who may be dying and a girl whose heart is dead. And who am I to lead them?* he wondered. There were no answers to such questions. Perhaps there were no answers left in the midst of the madness they fled. Ramond rubbed his eyes. It didn't matter right now. He was cold, and his head pounded with fatigue.

"We're here."

The little boy clung more tightly to him in protest. Ramond reached back for the canteen in his pack. It was only halfway full, but tonight they had nothing else. "Here, Adina." She took the canteen from his hand quickly, as if afraid he might draw it back. It was hardly any lighter when she returned it a moment later. Carefully, Ramond poured some of the precious liquid into the tin cup he'd been using for Hirschel. "Sit up for a moment, Hirschel. Good. Good boy. Now take a drink of water. And another..." Despite Ramond's coaxing, the little boy took only a few swallows before pushing the cup away. Ramond drained it in a single gulp. He could not help being near the sickness, he reasoned, but Adina must have every chance of staying well. It was better that she have the canteen to herself.

Ramond replaced both cup and canteen in his backpack. Food was not a problem, at least. He had purchased as much as he could carry in a tiny village they'd passed through days ago. Could he have gotten help for Hirschel there? Should he have tried? But a circumcised child would not be treated at any hospital in the Reich.

Ramond closed his eyes and leaned back against the cliff, exhausted by the weight of his ill-fated responsibility. He suddenly wished for a book, a story with a good plan that characters did not fall so colossally short of—

"Will he end?" Adina's voice was as gray as the mountains.

"I don't know. He's—I don't know."

Ramond blinked and looked down at Hirschel, lest Adina see the truth written in his eyes. *Nothing but a miracle will save your brother. And there are no miracles to be had among these silent rocks.* He drew a ragged breath and looked at Adina again. She was crying silently, the first tears she had shed since this terrible journey began. Had he spoken his thoughts aloud?

"We can hope," he offered clumsily, cringing at the trite sound of the words. Adina had lost hope a long time ago, he knew. And perhaps he had as well.

Commit Whatever Grieves Thee

A BRISK WIND HISSED down from the mountains, rattling the windows of Villach's elegant shopping district and tearing the last brown leaves from the trees. Eva wrapped her black coat more tightly around her and pressed forward. Cold as it was, she was almost grateful for the wind today. No one stopped long enough to stare at her with that frightened, aloof interest she had come to hate. The breeze stole cruel comments from speculating lips and hurled the words far into the rock and snow above the city. Yes, today was a good day to be out. Eva let her gaze linger on the pastel storefronts as she passed. Cafés. A boutique. Bakeries. The watchmaker's shop. With just a small stretch of the imagination she could make the *Juden Verboten* signs vanish, and the world seemed almost right again.

Soon pink and blue and yellow edifices gave way to rows of stately apartment buildings. Katrina's flat was just around the corner.

"Where do you think you're going in such a hurry?" demanded an insolent voice behind her.

Eva whirled, startled.

"I said where do you think you're going?" The speaker was a teenager, barely fourteen. Eva recognized him at once.

"Otto?"

He jerked his head once, and four other boys fanned out around her.

"Klaus! Herbert! Rolf! Johan!" She exclaimed, identifying each youth in turn. They were all boys who had been in her Sunday school class once—but they were different somehow. Harder muscles. Harder eyes.

"What do you want?" she asked, confused.

Otto sneered something incoherent in reply. Eva edged backward, suddenly afraid of him.

"They sent us to warn you—"

"To warn you filthy Bolshevik—"

"You're not welcome here!"

The angry words fell like blows. Eva glanced from face to face, too dazed by the sudden onslaught to offer any reply.

"The Red is dead." Johann, the youngest of the group, said it so softly that at first Eva didn't hear. But soon the other voices had taken up the cruel chant.

"The Red is dead! The Red is dead!"

"Reinhardt—" Eva's stricken whisper was lost beneath the vicious words. She stumbled back until the wrought-iron fence dug into her shoulders. The boys laughed and circled dangerously close.

"And we're better off without that cowardly traitor!"

Something inside Eva broke as the attack shifted from her to Reinhardt. She was shaking now, leaning against the fence for support. Their spiteful chorus rose higher, a dark current threatening to sweep her away.

"Bang! Bang! That's what happens to anyone who doesn't serve Hitler—"

And then Katrina was right beside her, fire blazing in her eyes. "Go home," she demanded.

"You can't make us!"

"I know each of you. I know each of your mothers. You *will* go home right now, or I will tell each of them exactly what your precious Hitler *Jungen* do in their spare time." The words were deliberately quiet but spoken with an anger that shook the group's bravado.

"Doesn't matter. We belong to Hitler," Otto insisted, but he seemed uncertain now.

"We can tell the Gestapo," Klaus muttered sulkily, but Katrina only narrowed her eyes and glared more fiercely.

Slowly, reluctantly, Eva's tormentors dispersed. Katrina did not speak again as she guided Eva toward the safety of her apartment. Not until they had ascended the two staircases and shut the door behind them with a comforting click did she venture to look into Eva's face.

"Eva? Are you all right? They've gone now; gone away."

There was no response.

"Eva—" She rested her fingertips on Eva's shoulder. The gentle touch brought Eva back. She began to cry, silently at first, and then sobs that shook her from head to toe.

"I'm so sorry, Eva. They've gone. It's all right. Oh, Eva, Eva ..." Katrina whispered. She hugged her friend tightly. "Believe me, please! It *will* be all right. Someday ... God will not forget us here in the shadow of death. Someday, Eva ..."

The flow of tears became a trickle and eventually stopped altogether. Eva pulled away from Katrina and stood on her own, looking very lost in the center of the foyer.

"Sit down." Katrina guided her friend through the living room into her kitchen.

Eva gingerly lowered herself into a chair as Katrina set the water on for tea. "I know them, Trina. I know them. I taught them at church. They were all at our house once, for Reinhardt's birthday. They knew him." She fell silent as their ugly taunts echoed in her mind. "What ... what happened?" she pleaded at last.

"I—I don't know. I wonder too. Where are the people—neighbors, friends, even—that I used to know? How have they fallen so far? They were ordinary ... we were ordinary once." Katrina shook her head and sat facing Eva. "But then I think that perhaps ... perhaps we have always been this way. Always completely capable of evil—only some of us have been rescued from ourselves. Once, on the outside, we all looked alike. Now we are divided like day and night. Light and darkness ..." Katrina lifted a hand and studied it, as if her fingers might untangle the jumbled thoughts.

Finally she sighed and leaned toward Eva. "Somewhere it is written that love never fails. And so it is. When light and darkness collide, does the darkness ever overcome the light? The first star, the hint of dawn—a candle flame. As long as even a single light glimmers, the night cannot claim victory. But you are not that single light, Eva. Not alone, though I know it must feel that way. At least we are together."

Eva woke that night from nightmares of a dark avalanche pouring across the city. *Trapped! Dear God! Buried alive!*

She hummed softly, trying to dispel the terror of the dream. The soft glow from the streetlamps seeped through the lace curtains and cast the room in pewter shadow. Eva stared the dark shelves silhouetted against the wall. She knew they contained Katrina's most prized possession: her books. She smiled at that reminder of her friend. There was nothing to fear here. Katrina slept soundly in the next room, and they were … safe.

Suddenly the afternoon surged back with terrifying clarity. *They sent us to tell you …* There was malevolence in the words that made her cold all over. She lay awake until the dawn rose to drive away the shadows of dread.

The world beyond the pass would have been breathtaking, if Ramond had had breath to admire it with. Fragile wisps of cloud broke the sunlight and sent it scattering over the topaz of the rolling earth. Dark pines pointed up the golden-orange slopes, like a waterfall flowing backward to the sky. Another day Ramond might have called it beautiful. If the injustice of Hirschel's sickness had not shut out all thoughts but the silence of the bright and cloud-streaked heavens, he might have found something to praise.

Ramond slowed to a weary stop as the dry grass dipped into a little hollow.

"Adina? We'll stop here for lunch."

The girl dropped to the ground without a word. Ramond sat slowly across from her, careful not to jar Hirschel.

"Are you hungry?"

She nodded sharply, like a little bird. Ramond laid Hirschel down and fumbled with his backpack. Bread. Cheese. Muesli. It was hardly enough for a bird, but in the empty beauty of these mountains it would have to be enough. He passed the food to her and closed his eyes. Certainly he should eat as well, but … He tore off another hunk of the dark brown bread and offered it to her.

"Here. Take it … extra." Why did it take such effort to talk?

The little swallow-hand darted into his and snatched the bread.

"You're welcome," he mumbled, leaning back against his pack. He wasn't hungry, at least. Dizzy and tired and cold, yes, but not hungry.

"Hirschel?" He sat up again to try and wake the child. "Hirschel, you should try and eat something."

A faint but stubborn *no* responded, and Ramond sighed. What did he know about sick children?

"When you're finished, Adina, we will go."

The insistent tapping dragged Ramond from sleep to surprising darkness. A faint red halo outlined the mountains beside him and the sky was indigo with the coming night—Ramond sat up abruptly. How was it night? They had stopped for lunch, and suddenly everything was dark!—

It was a moment before he located Adina in the dusk.

"What happened? Why didn't you wake me?" Her slight and silent face wavered in his vision. "Why did you let me sleep?" he demanded again, almost shouting in the still night. "Without camp or shelter or fire or—" His tirade suddenly dissolved into a vicious fit of coughing. He couldn't breathe. Couldn't see. He kneaded the earth with his fingers as the spasm worsened and then passed.

"Herr Ramond?"

For a long minute he said nothing. Then: "I'm sorry. I'm sorry. So sorry …" He continued to apologize, first to Adina and to Hirschel and then to the God, who, if He could hear at all, had surely turned His back on them long ago. He began to cough again as the wind picked up and ran howling around them in the dark. "So sorry …"

Eva studied the pale blue and white china teacup as if she had never seen it before. She ran her finger lightly over the rim, tracing the swirls of indigo vines and flowers with an ease born of habit. The cups had been a wedding gift from a family at the church. The last present to be opened, this set had brought her a reminder of the elegance of her childhood home in Vienna.

It was Frau Haupt who gave them to us, Eva remembered. She sighed at the memory. Frau Haupt and her husband had been gone since early March. One of the few Jewish families to heed Reinhardt's warnings, they had left the country only days before the Anschluss. *When they left,* Eva thought wryly, *human lives were still valued more than china. And existence here was far less fragile.*

The angry taunts of the Hitler Youth returned to her mind, and she set the cup down decisively. A quiet morning locked in memories was not so appealing after all. *This morning I promised Katrina I would stay busy.* Eva smiled faintly at the thought of her friend's concern. Today she had decided to go back Christ Church to practice on the organ. She had not played in church since Reinhardt's death, but now, strangely enough, she felt ready.

Eva fingered the key in her pocket as she walked to the door. Reinhardt's key. She had offered to return it to the deacons one day when the sight of the church was enough to break her heart to pieces again, but they had refused it. Now she was grateful they had. Today she would play in the solitude of the old building until the music filled her heart and lifted her prayers to heaven. And then tomorrow she would do it again, the congregation with her.

It was a terrible day for even the short walk from the Gestapo building to the church. The wind that raged beneath the slate-gray clouds was raw, and a fine sleet stung the faces of anyone foolish enough to venture outside. Karl shoved his hands deep into the pockets of his overcoat as he trudged forward, trying to remember why he had not simply driven a car across the street. *Someone might have been curious. Someone might have asked to come along.*

"Someone like Thomas," he muttered out loud. The burly agent had been unusually nosy during the past few days, filled with questions about everything from Karl's family in Berlin to the night of Reinhardt's execution. Karl was quickly growing to resent his probing company. He was grateful for the solitude of the short walk, at least. Even Thomas had not been keen on accompanying him for a routine visit to the suspect Christ Church today.

Routine visit. As if I were a doctor instead of a professional eavesdropper. Karl remembered the kind doctor who had visited them so often in Berlin before his mother died. His free medicine and advice hadn't saved her, though they had somehow comforted the little boy watching his mama fade away. *Someone was watching,* he had believed. Somewhere, someone cared.

It was a bad comparison, Karl decided as he jogged through the park. Someone was still watching—that would be him. Watching the church. Coming to prowl around an empty building, because … well, perhaps he cared. In some strange way, he was involved in what happened to Gottlieb's church. But Fredrik cared more. He would eventually make his victory over the church complete, Karl knew. The Inspekteur always won in the end. Always.

The silence of the empty church was as familiar as the voice of an old friend to Eva. She exhaled quietly as she stepped out of the cold and shut the door. All her apprehension, all the fear she had carried since yesterday melted away in the peace of this place. Though she knew this church was one the buildings most reviled by the Nazis, she was strangely unafraid. She did not even bother to lock the door as she entered the sanctuary.

Her feet sank silently into the soft red carpet. The stained-glass windows transformed the harsh white daylight into a glittering cloud of witnesses. On her left, Moses carried the tablets of the Law down from Sinai. Beside him, Elijah stood before the altar of the God of Israel as fire fell from heaven on his sacrifice. An inscription at the base of the portal proclaimed, "Jehovah, He is God!"

Eva pivoted halfway around to face the most glorious portrait of all. An image of Christ—a painting, not stained glass—beckoned above the high altar. His hand was outstretched, and there was a gentleness in His face that made Eva want to simply stand and gaze for hours. "Come to Me, all you who labor and are heavy laden, and I will give you rest. Take My yoke upon you and learn from Me, for I am gentle and lowly in heart, and you will find rest for your souls. For My yoke is easy and My burden is light." Matthew 11:28-29 She smiled at the familiar invitation as she turned to climb the stairs to the loft that housed the grand pipe organ.

Eva opened the worn red hymnal on the music stand and searched the table of contents. *Commit Whatever Grieves Thee … page 263.* She quickly flipped to the page and scanned the first verse, wondering if the words had been written especially for her.

Positioning her feet above the correct pedals, Eva pounded out the majestic opening notes. Her hands danced up and down the keys as she picked up the melody. The rich voice of the old organ seemed to match the hues of the windows in the sanctuary. Almost without thinking, she lifted her voice to sing the promises aloud.

> Commit whatever grieves thee
> Into the gracious hands
> Of Him who never leaves thee
> Who heaven and earth commands …

Karl clapped his hands, trying to restore feeling to his numb fingers. He picked up his pace as he hurried around the side of the storybook church. *Nearly there!* Right now, Karl could not imagine anything better. The prospect of being indoors was a cheerful one.

As he slowed to a stop in the empty gravel parking lot, it occurred to him the building was probably locked. Why shouldn't it be? No one would be there on Saturday. And after the execution of their pastor and the increased scrutiny of the Gestapo, the people of the church had every reason to be wary. It was dangerous enough for them to open their doors every Sunday morning; only foolishness would prompt the congregation to leave the building unlocked during the week.

Karl stopped short of the black doors and decorative columns, angry at himself for not thinking. The futility of this visit caused him to turn and look back toward the Gestapo headquarters. *Thomas and Fredrik are there,* he remembered. He looked again at the arched entryway.

"It cannot hurt to try," he murmured as he walked the few remaining steps to the building. He grasped the cold brass handle and pulled—and to his surprise, the door swung open.

Feeling as if he were somehow intruding, Karl stepped inside and gingerly shut the door. He was not alone. The resonant music of a pipe organ filled the air. Karl stepped quietly into the sanctuary, hesitating just beyond the entrance. Now he could hear a woman's clear soprano singing with the organ.

> Who points the clouds their courses,
> Whom winds and waves obey,
> He will direct thy footsteps,
> And find for thee a way.

The song stopped, and Karl pivoted in the empty sanctuary. For a moment the pictures and light overwhelmed him, and then he found the organ loft and recognized the woman who had played with such beauty. *Eva Gottlieb!*

She saw him at the same instant. Karl watched the color drain from her face and silently cursed himself for slipping in so unannounced.

"That was very good, Frau Gottlieb," he called up honestly after a moment's pause.

"Why—what do you want?"

Karl simply stared at the woman for a moment. Her hands trembled above the keys, and there was a fear in her eyes that filled him first with sadness and then regret. It would be cruel to ask her the questions that tormented him.

"Nothing." His reply was curt, but he could not help it. Glancing once more at the image of Christ above the altar, Karl spun on his heel and walked out.

The Good Shepherd

It was a bitterly cold morning in the middle of nowhere. Ramond left the campfire burning until the last possible moment as he broke up the camp. Even after his backpack was packed he lingered beside its heat. It would be so much easier to stay here. He glanced at Hirschel, almost invisible beneath Ramond's blanket and his own. He had not been conscious in two days.

"Adina?"

The girl looked up from her work of tearing and sorting the brown grass.

"It's time—" he broke off, coughing violently.

Adina returned to her broken garden until Ramond shoved himself to his feet. "Time to go." An unfamiliar liquid was warm in his mouth. He turned and spat and then tried unsuccessfully to kick frozen dirt over the red stain.

"Hirschel? Are you ready? We are leaving now." He did not expect an answer, but silence was an admission of defeat. Stooping slowly, he hefted first the backpack and then Hirschel. Finally he stamped out the fire.

"We will walk and be warm, and then when we stop there will be another fire." The pretended optimism sounded foolish even to Ramond. They would not be warm today no matter how far they walked, and when they stopped it would take another grueling hour or two to find firewood enough to fuel the smallest fire through the night. Still, it was only twenty-five kilometers to Villach…

The white circle of sun had nearly reached its cheerless height when another fit of coughing drove Ramond to his knees. Even after it passed he lingered on the ground, trying to regain his breath and control of his shaking limbs. A memory from university last year played absurdly through his thoughts. He had stolen a picture of a friend's sweetheart after supper one night and ran laughing down the stairs onto the frosty street with the deprived lover in dogged pursuit. He could hear his classmates' cheers as he danced just out of the reach of his friend's clumsy lunges: "Run, Ramond, run! Run!"

He staggered to his feet. The wind had picked up, adding its voice to the echoes. *Run.* He stopped again, fighting the dizziness that made the barren hills roll like waves. He had tried so hard to protect these two children, to fight for them against the evil that sought to crush them and so many other innocents. He had run as far as he could.

Coughing again, Ramond stumbled forward, still trying to carry Hirschel, still trying to walk. It was no use. No use. Adina turned away as he sank to his knees.

"Rest ... for a few minutes, and we ... will keep going," he panted.

She nodded silently, and Ramond wondered if she knew it was a lie. He surveyed the desolate land around them. A twisted, weather-blasted pine stood like a lonely sentinel above the brown and rocky hills. It would make a decent camp, if they were inclined to set up camp at noon ...

Ramond closed his eyes, deciding. He was not certain he had the strength to make it to the tree, much less past it. But to waste a precious half day shivering beneath a pine tree because he was too tired to walk ...

Hirschel's breath rattled in his throat, and Ramond shifted his arms to hold him closer. They would need an early camp today after all.

"Herr Ramond?"

"The tree ... is where we will camp today." Ramond struggled upright. Had Adina heard the sound in her brother's breath? Did she understand what it meant, that today was the end?

The rippling land had taken on a decided slant by the time Ramond reached the pine. He collapsed in its shadow, shaking and desperately cold. Adina slipped away to comb the ground for firewood, and he unbuttoned his coat until he could see Hirschel's ashen face. "I'm sorry, Hirschel. Hold on. Please. I know it hurts. I know..." He was talking much like he prayed, striving only to keep the silence at bay. But it returned when he stopped for breath, and in the emptiness that followed he knew there would be no answer.

Adina was frightened. Tonight she remembered the last terrible day in St. Michael. She could hear the shouts of the men who came to take Mama and Papa away, see them standing alone in the center of the square ... and then everything *ended*.

There would be endings tonight too. She knew Hirschel would be gone when she woke up. She had seen the certainty of it in Herr Ramond's eyes as she came back with the firewood this afternoon. He had been sad and angry. *And sick.* Adina swallowed against the tears that filled her eyes. Probably he would end soon as well.

She tried to curl into a tighter ball beneath the rough blanket. The cold wind that had scattered smoke and ash from the fire and made Herr Ramond cough so hard during the afternoon was gone, but the night was still freezing. She tugged the blanket over her head until there was only a little hole left for watching Hirschel. Like a turtle, Herr Ramond had said. But turtles were lonely and not very warm. Two weeks ago she and Hirschel had shared this blanket, which was lots better than being a cold turtle ...

Hirschel coughed suddenly, and she cried out with him. The dull light of the dying fire made him look almost invisible, like he had already gone away and there was just a shadow left. He whimpered softly and kicked against the cold. *Don't end, Hirschel!* she cried silently. *Please!*

Slowly his frail body relaxed; the ragged breathing stopped completely. Peace enfolded him, replacing the exhausted terror that had long marked his fight with the illness. Adina could not move. *The end,* she thought numbly.

And then Hirschel rolled over. He opened his eyes and called out across the embers that separated them.

"Adina? Are you awake?"

Hope came rushing in on the heels of paralyzing fear, leaving Adina trembling. She struggled to keep her voice at a whisper as she replied. "Yes, I'm awake."

Hirschel continued as if there was nothing wonderful or spectacular about his awakening.

"I had a dream. Mama and Papa were there, and Mama was singing to me."

"A good dream, Hirschel."

"Then they disappeared. At first I was scared, except then another man came and carried me and I was not scared."

"Was it Herr Ramond?"

Hirschel squeezed his eyes shut and then opened them wide. "I don't think so. It did not look like him. He had a nice face and his hands were hurt and also his feet. And he talked to me, and I didn't hurt anymore."

"What did he say?"

"L'Chaim. To life. Like the rabbi said at a bris at the synagogue." Hirschel grinned, and Adina thought she would break with happiness.

Not a dream! Joy, real joy, surged through her, and she laughed aloud. The turtle blanket was suddenly a robe, trailing behind her as she ran to her brother. He was *different,* she realized suddenly. Not only *not sick,* but laughing and smiling like he had before the ending!

Adina spun him in a circle and then leaned over to shake their sleeping guide. "Herr Ramond! Herr Ramond! Wake up …"

Ramond sprawled against the boulder that sheltered the fire. It burned brighter tonight than it had in since Hirschel fell ill, fed with the wood gathered by two sets of energetic hands. Ramond blinked hard and watched Hirschel through the dancing flames. He was well, whole—what was it he had said about the man who made him well? Adina whispered something in his ear, and they both laughed.

Ramond watched them with quiet amazement. Last night he had gone to sleep expecting to wake up and find a corpse. Instead Hirschel had woken him, jumping and laughing and bubbling with excitement about a nice man with hurt hands and feet who made him not scared and then not sick and then …

A miracle. Ramond winced as his chest tightened. His breath was white in the dark air, though the children didn't seem to feel the cold. *Why not*

both of us? he wondered tiredly. If Hirschel could be healed, then why ...?
He shook his head, dully resisting the questions he did not have the energy
to ponder. Today's journey had been grueling for him even without having
to carry the boy.

"Herr Ramond, are we really going to get to Villach?" Adina's thoughtful
voice cut in on his silence.

"Certainly."

"How much longer?"

He frowned, calculating the pitiful distance they'd covered today. "I
think ... maybe two or three ... more days. Four, at the ... most. We may
even ... be able to see ... the city when we camp tomorrow ... night."

Adina nodded in satisfaction and returned her attention to her
brother.

Privately, Ramond wondered what sort of a welcome they could expect
in the city. He had pinned all their hopes on the stories he had heard of
Reinhardt Gottlieb. Reinhardt fought the Gestapo for the release of a
member of his congregation, Reinhardt resisted all the false friendships
and hidden daggers of the German Reich Church, Reinhardt spoke only the
truth, and lived it as well ... but would the pastor take in two Jewish orphans
and see them to freedom? Somehow, Ramond believed he would.

But if not ... doubts lingered in his fever-wearied mind. If Reinhardt
would not help them, there was no hope left. Ramond coughed suddenly
and stiffened with the pain. He ran a hand distractedly over his ragged
beard, trying to think, to come up with some plan in case everything went
wrong again in Villach like it had at Tamsweg ... It was futile, he knew. He
could not take the children farther than Villach—assuming he got them
there at all.

He closed his eyes and leaned back against the rock. Perhaps he should
explain the map to Adina. She had been so full of questions and life today:
Why was it so cold when there wasn't any snow? How did the birds fly
without moving their wings? How far away was Villach? And why couldn't
Herr Ramond keep up with them ...?

He nodded decisively. While the fifteen kilometers might be too much
for him, two healthy children would be able to cover that distance in two
days. *Healthy children.* He smiled and then frowned in concentration,

reducing the instructions to their simplest form. *By tomorrow afternoon we will see the road. Follow it, but stay in the hills as long as you can. When you get to the city find a church and ask about a man named Pastor Gottlieb.*

The words were never said. They were on the tip of his tongue, and then—then he was doubled over on his knees, choking on the taste of his own blood. *Drowning! God!* In the throbbing light he thought he saw his father as they led him away. He tried to call out, to get his attention long enough to say I'm sorry and I love you and good-bye. He couldn't breathe. Hirschel and Adina were alone by the fire, alone without directions or a guide and there was nothing he could do. *Helpless!* He strained to focus on the bright campfire as the world flickered and dimmed. How could a day born in such hope end ... end? His strength spent, Ramond lapsed into darkness.

Somewhere in the night, a voice was speaking. "All flesh is grass, and all its loveliness is like the flower of the field. The grass withers, the flower fades, but the word of our God stands forever. He will feed his flock like a shepherd; he will gather the lambs with his arm, and carry them in His bosom, and gently lead those who are with young." Isaiah 40: 7, 8, 11

The quiet words ran together like water, cool water on the parched sands of his soul. Somewhere in the back of his mind he realized he could breathe again.

"Have you not known? Have you not heard? The Everlasting God, the LORD, the Creator of the ends of the earth, neither faints nor is weary. His understanding is unsearchable. He gives power to the weak, and to those who have no might He increases strength. Even the youths shall faint and be weary, and the young men shall utterly fall, but those who wait on the LORD shall renew their strength; they shall mount up with wings like eagles, they shall run and not be weary, they shall walk and not faint." Isaiah 40: 28-31

As the last sentence echoed, Ramond saw once more the rugged grandeur of the mountains and beheld the glory of the heavens. *Have you not heard?* Was he so quick to forget? Only yesterday the nail-scarred hands of the Everlasting God had reached out to hold Hirschel and bring him back from the brink of death.

Ramond felt himself shrink under the magnitude of galaxies that wheeled above him. So it was true after all. The God Who Is Near *knew*—and in His knowing, there was peace.

"Herr Ramond! Herr Ramond!"

A chorus of anxious voices assaulted him as he blinked and gasped and struggled to sit up. Adina and Hirschel knelt over him, wide-eyed with fear.

"We thought you ended!" Adina sounded close to tears.

"'Cause you didn't wake up when we called your name except now! Don't go 'way again!"

"Promise, Herr Ramond? Please?"

Ramond rolled over and spat and drew a ragged breath.

"Herr Ramond?"

He nodded slowly, ignoring the fire than seemed to be smoldering in his lungs. "Yes. I—" He closed his eyes again and dragged himself upright. "I promise." Cautiously, he tested his heart. The peace remained. He let it wash over him again like a wave, breaking and baptizing on the edge of the sea.

Castles and Angels

THE LAST DAY OF Hirschel and Adina's journey dawned sharp and cold beneath a granite sky. There was no food left, but today it did not matter. Last night the glow of Villach's steeples had illuminated the sky behind the papery November leaves in the grove where they camped. That light had outshined the stars and their campfire combined. And the bells! They had cut the long cold night into hours and brought the morning in with a celebration of sound. Hope was here, sprawled out behind the next hill in a patchwork of cobblestone and brick!

But Adina's thoughts had not yet mounted that final hill. More than anything, she was cold. She knelt beside the sullen red embers of last night's fire. Cupping her hands, she blew on the coals and was rewarded by a single wavering flame. Carefully she laid the last dry branches around it like Herr Ramond did, and soon the fire crackled cheerfully. It was nice, she decided, to be the only one awake in the morning when it wasn't so cold. And today the miracle of joy in her heart burned warmer than the dancing flames.

As if summoned by her thoughts, Hirschel rolled over and settled beside her. Was it really true? For the hundredth time she smiled into his clear brown eyes and listened to the gentle music of his untroubled breathing. For the first time since that terrible dawn in St. Michael, her long-silent heart found a voice to pray. *Blessed are you, O LORD ... who does miracles!*

"Adina?" Hirschel was watching her with curiosity.

"Yes?" He could really talk again!

"Is Herr Ramond an angel?"

Adina turned to see him looking at Herr Ramond with a mixture of wonder and concern. Their guide was asleep sitting up with his back against a tree. Last night she had asked him how he didn't fall over when he slept like that, and he had just shrugged and said it made it a little easier to breathe. So she still wasn't sure how he did it.

"Adina?"

"I—I don't know. He *has* watched over us, but I don't think angels can get sick."

"Maybe he had to get sick when I got sick so he could carry me. And now he will be well again. That man will make him well." He pronounced the last sentence with a faith that could have shaken the mountains.

Adina bit her lip, deep in thought. Hirschel had not watched Herr Ramond get sicker and sicker and keep pretending nothing was wrong. He had not seen how scared their guide's eyes looked when the cough made him fall down, or heard his angry whisper-prayers as he stood up again and kept walking. Adina doubted even an angel would agree to suffer so … but until five nights ago, miracles had been as impossible and unattainable as the distant stars.

"Maybe … maybe so," she conceded.

Both children fell silent as the subject of their conversation blinked and groaned.

"Herr Ramond!"

"You could have … woken me." His voice cracked with fatigue.

Adina shook her head. The hope from Hirschel's words made her feel light.

"We will be in Villach today," she reminded him.

Ramond nodded tiredly. "Ja. Villach." He attempted a smile.

There was little to break up at camp. Adina folded their dirty plaid blankets and shouldered the enormous, empty backpack. Then, a little bit sad, she kicked dust over her small fire. Ramond followed her movements with grateful eyes.

"There is … no more … food?"

Adina shook her head.

"Sorry …" For some reason Herr Ramond looked sad.

"But I am not *so* hungry," she added quickly.

"Me neither. I will not *ever* eat hard bread and sausage and stinky cheese again!" Hirschel declared.

Ramond nodded. "Good boy. Good—" He braced himself against the tree as a fit of coughing shook him like a brittle leaf.

"Can you get up, Herr Ramond?" Adina asked softly when it had passed.

He gave a terse nod and closed his eyes in concentration. Slowly, he pushed up until he was leaning on the trunk.

"If you want to you can hold my hand," Hirschel offered.

Ramond smiled as he tried to regain his breath. "Thank you. That … would be good."

"Is it that way, Herr Ramond?" Adina pointed at the last hill.

He nodded slowly. "Are you … the guide … today?"

"Ja. Follow me but not too far behind, and we can stop and take breaks if you need them but not too many because we don't want to be late!"

Ramond bowed slightly at the echo of his own instructions. "Certainly. I am … following, Adina."

And so with the reminder of a miracle and the hope of a promise, the ragged band ascended the final hill of their journey.

Lists, Karl thought wearily as he read again the request that the records of Jewish-owned businesses in Villach be reexamined for accuracy. It was not a strange order in and of itself, but this was the third time in a week! *Diplomat Vom Rath dead in Paris, the Fuehrer in a rage, and Berlin orders that our accounts of Jewish commerce be updated?* It made no sense. But then again, less and less was making sense in the Reich these days. Karl scraped his chair backward and stalked out of the room.

He had crossed the dim hallway and made it as far as the door to the archive room when Thomas's voice sounded behind him. "Heil Hitler, Karl." The swarthy man exhaled the words in a single breath and then paused, as if he had not yet pondered what to say next.

Karl flatly returned the greeting. "Heil Hitler."

"What are you doing?" Thomas asked at last.

Karl turned to face him, reading an edge of suspicion in the agent's inquisitive stare. He considered asking Thomas what *he* was doing, following him like an unwanted stray, but immediately thought better of it. "Orders," he replied curtly, thrusting the paper at Thomas's barrel chest.

The bulky man gave the paper a cursory glance before blurting, "Are you ready?"

"For what?" Karl scowled. "To read through three pages of shops owned by Meyers and Cohens and Levys? I did that yesterday and the day before as well."

Karl's intentional rudeness did not dampen the enthusiasm of the other agent. "They're preparing for something big, you know."

"Of course. When has our Fuehrer ever done anything small?"

Karl opened the door and stepped into the cool darkness of the archive room. Flipping on the light, he inhaled the sharp scent of paper and ink.

Thomas followed him and did the same. "But you must have heard the rumors."

Karl shrugged noncommittally, wishing Thomas would take his rumors and go somewhere else. Somewhere far away, like England or France. *And if he happened to get arrested in the process ...*

"In Paris." Thomas was saying.

Karl's head snapped up in surprise. Had he mumbled his wish aloud?

"And now that he is dead—"

No. He is talking about Vom Rath again. Concentrate, Karl! Nod and act like you care what he is saying!

"The Fuehrer has not said anything publicly yet, but of course we are all being put on high alert. There is to be a great demonstration tonight, all across Germany!"

Karl frowned, conscious that for once Thomas was saying something important. "Yes?"

Thomas nodded.

Ignoring him, Karl walked a few paces farther into the too-bright caverns of card files. *Jewish commerce. Section B4. It should be on the right.* He found the file he needed and turned back.

Thomas was still staring at him, close-set eyes narrowed with mistrust. "You are not pleased with this news."

It was not a question or even a statement; it was an accusation. That realization raced through Karl like a bolt of electricity just as he opened his mouth to reply. *Spy!* He held his tongue and glared at the man in front of him.

"Tell Fredrik I will be wherever I am needed."

The men eyed each other warily for a moment, like two lions uncertain of whether to attack. Then Thomas's animosity slipped beneath the surface again, replaced by a condescending smirk.

Karl lifted his chin angrily. "Is that all, Thomas?"

"No. You need to come with me."

"Where?" Karl's voice was harsh, but this time the gruffness covered fear.

"With me," Thomas repeated, indicating with a jerk of his large head the direction they were taking.

Karl looked down at the folder in his hands, suddenly preferring the lists to another second in the company of Fredrik's spy. But it was an order. He slowly replaced the file and followed Thomas down the dark corridor.

Eva wanted to turn off the radio. As the recorded voice from Munich dealt out judgment on the innocent and held out steadfast promises of destruction, she wanted nothing more than to flip the dial and fill her house again with sweet silence.

But she did not. Something held her breathless in horrified apprehension as Germany's Minister of Propaganda raged on and on. From the handful of details scattered throughout the impassioned rhetoric, Eva gathered that a young German diplomat had been shot in Paris—by a Jew.

One man. How dare they care for one life among the thousands they have crushed? But it seemed Germany cared very much about her own. With cold dread she listened as Goebbels called for a righteous vengeance against the Jews, those "stained by the blood of a brave son of the Reich!"

Mercifully, the speech was over. Eva looked down at her shaking hands and silently blessed the harsh military music. Outside the window, the bell tower of St. Jakob's was visible over the trees that separated her from the city. Surely the turmoil of Germany would not reach them here. The promised storm would blow above them, and they would be safe in the shadow of the mountains …

The abrupt return of the news bulletin shattered her wish like the snowflakes dashed against the stony cliffs.

"This monstrous and dastardly attack on the Reich cannot go unchallenged!" The normally bored voice of one of Villach's newscasters trembled with rabid excitement. "We cannot let this deed go unpunished! We must show the Jews the justice of Germany!"

Eva lunged forward to silence the radio and then fell back, shaking. *The justice of Germany.* The phrase echoed evilly in the placid living room. Germany's justice was murdered husbands and broken hearts.

She looked out the window again. Now the mountains rose to form the walls of a giant bowl. The coming darkness would not pass above the valley, it would fill it up. And there was no place to run.

Villach had been a word of hope for weeks now, but neither child had expected such a sight. Rising from the trees directly in front of them, the stone walls and towers of an ancient castle reared over the city of their promise. Adina and Hirschel stopped short in awe.

A smile lit Ramond's eyes at the children's surprise. He had been only a few years older than Adina when his father brought him here. "Landskron … Landskron Castle," he panted.

The name seemed to take on a magic of its own as both children whispered it reverently. Ramond wished he had the breath to talk, to tell them the long-forgotten stories of this archaic fortress. As they approached, the castle began to show signs of age. The ground was scattered with fist-sized stones from the crumbling walls, and the entire roof had fallen in.

Ramond thought of a decrepit guard, fading and broken but still standing watch over its charges. *Still standing.* A weary smile flickered across his face. "Almost …"

"Almost there," Hirschel finished for him. "Herr Ramond, when we get there will you be at a hospital?"

Ramond started to shrug in reply when a sound made him freeze.

Voices! God, not again— Hirschel and Adina seemed rooted in place. With sudden strength he propelled them toward a gap in the wall.

"And I tell you, Inspekteur Schmidt will be satisfied with nothing less than total affirmation from the church. The longer they hold out, the angrier he gets. I do not envy you, Karl. Bad luck to get stuck with such a stubborn lot."

"More stubborn than you know." The voice of the man called Karl was somehow sad. "Stubborn. Yes. A foolish courage."

The two speakers drifted away, leaving Ramond desperately cold. *There is no safety here! Not even here!* He was shivering now from fever and fear. *Foolish courage.* Was it such a misplaced hope that had brought them through the mountains? Had his deluded bravery led them from Tamsweg to here, to this end? Ramond looked miserably at the children. They were both frightened. Both hopeful. Both still wearing those ridiculous once-bright wool hats. They looked every bit the part of illegal refugees. There was no way they could enter Villach! Someone in the city would see. Someone would ask questions. And there were no answers ...

"But I AM with you. Never will I leave you; never will I forsake you. Ramond, do not be afraid! Lead the children as I lead you. Take courage, my son ... you are nearly home."

The sound of that Voice was deeper than the thunder in the mountains and clearer than the fire of a thousand stars. Peace returned suddenly—for who could not be at peace in such a Presence? Ramond exhaled softly and opened his eyes. Silence had fallen in the ruins, and Hirschel and Adina watched him expectantly.

"We will ... keep going. Almost home. You ... you will be safe."

He was still bent with exhaustion and pain, still fighting for the breath to speak, but something had changed. There was joy in his eyes. Assurance. Ramond did not know it, but in that moment he looked very much like an angel.

Refuge

"My feet hurt. Please carry me." Hirschel tugged urgently at Adina's arm.

"I can't carry you," she replied wearily.

"Herr Ramond—"

"Can't carry you either, Hirschel." Adina spoke in a rush, hoping Herr Ramond would not hear.

"But he did!"

"But he can't right now because ... just because."

"Herr Ramond?" Hirschel appealed to the higher authority.

"Adina ... is right. I can't ... carry ... you. You have ... to walk. To be ... a brave ... boy. Can ... you do that?"

Hirschel nodded and blinked back exhausted tears. Ramond wished he had the breath to explain that if it were at all possible he *would* carry him—but then again, if he could put a single sentence together without stopping for air, the little boy would almost certainly be in his arms. *Nearly home.* He swallowed hard, longing to share his joy with the children. *But it is a pastor we are seeking! He will tell them the story, and they will tell him of the miracles we have seen.* The thought cheered him.

"Let's keep going."

Adina resumed her role as pathfinder as they picked their way down the slope toward the city. Hirschel followed his sister, and Ramond stumbled behind them. Twice he fell on the brittle grass. *But those who trust in the LORD—are nearly home. Soon.* The words became anthem in his heart, urging him on.

At last the ground leveled, and they were on the outskirts of the city. Fear flashed through him until he remembered the promise. *Lead the children as I lead you …*

"I am following, Lord," Ramond whispered. "Show me the way." He hesitated for a moment at the road, and then, not knowing why, turned to walk alongside it. Suddenly he remembered that he did not know the pastor's address. For some reason that thought made him laugh. The laughter dissolved into a fit of coughing, but when he could breathe again he realized it was still funny. It was indeed a joke of sorts: to wander into a city a hundred kilometers from where they should have been in hopes of finding a pastor he had never met who would help two children who shouldn't be alive. Ramond was certain they would find him.

For a long time they walked along the shoulder of the road. There were no cars. Just trees and the faint tolling of the bells—fainter now than they had been an hour before. At last he saw the small, stone-fronted cottage. He stopped for a moment in the road. He didn't know how, but he *knew*—this house was both punch line and punctuation of the long and desperate journey. Smiling, he slowly climbed the stairs and raised his fist to knock.

Once. Twice. Three times, and Hirschel and Adina held their breath. Just as he prepared to knock a fourth time, the door swung open to reveal a young, sad-faced woman.

"This is … the house of … Reinhardt Gottlieb?"

"Who are you?"

Ramond heard the fear drain from her voice as she took in their ragged appearance. He imagined what she must be seeing. *Gaunt bodies. Torn and filthy clothing. Hollow, hopeful eyes.* Could she see that hope? The fear and the trust and—yes, the laughter in it all? Could she see that, or did her vision stop outside their hearts?

"Who are you?" she asked again, gentler this time.

"Travelers … seeking shelter … can Pastor Gottlieb help … us?"

A shadow seemed to cross the woman's face, and the fear returned to her eyes. "Come inside." She motioned for them to hurry, her eyes sweeping the road behind them for any unwanted watchers. Ramond pretended not to notice as he stepped gratefully into the warmth. There was no wind, no biting chill in the air—the heat of the little house seemed like a miracle in itself! He gazed hungrily at the furniture in the room. A champagne-colored settee. Two lamps. There was even a piano in the corner beside the fireplace! Ramond smiled again, strangely amazed that the furniture was real. They were here, somehow, long after he had broken but maybe not failed ...

"I am Eva Gottlieb." Weary heads bobbed in excitement, and Hirschel and Adina looked up at Herr Ramond in awe. Perhaps he was an angel after all.

"Reinhardt ... was my husband." She paused, struggling to master the tide of emotions that swelled in her voice. So much regret and sorrow in those simple words! "He was killed—murdered—by the Gestapo ... three months ago, now. He is gone."

Ramond leaned heavily against the door frame as a terrible silence filled the room. His mind spun with confusion. Reinhardt dead? Then how—why—had they been led here? *Lord? I thought ... here ... You brought us ...* his fragmented prayer trailed off in incomprehension.

"I—I am so sorry," he managed at last. "These children ... orphans. To get papers ... Tamsweg. The SS ... was drilling. We ran. I thought ... your husband could ... help us. Nowhere else ... nowhere else to go. We were led ..."

Ramond knew he wasn't making any sense but was too exhausted for words. Whatever strength had sustained him through the last agonizing kilometers suddenly fled, and he sagged against the wall. He was coughing again: violent, racking coughs. *Take courage, my son.* For a fraction of a second, he sought Hirschel's eyes in silent apology, and then he crumpled to the floor.

Katrina had quietly braced herself for the worst when she received Eva's urgent request to come. Two refugee children and a dying man, however, exceeded even her expectations.

"You shouldn't stay long, Trina."

That had been Eva's greeting as she opened the door. Through the hurried explanation of the afternoon's events, her fear had not lifted.

Now Katrina stood above the bed where the filthy guide slept.

"The children call him Herr Ramond," Eva offered from the doorway.

Katrina nodded. "Ramond." She resisted the urge to release the barrage of questions that flooded her mind. *What are the symptoms? How long has he been like this? How has his condition progressed?* Those were the questions of a nurse, and she knew Eva did not have the answers. Instead, she laid a hand on his forehead. He was burning with fever.

"Ramond," she said again, sadly. Beneath the ragged beard, the bone-white face on the pillow looked very young. He was nineteen, she guessed, maybe twenty.

"He was coughing?" Katrina asked at last.

"Not at first." Eva's voice sounded weary. "When he talked ... it was very ... choppy, like ... this. He asked for Reinhardt. I told him he was gone, and he tried to explain ... something. I don't know. He was coughing terribly hard when he passed out."

"Was there blood?" Katrina did not look up to see Eva's pained expression.

"Some."

"And he has not come around?"

"For a few seconds ... but not again."

Katrina let out the breath she'd been holding in a long, quiet sigh. A single word whispered at the back of her mind, terrifying in its finality. *Tuberculosis.*

She was not certain, of course. Dr. Brandt would make that proclamation. But if it were true ... *To a patient in a sanatorium, they say "rest and pray." Rest for the body, to ease the pain of the disease. And prayer for the soul because there is almost nothing a doctor can do.*

But Katrina did not speak such thoughts aloud. She did not tell Eva even the name of the disease that she feared.

"Trina? What should we do?"

Katrina stepped away from the bed and turned back to Eva.

"Do you want me to take him to the hospital tonight? We will make up a story ... call him a beggar or a lost hiker we found."

"Not tonight." Eva's adamant answer surprised Katrina.

"Why not? He's very ill, and—"

"Haven't you heard the radio today? The diplomat in Paris ... something—I'm afraid, Trina."

Katrina frowned and considered Eva's words. The death of Ernst Vom Rath, coming two days after the young assassin's attack, had been passed from mouth to mouth all day in a buzz of speculation. Someone had heard something of the possibility of a demonstration somewhere—and so the rumors flew. The gentle Doctor Brandt had gone as far as to warn the nurses not to venture too far from home tonight.

Katrina would have gladly disregarded all this had she believed the hospital would afford any help to the stranger who lay so pale and still in Eva's guest bedroom. But she did not. And with Eva's safety to consider as well … she bowed to her friend's request and followed her quietly out of the room.

Eva sat on her bed, silently staring at the picture of her and Reinhardt's wedding. She knew Katrina was just behind her, but she did not move.

"I will take Ramond to the hospital tomorrow, Eva. But these children—what will you do with them?"

It was unlike Katrina to cut directly to the heart of the topic at hand. Tonight there were no dramatic flourishes, no long words or unnecessary adjectives. Any other day, this might have coaxed a smile from Eva. *What happened to your vocabulary, Trina?* But tonight she remained fixed in place. She could not turn to face Katrina, could not bear to let her see the fear and the anguish that she knew was written on her face.

"Eva?"

She quickly shook her head. "I don't know, Katrina." Irritation masked the tremor in her voice.

"Will you keep them here with you?"

"No!" The word was so like a cry of physical pain that Katrina flinched. "No," Eva said again, this time in a whisper. "How could I keep them here?"

Katrina sat beside her and started to respond, but Eva cut her off. "When he—Ramond—came, he asked for Reinhardt. And Reinhardt is gone … dead. He would have helped them. But … I'm not Reinhardt, and—I can't." She finished abruptly, shoulders shaking as she fought against the tears that threatened to break her control.

"Eva. Eva." Katrina said her name gently, like a mother whispering away the fear from a nightmare. But it was too late to stop the weeks of pent-up grief and anxiety from spilling over.

"Reinhardt loved people like this. Reinhardt gave his life to save a family like this. Reinhardt—not me. I'm not a hero. Only alone. And I can't help these children. I don't know how. I'm not strong enough. And I don't want to be strong enough! I only want Reinhardt back!"

Eva covered her face with her hands, trying to muffle the sounds of her weeping from the children sleeping in the sitting room.

"You can cry, Eva. It's all right." Katrina embraced her tightly. "But you are not alone. No. Christ is here. He is watching over His own, even here where darkness falls."

Eva shook her head and pulled away. "You've always seen His hand, Trina. Always heard His voice. Maybe I'm blind; maybe I'm deaf. But when I look around, I cannot see anything—nothing but the evil and the fear. And I'm afraid." She looked miserably at Katrina, expecting to see reproach in her eyes. Instead there was only bright compassion.

"Eva. Eva. I know. There is so much to fear here. The mountains are falling into the sea, and yet … somehow we are secure. If you can't find the strength to trust the promise of His love, will you at least trust me when I tell you it is still true? God could not abandon you or me any more than a mother could forget about the child she holds in her arms. And even if… if she were to forget, He would go on loving!"

"I wish I could believe that," Eva whispered bleakly.

"Look at me," Katrina murmured, clasping Eva's hands between her own. "You haven't lost your faith. No. I know your heart is broken, but … He is the Healer."

"I hope you are right."

Katrina bit her lip and nodded. "And these children—I will keep them if you cannot. But tonight …" She glanced from her watch to the window and back again. "Tonight they may be safer with you. Outside the town, ja?"

"I suppose." Eva's voice was hollow, as if all the life and hope had gone out of her.

"I wish I had a better answer to give you. Truly I do! But … one night.

Show them love for one night, even if you do not feel it. Perhaps you are entertaining angels, ja?"

"Perhaps." Eva smiled faintly at Katrina's gentle reminder. *I was a stranger and you invited Me in … whatever you did for the least of these brothers of mine, you did for Me.* Matthew 25:35, 40

Katrina stood suddenly and looked at the clock. "It's past eight. I should be going."

"Yes. You must. But Ramond—"

"I will come tomorrow after work and say I found him when I was walking up near the castle. Until then, keep him warm. If he wakes, give him soup; if not, let him sleep."

Katrina paused in the hallway to look back at her friend. "And Eva—"

"Yes?"

"Be careful."

Eva watched the taillights of Katrina's old Ford until they winked around a bend in the road and disappeared. Satisfied her vague sense of dread had not materialized into something dark and horrible in the night outside, she turned and pulled the curtains tightly across the window.

Hirschel and Adina had not moved from where they slept by the fireplace. Sprawled out side by side on the floor, they reminded Eva of the kittens she had raised in Vienna. She smiled faintly. Those cats had been the pride and joy of her seven-year-old heart. She played with them, petted them, talked to them … and then Mama had given them away when they got too big and boisterous. *I was at school,* Eva remembered. *I went to school and when I came back they were gone. How I cried for those kittens! I swore I would never forget them, forgive my mother, or be happy again.*

Eva smiled again, wryly. She had eventually forgiven her mother, though the cats were not forgotten. And she had been happy, with Reinhardt …

She returned her attention to the children. Remembered kittens notwithstanding, they would need food and hot baths tonight. *But which first?* she wondered. Her own stomach growled, and she squinted to read the face of the grandfather clock. *Already half past eight! Supper first then.*

She padded quietly past the two sleeping children and into the kitchen.

She had made potato soup this afternoon—rich and creamy and perfect for this cold, uncertain night. All that remained was to reheat it on the stove. She easily crossed the small kitchen in the dark and ran her hand over the shelf beside the oven, locating the matches by touch. She lit the burner beneath the pot of soup and quickly blew out the flame. Darkness seemed somehow safer tonight.

Invisible, Eva thought. *If no light shines from the windows, then we are just another boulder at the base of this mountain. Nothing strange. Nothing dangerous.* Indeed, she wanted to hide tonight. The presence of the two children and their guide felt like a beacon, a wide-open door that would let *something* in. Eva shuddered as she wrapped her hands around the warming pot. Suddenly she wanted nothing more than to go to bed and pull the covers over her head and wait for morning. *Or to talk to Reinhardt.* She groped for a spoon from the jar of utensils. *He would have turned on all the lights and thrown a party for these two children. And the guide, Ramond—he would have known what to do with him as well.*

She gave the soup a more vicious stir. Yes, she knew what Reinhardt would have done. And with him beside her, it would have felt safe and right. But now, tonight, alone … it was all she could do to cook soup in the dark for these ragged strangers.

And pray. She heard the words in Katrina's voice. It was no wonder—Katrina was forever reminding her of such things. Katrina, with her fearless love and unshakeable faith.

She sighed. Katrina could pray—and Eva hoped she *was* praying tonight. *But I don't know if I can.* The blackness of the kitchen pressed down on her like the fog that rolled in with a late-autumn thunderstorm, muffling hope and reassuring her no one would hear. *The mountains are falling into the sea, but we are secure …*

"Help, Lord," she whispered at last. But only silence replied, so she turned the stove off and went to wake the children.

It was just past midnight when four unmarked trucks halted directly in front of St. Jakob Church. Whispered instructions rustled through the ranks of young storm troopers hunched inside, were confirmed, and then repeated with enthusiasm. At precisely 1:20 a.m., the first shouts and angry footsteps sounded in Villach's streets like far-off thunder echoing in the mountains.

The tiny synagogue was the first to burn. From there the flames of greedy destruction lapped outward to ravage the city, a conflagration of organized chaos. And the low, cloud-laden sky reflected crimson as Villach woke from night to nightmare.

The muted roaring pulled Eva from a reluctant sleep. She opened her eyes and looked around, trying to remember why she had fallen asleep in the chair beside the fireplace. *Something ... Katrina was here, and—the children. Oh. Oh.*

Suddenly awake, she held her breath and listened to the noise outside. Too sharp for rain, too irregular for hail—what *was* it? She frantically searched the room, suddenly possessed by a nameless fear. At last her gaze rested on her piano. A sliver of dull light reflected on the wood's dark patina—light? It seemed to grow brighter in the darkness of the living room. Shrugging the blanket off, she drifted toward it and laid her hand in the glow. *Red! But why—*

Eva snatched her hand from the bloody light and stood trembling in the center of the sitting room. Something *was* coming, *was* happening, was already here—she shook her head and breathed deeply, trying to muster the courage to walk to the window. *A meter and a half. Just to see, to know ...*

She shuffled forward, brushed the curtain aside a fraction of an inch ... and simply stood. Stared at the wild light and tried to comprehend. An unnatural dawn illuminated the sky beneath the city half a kilometer away. It pulsed and ebbed with the tide of terrifying sound.

"*Bitte*—"

Eva jumped and dropped the corner of the curtain before she remembered the strangers who were here with her. She stilled the swaying fabric before running toward the front bedroom. The guide was perched on the side of the bed, trying to stand.

"Help me," he whispered hoarsely, nodding toward where the lace curtains pulsed with the evil light.

Eva hesitated, uncertain whether to draw the curtain or help the man stand. At last fear decided. She would not let in any more of this terrible night. Guiding his arm around her shoulder, she lifted him to his feet. He leaned heavily against her as they made slow progress to the window. His breath came harsh and unsteady, loud even over the shrieking wind outside.

"What—what are they ... doing?"

Eva let the drapery swing back from where she had been holding it. Meeting the guide's eyes for the first time, she simply shook her head in anger and helplessness. *They are destroying. What else? This place is no different than wherever you fled. No safer. No better. Not at all.*

He seemed to read the bitter words in her face. Or perhaps he simply heard them in the screams of the furious storm outside.

"Where ... can I go?" The words were barely a whisper.

Nowhere! Nowhere is safe for you, for me, for these children you have brought!

"Where can I ... go ... from Your presence? Where can ... I flee, but You, God ... You are there?"

Eva stared at him in disbelief. Where did he find the strength to hope in that promise tonight? To trust? The world was burning! Dark! There was no more hope! And yet ...

"Even there—here—Your ... hand shall ... lead me. Hold me."

Just then the little girl appeared in the doorway.

"Herr Ramond! They followed us!" Adina's voice trembled on the edge of panic. Without waiting for an answer, she ran to Ramond and buried her face in his side.

"No, Adina." His instruction was scarcely louder than his prayer as he wrapped his free arm around the child. "No. We are ... safe. Here ... hear Him. We are safe."

Eva closed her eyes and said nothing. How could this man named Ramond promise such things? There was nothing to keep the shadows in the street from coming here too! No guarantee the fire would not also set them ablaze!

But she did not speak, and in the silence they stood to wait for morning.

The Promise

THE STARS HAD VIEWED centuries of triumph and terror since the beginning. Tonight they gleamed distant and cold as lives were shattered like so much glass. Beneath them, the flames of dying synagogues dotted the Greater Reich in a constellation of human suffering.

At last the darkness began to recede, and the icy points of light faded in the first wash of dawn. A gust of frigid wind swept over the open platform of Villach's freight train station, sharp with the acrid stench of hope gone up in smoke. Of the sixty-five men who stood shoulder to shoulder there, many stared ahead in numb incomprehension. A few cast longing looks back to the town where wives and children doubtlessly huddled in uncertain terror. One kept his gaze trained on the cobalt sky, beseeching the silent witnesses there to remember.

Karl paced around the group with tired steps. He felt the eyes of some of the men following his meaningless journey. Back and forth. 'Round and 'round. Like a sheepdog keeping an unruly flock in line—only these men did not resist. Did not struggle.

It would be pointless, Karl knew, as he eyed the line of stony-faced SS guards. Ten stood with their backs to the train tracks, machine guns loaded and trained on the center of the group. Two sleek German shepherds strained and growled at the end of their leads, completing the savage picture.

Wolves, Karl thought darkly, veering closer to the prisoners to avoid the reach of one of the snarling dogs. The owner grinned at his discomfort.

"Do not worry, Agent Zehr," the man called loudly. "Our dogs will not harm you. They like only the taste of *Jewish* blood!"

Laughter rippled up and down the platform, sounding somehow hollow and dead in the gray light of day. The owner of the dog suddenly gave his beast a meter more lead. The animal lunged toward the prisoners, fangs bared. Cries erupted as the men surged away from the savage creature.

Now the laughter among the guards was uproarious. Karl hurried his steps until he was behind the group of prisoners, not lifting his gaze from the weather-worn boards of the platform. He felt his face grow hot in the cold air. *We are the wolves,* he realized as another guard fired his gun into the air and screamed for order. The men froze and fell silent again.

Order. Orders. It was my orders to be here and witness this madness. My orders to help carry it out. He clenched and unclenched his fists, suddenly furiously angry. Angry at people like Fredrik and the monsters and their dogs, who took pleasure in this punishment of the innocent. Angry at the prisoners for enduring their persecutors' sport in submissive silence. And angry at himself most of all, caught between the SS and the prisoners and on the side of neither. *This is the cause I am sworn to! This—to inflict terror and take life! And this ... this is my victory.*

The clashing of metal on metal announced the approach of the train that would carry the prisoners away. Karl grimaced as it came into view. It was a freight train—a string of metal boxes being used to transport men. No sooner had it ground to a torturous stop than the guards were yelling, herding the group of men into a car near the engine.

Karl turned away in utter disgust as blows and curses rained down on the stumbling prisoners. For him, the ordeal was over. He was free to go.

✶

Eva woke on the floor of her own bedroom just as the first gleam of day found its way through her curtains. Stretching her stiff muscles one by one, she silently blessed the watery light. It was natural, real, the morning after the long nightmare.

The night. The cry of a departing train was piercing and cold in the gray dawn. In it was the last echo of the burning, the smashing, the destroying storm. A moment longer, even that sound faded. Villach was quiet—not the quiet of a town asleep but rather the empty, final silence of a tomb.

In the calm Eva wondered about Katrina. Had she been caught in the riot? What if—Eva closed her eyes. She would not, could not consider that possibility. Not yet. Before eight o'clock she would find some pretext for calling her, to make sure, but for now she would only let her concern travel as far as the three people within her walls. *The children may be safer with you … outside the town.* Despite her resolve, Eva felt worry churning in the pit of her stomach. Why, *why* hadn't she asked Katrina to spend the night here?

Because I didn't have enough beds. We could have both easily slept on the floor, but I was worried about beds. She shook her head as she stood and took her robe from its hook on the door. In reality, even her worst imaginings had not come close to the terror of the riot last night. She hadn't foreseen—but no one had, for that matter.

"But here we are safe." She whispered the sentence, a benediction over the two children asleep in her bed. Ramond's words had proven true after all. And although she did not call it a miracle, she was grateful, as grateful as she was for the new morning.

Eva quietly opened the heavy door to her room and slipped out. The silence was still oppressive. Even the birds had the wisdom not to sing this morning. She felt her way down the stairs in the semidarkness and then stopped, wary of the openness and the light of the front room. Upstairs, in the single room on top of the house, the illusion of safety had been stronger. *But it is over now,* she reminded herself.

Unwillingly she remembered the vigil they had held in that terrible light. For more than an hour they had stood, silent, as the glow of the burning buildings bathed the room in unnatural radiance. Eva had been silent, at least. The faint murmur of Ramond's prayers had not ceased until his knees buckled in exhaustion. Only after that had Eva convinced Adina that it was safe to sleep.

Now Eva opened the door to Ramond's room hesitantly. Half-afraid the guide would have stopped breathing altogether, she listened with relief to the sound of his shallow panting. He was not dead but asleep. *And not sleeping quite that deeply either, thank goodness.* Eva permitted herself a half smile as she padded across the room and settled into the old rocking chair beside the bed. That was the type of humor Reinhardt had loved. A hidden reference here, a quotation there—all of it flowing directly from the Scriptures. *As did everything else,* Eva reflected. How she missed that unwavering faith! Reinhardt's belief had been the hands cupped around her own unsteady flame. But now …

Perhaps that was why she was sitting in Ramond's room in the bleak light of the November morning, hoping against hope he would wake up. The trust he carried comforted her, somehow. It was easier to believe in the guiding hand of God while looking at a wanderer who had found shelter just in time—even if that shelter was as imperfect as her home.

She did not have long to wait. A low, racking cough shook the guide's thin frame, and then he was awake, blinking at the flower-speckled wallpaper in a sort of dreamy incomprehension.

"Ramond?" Eva timidly ventured.

He turned toward her with difficulty.

"Did you sleep well?" She felt entirely foolish now, coming into his room and practically waking him only to ask mindless questions.

"Certainly." A dip of the head, the flash of a joke … for an instant he reminded her of her younger brother, Stefan. Then he coughed again, hard, and the illusion vanished. "So good … to be warm. Thank you."

"It is nothing." Eva was embarrassed by his gratitude. "Anyone—"

"No. Not … anyone. You must be … very like your husband … was."

Eva smiled sadly. *No. I am not like him. For your sake now I wish I were, but I am still only Eva. Still only alone and frightened and powerless to help you or the two little ones you have brought.*

The silence stretched on into one minute, then two, and Ramond seemed to be drifting back toward sleep. Suddenly he fixed his cobalt eyes on Eva's with pressing urgency. "Frau Gottlieb—the children …" He paused as another spasm of coughing gripped him.

"Fast asleep upstairs." She tried not to look at the blood on the sleeve he pressed to his mouth, already half-dreading what his real question would be.

"Will you … take them in … out of the Reich? Somewhere … safe?"

So that was it. The *question.* The one thing she had said she could not, *would not* do. There were ten reasons—no, fifteen! Twenty!—why she couldn't do what he asked. *I am the widow, not the hero! I was never involved in Reinhardt's refugee work—I know less of it than you do! And do you think two skin-and-bones children would not be noticed if they suddenly appeared with me? I am already watched by the Gestapo! No. It is impossible. Ask someone else. Not me.*

Eva bit her lip and looked at the ceiling in anguish, wondering how to put into words her refusal. *No, I cannot, but we will find someone else ...*

Who, Eva? The silent demand was jarring. Eva glanced down at Ramond to make sure he hadn't spoken it. But he was still watching her, pleading wordlessly for the children.

Who? Who indeed? If not me ... then who? And so in trembling obedience Eva spoke the impossible. "Hirschel and Adina ... yes. I will."

For an instant the joy that lit Ramond's face made her forget her shaking hands and racing heart.

"Yes. I see now. Thank You," he breathed. "And thank you, Eva ... Gottlieb. So much ... but they are miracles." He smiled, oblivious to her bewilderment. "Ask them. We have seen ... miracles. Hirschel—" Again the cough cut him off. "Ask the children," he implored, when he could speak again.

Eva nodded. "Shhh. Yes, I will ask them. But don't try to talk. I'll make breakfast and bring it to you, if you are hungry. Then I will call Katrina ... and then I will ask Hirschel and Adina what miracles you have seen."

She smiled hopefully, but Ramond was already asleep.

Heaven is trying to put out the fires. That was Karl's waking thought as he opened his eyes and blinked out at the curtain of falling snow.

He rubbed his eyes and slowly sat up, certain now that his two-hour nap had done more harm than good. His head pounded with tiredness, as if no time at all had passed since he stumbled up the cold stairway to his apartment in the early morning hours. In the tiny bedroom, nothing had changed. His desk to the left of the door was still threatening to collapse beneath the mountain of clutter atop it, and his smoky clothes lay where he had thrown them.

Heaven is trying to put out the fires. Karl frowned and pulled the coarse red blanket more tightly around his broad shoulders. It trailed behind him like a bedraggled cape as he shuffled to the window. The snow was falling thickly now, silent and pure in response to the angry sparks that had invaded the sky last night. *Last night …* Karl groaned. More than anything, he did not want to think about last night. Didn't want to remember what his precise, meticulous lists had done in the hands of the crazed storm troopers.

They arrested sixty-seven men. But only sixty-five were sent to Mauthausen this morning …

The images were vivid in his mind. *A boy and his father. The boy was crippled. When they took him he couldn't keep up. He fell in the street, and the father stopped …*

Karl pressed his face against the cold glass. How he wished he could simply freeze the memories, bury them in the snow outside and sleep! *The storm trooper was probably the same age as the crippled boy. But he was stronger. And he started to beat them. I yelled at him to stop and he laughed. And then it was too late …*

Sixty-seven. Sixty-five. Karl remembered the train platform this morning: the mocking, the shouting, the silence. If heaven was indeed trying to intervene, the snow was too little and much too late. The fire had already burned and devoured and destroyed. What good was it to simply cover the ashes?

Without warning, Reinhardt's words cut through the fray of his ragged thoughts. *In the end, Truth is all that will remain, shining in the midst of these shattered lives and your broken promises, calling men and women to Himself.*

Himself. But who is He, this One called Truth? Karl rubbed his deaf ear almost desperately, as if the answer to this riddle might be whispering behind the silence. He remembered the day he had found Gottlieb's wife playing the organ in the empty church. For a moment the music and the stained glass murals had fused into one bright, dazzling beauty—almost blinding in the gray of his life. And just as it ended, he had seen Him. *The one they call Jesus.* The picture was as clear in his mind as the memories of the violence last night. *He stood in the center of the portals, arms open. Living. Calling …*

Karl sighed quietly and turned away from the window. The portrait in the church was just that—a portrait. It—He— changed nothing. The synagogue had burned last night. Two men had been murdered on the street, and over sixty more had been jammed into a freight car and sent to Austria's most notorious labor camp.

And Karl had been part of it.

The eggs were boiling by the time the children came downstairs. Eva had just turned from the stove to the counter to slice bread for toast when she saw them wavering in the doorway.

"Good morning!" Eva greeted them with a cheerfulness she did not feel.

Hirschel smiled shyly in reply.

"Come and sit down. Breakfast is almost ready—do you like hot chocolate?"

They nodded gravely.

"Good. I will just heat the milk up, and there will be enough for all of us. I don't usually drink hot chocolate at breakfast, but today is a good day to have some. Do you think so?"

By this time both children had settled cautiously at the table. Eva smiled brightly as she busied herself with making the hot chocolate.

"Frau Gottlieb? Will the bad men come back?" Adina asked in the silence.

Eva laid the wooden spoon down and turned to look back toward the children. "No. They did not come here at all, and they will not come out again," she declared more firmly than she believed. "And today is—"

"Snowing!" Hirschel announced happily.

"What?" Eva pivoted to face the living room window. The little boy was right—the first snow of the winter was falling fast. *Snow already! But that means—the river … Oh no.* Mechanically she fished the eggs out of the water and set them on a plate. *Snowing!* Reinhardt had never said much about where his refugees went, but she knew the Drau was always involved. *The river. He always took them to the river. But if it freezes in the snow …*

The hot chocolate was done now, so she ladled the sweet liquid carefully into three mugs. Just as carefully, she carried them to the table and sat.

"Is the snow bad, Frau Gottlieb?" Adina was watching her worriedly.

Yes. Very bad. This storm may have trapped you here. In any case, I don't even know who I can ask to help you! I was very, very foolish to promise that I would take you in. But Eva could not tell the children such things. Miracles or not, they had been through too much already. So she simply shook her head no.

"It is very good that you came to my house yesterday. Today it is far too cold to be outside."

Satisfied with her answer, Adina nodded and bowed her head. A moment passed in uncomfortable silence before Eva realized the children were waiting for her to pray. She offered up a hasty blessing before setting the basket of bread on the table. Then, pursued by her false words of gratitude, she hurried from the kitchen to her room.

It was thirst that woke Ramond from his heavy sleep. Not painful, desperate thirst, but rather a half-dreamt longing for water. In the curtained twilight of the room he weighed the desire against the effort it would take to call Eva's name. At last he decided in favor of it.

Mustering his strength, he breathed as deeply as he dared … and then the bedroom transformed itself into a mosaic of darkness and dancing bright spots. In the back of his mind he realized he must be coughing, but he could not hear the noise. There was only the pain in his lungs and the salty taste of blood. *As a father pities his children … so the LORD … pities … those … how long, Lord?* Psalm 103: 13

He felt rather than saw the hand that guided him back toward the pillows. A cool cloth was between his arm and his mouth, washing him. *Soon, Lord?* This time there was no darkness to receive him. The feeble light that bled through the curtains remained constant, throbbing behind his eyes.

"Ramond?" Eva's voice was small and far away. "Ramond, breathe. Yes, that's it. Another breath now. You're going to live. Can you hear me? You're going to live."

No. I'm going home. Soon. But he listened anyway. Took shallow, careful breaths until the ringing stopped and he could hear again.

"Eva—"

"Shhh. Don't try to talk. My friend Katrina will be here in a few hours. She's a nurse, and she's going to take you to the hospital. She will tell them that you are a lost hiker. She found you up near Landskron Castle and brought you straight to the hospital. Alone. Do you understand?"

Her blue eyes were bright with sympathy and purpose. *And fear,* he realized slowly. Still, she glowed like a piece of summer sky in the gloomy room.

"Do you understand, Ramond?"

He nodded wearily. "No children. No house. Just—"

"Shhh. Yes."

"May I ... tell Hirschel and ... Adina ... good-bye?"

Grief sent a shadow flitting across the face of the sky. But she nodded gently. "Of course. I'll bring them in."

"Eva?" She stopped halfway and looked back at him. "Hirschel ... was like me. Worse. Ask them."

She gave a quick, confused nod and left the room, leaving the door half-open. Ramond held his breath and listened to the quiet voices in the hallway beyond. Eva's words rose and fell gently, and then he heard Hirschel sniffle. Adina was predictably silent. *Hard, Lord. What can I tell them?*

But he received no answer before the door scooted open and the children appeared. They were not wearing their old and dirty traveling clothes, he suddenly realized. Where had Eva found things for them to wear? He was grateful she had. They looked more like children now, instead of ghosts or wandering refugees. *But so sad. Show me, Lord.*

Adina edged forward until she was standing at his bedside. Hirschel clung tightly to her hand.

"Will you be all right, Herr Ramond?" she asked in a trembling voice.

Home. Yes. He smiled at her. "I will be ... very well. Hirschel ... the man who made you ... well. His name ... Jesus. And I will be ... with Him."

"But when do we see you again?" Hirschel whimpered.

"It will be a long ... long time. Because Frau Gottlieb ... will take care of ... you, and then ... you will leave ... Austria."

"But where will we go?" Adina's eyes were wide at the idea of leaving this new place without their guide.

"I think ... Italy. Somewhere without ... the bad men. Somewhere good."

"And you will be somewhere good?"

Images of his father and mother and friends from Salzburg and Vienna suddenly flooded his mind, but he hesitated only for a moment. "Somewhere ... very good."

Adina nodded and blinked away the tears that trembled on her eyelashes. "We will miss you," she whispered.

"I'll miss you ... too. But promise me ... you will be brave ... and good for ... Frau Gottlieb."

Both children nodded miserably.

"And tell her ... what Jesus ... has done."

"We will," Adina promised softly.

"Good." Ramond smiled at them, even as he felt his strength ebbing to exhaustion once more. *Hirschel and Adina ... we made it. Here is where You led them, here they will be safe. And I will not stop praying for them, until ...*

"You are loved," he whispered. "Under ... His wings ..." He was tired, so tired, as he fought to make his tongue form the words. The promise come true seemed trapped beneath his unsteady breathing, locked in a throat made bloody by this brutal cough.

"You will ... be ... safe. Hiding. Refuge ... in Him."

Had they understood? Adina was nodding, her bright brown eyes never leaving his face. He tried to speak once more, to say good-bye and thank them and tell them to smile for him because it was over at last and he was free ... it was too much. He felt Hirschel's small hand grab his own in one final plea to *stay*, but then the darkness washed over him again and he was asleep.

"My Hope Is Built on Nothing Less"

KARL WAS NOT SUPPOSED to be in the plaza. He had left the Gestapo headquarters on the pretense of meeting with an informant from Christ Church, and now he wandered through the heart of the old city without any real purpose. The street suddenly widened into the plaza dominated by St. Jakob. Karl stopped his perusal of the cobblestones long enough to glance up at the magnificent bell tower, and then dropped his gaze just as quickly as he remembered the storm troopers assembling in its shadow three nights prior. Frozen snow—or was it glass?—crunched beneath his feet as he approached the door.

Yes. It was here. Did Fredrik choose this place simply to prove that no power can interfere with the might of the Reich? He had been right, Karl admitted with a disappointment that bordered on anger. He sighed and risked another glance upward. A few intrepid pigeons preened among the eight distant crosses of the bell tower. *If it is true, then shouldn't something have stopped them? Us? Fire from the sky, a voice of judgment—something?*

Karl stopped just outside the shelter that joined church and bell tower and shoved his hands deeper into his pockets. His frozen breath rose like smoke from the smoldering buildings. Somehow he could not make himself believe that the silent heavens meant Fredrik's cause had won. For the hundredth time he remembered the night of the pastor's execution. *Gottlieb knew something—had something—none of us did. And in dying, he was somehow victorious. Even the silence did not diminish that.*

He glanced back at the too-quiet facades of the pastel buildings on the square and then strolled up to the door as if he cared nothing about two-faced agents or the Gestapo's ubiquitous informers. Possessed by the sudden thought that that strange peace of Gottlieb's would somehow diminish the importance of the watchers, he pulled open the heavy black door and slipped inside the sacred gloom of the church.

For a moment, the contrast of light and dark within the church wreaked havoc with his vision. Then, gradually, the images began to clarify into shadowy, candlelit enclaves and dazzling windows. It was the windows that drew him in. Outside, they had been three dull brown floor-to-ceiling inlays on the sandstone walls. But here in the sanctuary the weak sunlight transformed them into shimmering columns of color. There were no pictures in the glass, Karl noted with vague disappointment. Just colors. Patterns that shifted with the light outside and reflected blindingly off the elaborate gilded altar.

He blinked hard and took a few cautious steps into the interior. Racking his mind for whatever scraps of information he had read in the Gestapo file, he seemed to remember that this building had become Austria's first Protestant church. *And then later it was converted into a Catholic one.* Karl shook his head as he found the narrow stone staircase on the right and made his way up. Such conversion and reconversion had been fairly common in the past few centuries, depending on the religious leanings of whomever held the most power. That much he remembered from school, from before they had stopped teaching church history in Germany. *And so the swastika will be ... there.* His trained eye easily found the black symbol, tacked irreverently to the feet of the crucified Christ. *A few centimeters lower,* Karl thought derisively, *and He would be stepping on it. I wonder if anyone would notice?*

He was not surprised to find the swastika here. St. Jakob had been most extraordinarily helpful in its compliance with the new Nazi laws. Not only had the church acquiesced to each decree, it had even urged the other churches to follow suit! Karl scornfully shook his head. From his perspective, the whole act was as ridiculous as the swastika on the altar. The obeisance of these priests had only served to placate the Gestapo's immediate scrutiny. Should they attempt even the most pitiful defiance, the retribution would fall just as mercilessly on them as it would on Christ Church.

They have gained nothing, Karl realized as he stared out over the great empty sanctuary. Above him, the intertwining red molding on the vaulted ceiling gave it a sinuous appearance, as if it were the wing of a giant dragonfly or the veins of a beating heart. But the appearance was just that—illusion. There was no more life here than there was in the boarded-over streets of the Jewish neighborhood. Frustrated and strangely dissatisfied by that realization, he stood abruptly and clattered down the stairs.

It could not be put off any longer. Eva quietly shut the cabinet. *Flour and vanilla extract and four potatoes.* She pivoted slowly, searching the kitchen. There were also three soft apples in a basket on the counter. Enough for a snack, perhaps, but certainly not another meal. *I will have to go out today.* For some reason the thought terrified her. She had not left the house since the day of the pogrom. Katrina had come and taken Ramond to the hospital, but Eva had gone no farther than the front step. For three days she had cooked, cleaned, and played with the children, trying to forget and praying the world had forgotten about her.

But today the food had run out. She sighed quietly as she resigned herself to leaving the safety of the house. Tomorrow was Sunday; nothing but the churches would be open. *And the Gestapo office and the prison.* Eva crossed the kitchen in three steps and picked up her handbag. She would not let herself think about such things. Like the widow who had fed the prophet Elijah so long ago, she would offer what she had and trust—hope— that God would provide. *Although it is not food that we need so desperately,* she realized as she counted the marks in her handbag. The church had graciously provided for her in the months since Reinhardt's death, giving her each month the same amount they had paid him. It was more than what she needed to live on, and more than once she had given the unused portion back in the offertory. Now the sum would be just enough.

No, money was not the problem. Safety was. *If these children are seen, if they appear without papers ...* The thought of the Gestapo and the prisons returned abruptly. With an effort she pushed it back, recalling the story of another prophet in its place. *Elisha and the angel armies. More are with us than with them.* Could she hope for that same protection today?

Eva crossed the kitchen and opened the cabinet again, halfway hoping food had been miraculously provided. The shelves were still bare. *No bread,*

God, she prayed silently as she glanced out the window. *And no ravens, either, so today it must be angels, yes?*

"When do you come back?" Hirschel's lower lip trembled with concern. Herr Ramond had gone away three days ago, and he had not even come back at all!

The pretty lady named Eva squatted to look him in the eye. "I will be back in two hours. By lunchtime," she said firmly.

"She will come back, Hirschel." Adina nodded wisely. She looked like she knew about going to hospitals and going shopping and going away forever, and how they were not the same thing.

"Yes. We need food, ja? But I will be back to make lunch," Eva promised.

At last Hirschel nodded, and Eva smiled brightly. "Good. But when I am gone, I need you to be very quiet. Like little mice, ja?"

"Ja, Tante Eva," Hirschel said quickly, just like they had practiced. He did know about hiding like a mouse. They had done that a lot after the bad men came in the spring. And then Herr Ramond had come and helped them. The last thought made him sad inside, because Herr Ramond was gone. To a hospital, Adina said, but maybe forever too!

"Will you see him, Tante Eva?" he blurted.

She stopped and turned around. "See who?"

"Herr Ramond!"

She looked sad too, the way Frau Dreher had looked when he'd asked about his parents. Herr Ramond really was going away forever, he guessed.

"*Nein*, Hirschel, I will not see him. But my friend Katrina is coming for supper tonight, and she will tell us how he is."

"Can he come too?"

"No, because he is very sick right now. He needs to be in the hospital."

"But I was sick!" Hirschel cried, still not understanding.

A strange look crossed Eva's face, and then she repeated her promise to return and hurried out the door.

Yesterday's shopping trip had passed without incident, so today Eva had gathered her courage and come to church as if nothing had changed. From her perch at the organ she watched the backs of the churchgoers as they trickled in to the pews. There were many missing in the congregation today, she realized with a mixture of dread and grief. As if by some unspoken agreement, nearly all the people present wore back. *We are in mourning today,* Eva thought. Hushed in holy stillness and bathed in the colors of the stained-glass windows, the atmosphere in the little sanctuary was nonetheless very much like that of a funeral. *We weep for friends today. For neighbors and for strangers, and for our helplessness to do anything at all.*

The bells began to toll, announcing the beginning of the service. *The Cohens are here! A miracle!* She smiled with momentary relief as the last Jewish-Christian family remaining at Christ Church hurried to take their seats near the front. The stocky Herr Werberg slipped quietly into the last row, and that was all. *Three hundred here. But we have nearly fifty more!* She whispered the names of the missing in a helpless prayer as she adjusted the music in front of her and poised her fingers above the keys.

Herr Thaer on the front row, with his thick spectacles and massive Bible. The entire Werthiem family: all three boys and their parents. Spirited Frau Mader, who claims to have outlived the Fuehrer twice and plans on doing so once more. These and others were gone this morning. Eva felt their absence like the breaks in a student's stumbling music: loud and jarring silence. *Were they arrested?* she wondered. Or simply hiding until the storm abated?

There was no way to know. There was a rustling noise as the congregation stood, and then a half second of silence before she began to play.

> My hope is built on nothing less
> Than Jesus' blood and righteousness
> I dare not trust the sweetest frame,
> But wholly lean on Jesus' name.

The music was light, rippling, but somehow not out of place as it soared up on the voices of three hundred somber churchgoers. All other frames had blazed and then crumbled to ash on Wednesday night.

> On Christ, the solid rock, I stand,
> All other ground is sinking sand.

Had that promise ever been so needed as it was today? Eva watched in amazement as stoic members of the congregation bowed their heads and wept. Others looked upward: praying, surrendering, adoring. She raised her voice to join the song as the second verse began.

> When darkness veils His lovely face,
> I rest on His unchanging grace—

Grace. Yes. It flooded the sanctuary this morning, the very Presence of heaven pouring over the small and frightened flock gathered in the shadow of death.

> In every high and stormy gale
> My anchor holds within the veil.

Here was hope, true unwavering light in the suffocating darkness that threatened! Had any hoped in money before? In power, or position, or pleasure? Such things seemed utterly ridiculous now, more useless than the charred walls and broken glass that littered all of the Greater Reich. In the fires of Kristal Nacht, in the portent of what the future would surely hold for the Jews and all who stood with them, the last illusions and fragile hopes of this church were burned away. Now only one thing remained.

> On Christ, the solid rock I stand,
> All other ground is sinking sand,
> All other ground is sinking sand.

From the far left corner of the sanctuary, Karl watched the change uncomprehendingly. Something was *happening* as the churchgoers sang their words of bold defiance and hopeless hope. For once he was forgotten at his post at the back of the church. He searched each face openly and was not caught in the act. There were tears on many cheeks this morning.

Karl focused on the dignified form of Klaus Pieters, the man who had been acting as the pastor since Gottlieb's death. Pieters's eyes were closed, his expression intense as he turned his face toward heaven. His lips moved silently, faster than the words of the song. *Praying*, Karl realized.

Tears. Prayers. Songs that spoke of unshakeable hope and unchanging grace. The peace in the sanctuary was unmistakable, and as Karl turned toward the image of the shining, living Christ he felt his throat tighten with impossible longing.

But it cannot be, he reminded himself sharply. No. It could never be. He stood in the sanctuary today as an enemy of the people who served this Christ. He hated the side he had chosen, but he *had* chosen it. He served darkness. How could he ever hope to belong to their God of light? The hope, the promises—they were for the people he hunted. Not for him. Never for him.

Though he had known it all along, the clarity of that realization was suffocating. Suddenly Karl could not bear the sound of the singing any longer. With one more glance at the worshippers around him, he slipped out of the light and music of the sanctuary and back into the sand.

It was the second night in a row that Katrina had eaten supper at Eva's house, but that was not unusual. Katrina had been a frequent meal guest in the Gottlieb household when Reinhardt was alive; she was here more often since the terrible summer. She and Eva had even devised a system for such occasions. Eva would call her the day before with whatever meal she was planning, and Katrina would go out and buy some of the ingredients. Dropping them off on her way to the hospital, she would return after work and eat with her friend.

It was a good system, Katrina reflected. She was utterly useless in the kitchen unless a kettle and a teabag were concerned—Eva had graciously pointed that out on several occasions. So she bought, Eva cooked, and they were both happy. *Like sisters*, she thought with a smile. *We eat together, laugh together, weep together, pray together … if I moved in with Eva, I would save hours of time driving. I'm here nearly every day anyway!*

Eva had hinted at as much once in the past few months. But the arrival of the two refugee children dispelled that possibility. *There is not room enough in this house,* Katrina realized as she stood to help Eva clear the table. The two children watched her with shy interest. She smiled back at them and followed Eva into the kitchen.

"I should bring my cat," she murmured, more to herself than to Eva.

"No." Eva's tone left no room for negotiation, but Katrina pressed on with her idea.

"Children like animals. More than pianos, you know."

"Animals, yes. But your cat—no." Eva firmly shook her head, picturing the moody, long-haired "Maestro."

"He's a good boy! He likes people—"

"For food."

"And he's very social," Katrina defended.

"Mm. Social like a Gestapo agent. Which, by the way, is not a bad idea. You could take him to the Gestapo station downtown, and all our problems would be solved!" Eva smiled brightly as Katrina made a face.

"My poor Maestro. I won't bring him here after all. I'm afraid of what you'd do to him."

Eva denied nothing as she handed Katrina a towel. "You dry."

Katrina laughed at the smirk on Eva's face. "Plotting the end of my innocent kitten. Shame on you, Eva Gottlieb."

"It was not such a bad idea. Probably they would give him to the SS. He could become an honorary German shepherd."

Katrina merely shook her head. There was too much reality in their jokes, and her laughter died at the thought of the news she'd brought Eva tonight. She dried the dishes in silence for a moment before Eva noticed the change.

"Trina?"

Katrina shook her head and glanced toward the table where Hirschel and Adina still sat. *Not around them,* her look seemed to say.

Eva nodded as she plunged the last plate into the soapy water. Then she handed it to Katrina with a flourish and sighed dramatically. "I don't know what to do, Trina!"

"Why, whatever is wrong, Eva?" Katrina replied, joining the game with enthusiasm.

"I made jam cookies this afternoon, but"—Eva drew the word out and spread her hands in confusion—"I don't know *anyone* who likes jam cookies!"

"We do!" The vote from the dining room was passionate and unanimous.

"You do?"

Katrina shook her head and busied herself with putting away a plate, lest she burst into laughter and spoil the perfect expression of serious surprise on her friend's face.

"Ja, Tante Eva!"

"Really? You will help me eat them?"

Katrina did laugh as the two dark heads nodded in earnest agreement.

"I will too, Eva, if you don't mind," she called as she returned to take her seat beside Adina. "Your Tante Eva's jam cookies are the very best in all of Austria," she whispered conspiratorially.

Again she received no reply from the children, but Adina smiled happily back at her, as if to say cookies were good and it had been a very long time since she had had one.

The jam cookies had been eaten, the last plates washed and stacked again in the cupboards, and the children put to bed. Now Eva sat across from Katrina on the red settee. The fire popped and hissed in front of them, and Eva blew into her coffee and inhaled the steam before turning to Katrina.

"You have news."

That much was clear from the end of their conversation in the kitchen. Katrina nodded once. "And it is not good."

Again Katrina nodded, wondering exactly how to bring up the subject. At last she decided on a direct approach. "It concerns Ramond." She took a sip of her drink—tea, not coffee—before continuing. "He has tuberculosis."

Eva's face was tense in the firelight, but Katrina could see she had not understood the significance of the diagnosis.

"Dr. Brandt thinks ... perhaps a week. Perhaps a little more."

Eva drew her breath in sharply.

"The doctor will operate on him tomorrow. Collapse one of his lungs." Katrina winced as she spoke. "But he is so ill, Eva ..."

Eva stared into the fire for a long time, remembering the peace and the triumph she had felt in church yesterday morning. How far away that seemed now! "Adina and Hirschel will be heartbroken," she whispered at last, sadly. For some inexplicable reason she felt a kinship to the man who quoted Scripture and spoke of miracles even as he coughed his life away.

"How well did you clean that room, Eva?" Katrina demanded.

"Very well."

"And the bed linens?"

"I washed them twice and put others on the bed."

"It would have been better to burn them," Katrina murmured. "But I suppose you can't. The curtains?"

"I did not think—no."

"And you are sleeping there?"

"No. I have not. But the floor is rather hard—"

"Better the floor than a hospital bed!"

"What?"

"I'm sorry." Katrina sighed, dropping her gaze from Eva's to stare at the windows behind her. The lace curtains swayed faintly with the updraft from the chimney. Tiny, intertwining rosebuds seemed terribly incapable of holding back the dark.

"I'm sorry," she murmured again. Still she did not look at Eva. Her voice was flat, measured, when she spoke again. "Tuberculosis is highly contagious. Easy to catch and nearly impossible to treat. And if you or either of the children should come down with it and come to the hospital, *they* might very well make the connection between you and Ramond and the children, because there have not been many cases in Villach recently. You see?"

"If I get sick and the sickness does not finish me, then the Gestapo probably will. And if I do not get sick, then it is still rather likely the

Gestapo will find out about Hirschel and Adina because we can hardly hope to keep them hidden until ... until we have a way to help them escape. Yes, I understand." Eva was strangely unafraid as she spoke the words.

She smiled at Katrina and hummed the first few measures from the song yesterday. *My hope is built on nothing less than Jesus' blood and righteousness ...*

"We are secure even though the mountains are falling, yes?" she reminded her.

Katrina smiled wryly. "You remembered."

"Yes. And what else can we do? If it is as bad as you say ..."

"It is. And so we must." Katrina fell silent again, lost in thoughts that twined and glowed in the fire. "But there must be some way to protect the children ..."

Fredrik Schmidt was understandably angry. He had been called—no, *summoned*—from his duties in Villach and ordered to report to the Klagenfurt branch office to receive "directives." He hissed that word, along with several others, under his breath as he strode through the wide courtyard of the Klagenfurt headquarters.

Two tiers of stone and plaster arches created sheltered walkways along the edges of the courtyard. Above the second story of arches, rounded windows mirrored the gray November sky, the only variation in otherwise-featureless walls. By size alone, the *Alte Burg* was impressive. But the finer details of its architecture were entirely lost on Fredrik. If he noted anything about the building, it was that it was bigger than his own headquarters in Villach. The thought filled him with a strange mixture of envy and pride. Yes, the Old Castle of Klagenfurt was more commanding than his Gestapo office. But even Dr. Weimann, the head of this bleak courtyard with its grinning archways, could not boast of as much as him!

Villach was not as prestigious as Klagenfurt, but it was very nearly *Juedenrien*—Jew-free—thanks to the meticulous work of Fredrik Schmidt. Fredrik smiled and lifted his face into the biting wind. Last week he had personally organized the deportation of sixty-five Jewish males and seen to it that not a single shop or office owned by the swine had had so much as a doorframe left intact. Though there was not yet a directive to deport the women and children, Fredrik was confident that such orders would not be long in coming. In the meantime, there was satisfaction in knowing the creatures couldn't breed. They would soon be gone from Villach— from Germany—from Europe!—all together. And Fredrik Schmidt was confident he would receive part of the credit.

Such a prospect cheered him as he entered the stark black-and-white reception room. Bright-red banners draped the walls, and a portrait of Adolph Hitler glared ferociously at the back of the impeccable Aryan secretary.

"Heil Hitler, *guten morgen*," the woman said without glancing up from the paper on her desk.

"Heil Hitler." Fredrik snapped off the salute, though the lady had still not looked up. She was beautiful—blonde, blue-eyed, and perfectly proportioned. A model of Aryan perfection. *As should be expected here.* Fredrik permitted his gaze to linger on the line of her slender neck for a moment more before he cleared his throat.

"Sir?"

"I am Inspekteur Fredrik Schmidt, from Villach," he stated coldly, as if he were ordering an arrest.

The secretary smiled and nodded quickly, but not before Fredrik glimpsed the unease in her wide blue eyes. He waited for her to speak again.

"Up the staircase, second room on the left. You are early."

He jerked his head once and saluted again. Perhaps he would come back after the meeting.

Dr. Weimann was the only man present when Fredrik entered the room. He saluted without rising from his seat and then swept his hand toward the pot of coffee on the far end of the table.

"Herr Schmidt. I'm glad you are early."

The absence of his title was not lost on Fredrik. He caught the glint of condescension in Dr. Weimann's gray-blue eyes as he sat down. "It seemed important."

"Yes, in fact it is. There have been problems in your city."

Though the tone was still polite, there was an edge beneath the words. Fredrik let his own temper rise to meet it. "Problems?"

"Imprudent destruction of property. Careless handling of informants and prisoners." Dr. Weimann ticked them off from the paper he held in his hand. "And lastly, of course, the church."

"There are churches all over Austria!"

"Yes. But there is only one Christ Church in Villach. Formerly pastored by the late Reinhardt Gottlieb, I believe?"

"I did not wish to handle them carelessly," Fredrik replied icily.

"*Our* sources indicate that there are only 353 in attendance. You might have had them arrested during the pogrom."

"I tri—" Fredrik stopped himself, but Dr. Weimann had guessed what he was going to say. The aristocratic features hardened in mockery.

"You tried? Please, Herr Schmidt, tell me what happened. Perhaps we can assist you?"

"Nearly every churchgoer was on my list." Fredrik snapped. "And *your* storm troopers did not arrest them! By the time I received the names of the prisoners, it was daylight! The train was gone! Too late to make any more arrests!"

"Most interesting." Dr. Weimann absentmindedly smoothed his little moustache. "But we are not vampires, Herr Schmidt. We are quite able to walk around in the daylight. Even able to make arrests, I believe."

Fredrik glared at the man across from him. The head over the region of Carinthia, Dr. Weimann presumed to scold and order him like a slave! *Villach is larger than Klagenfurt!* It was sheer geographical accident that Dr. Weimann ranked higher than him.

"Not knowing the delicate atmosphere in Villach, you would not understand the … effects of such an action," he answered at last.

"And do you understand the ramifications of being ineffective and counterproductive to the unity of the Reich, Inspekteur?" Icy eyes narrowed in earnestness, and his voice dropped to a soft monotone. "You are not the only ambitious man in Villach," he finished indifferently.

The door opened before Fredrik could respond, and the heads from Grafenstein and Krumpendorf filed in. The conversation was finished.

Like a Child

The Christmas season would begin in less than a month. Already the mountains of Villach were dressed for the part. Each day the sun rose with blinding gold and pink from behind the snow-capped summits. At night the crescent moon made the peaks glow weakly against the flat blue sky. In a mere twenty-seven days, St. Nicholas Day would officially begin the month of Advent.

But the mood in the Gestapo headquarters was anything but festive. Sullen mistrust reigned as the many German agents wondered how the former nation of Austria would handle its first Nazi Christmas. It was not that the party leaders feared the babe in the manger—most simply discarded Him as an old fable, a myth useful for warming hearts and helping children behave. Their concern was more practical. Angels and babies notwithstanding, it was common knowledge that traditions united a people. After all, hadn't the Fuehrer used the revived Nordic practices to do just that? Bonfires, pagan dances, and cookies cut in the shape of swastikas marked the celebration of the holiday now. Peace on Earth was assured through the fulfillment of the Thousand-Year Reich, and there was plenty of goodwill toward men—provided those men were loyal and Aryan.

But it remained to be seen how these changes would go over in this new addition to the Reich. The impending holiday season weighed heavily on many minds in the Nazi hierarchy of Villach, and especially on the mind of Fredrik Schmidt. Acutely aware of the eyes that now watched his city, he urged his Gestapo into an unprecedented blur of activity. Arrests were made quickly and justified later, often by nothing more than the angry rhetoric of the accuser. But that was to be expected. Treason was in the eye of the beholder these days, and the Gestapo watched the public with hungry eyes.

It was in the midst of this chaos that Fredrik received a telegram from Berlin. He scanned the lettering on the outside and sneered. The German Evangelical Church was of no more importance to him than the mangy gutter cat that had staked its claim in the alley behind the building. A laughable mix of Christianity and Nazism, it lived solely off the goodwill of the Fuehrer. But the envelope was official, so Fredrik ripped it open and slouched further back in his chair to read.

By order of President Friedrich Werner, of the German Protestant Church, the name of the god of Israel is to be obliterated wherever it is displayed in Protestant churches. In addition, Old Testament figures and prophets must be removed. Appropriate measures may be taken against churches who fail to comply.

That was it. Fredrik laid the envelope parallel to the edge of his desk and smiled for the first time in days. Never mind the bumbling storm troopers that had somehow managed to leave Christ Church untouched ten days prior. The stubborn foolishness that had threatened his career would now bring the church directly into his hands.

Evening. Sandwiched between supper and nighttime, that magic hour-and-a-half had been Eva's favorite part of the day when she was a child. She could remember the long conversations and stories and games with her two brothers, before the invasion of school had relegated that time to quiet studies.

The whole family together. Images filled her mind as she gathered the dishes and carried them to the sink to wash. *Winter, like now. Christmas coming. The lights of Vienna painting the misty windowpanes bright gold and green, and the glow of the fire on all the faces around the hearth. Mama. Papa. Joseph and Stefan.* She smiled at the memory. Her two brothers were wrestling—or on the verge of it—just as Papa began to read the story of Joseph from the Bible. She could hear his voice perfectly: firm but amused as he coaxed the boys back to their seats. "Sit still, both of you. We are not a zoo. Joseph, this story is just for you, about another Joseph long ago ..."

Eva looked across the counter at Hirschel and Adina. They were still sitting at the table, waiting, doubtless, for dessert. *I would have been Hirschel's age then.* That realization made her sigh and ache again for those dear faces. If only Mama and Papa could be *here*, instead of Vienna, they would welcome these two little ones just as she had.

"Where's the cookies, Tante Eva?" Hirschel's hopeful voice piped from the dining room.

"Not cookies tonight, Hirschel. You helped me make the apple tart this afternoon. Do you remember?"

She smiled at the grin that lit his face. "I helped mix the sauce," he announced proudly.

"That's right. And I'm sure it will be delicious," Eva finished, as she retrieved the tart from where it warmed in the oven. That was as it should be, at least. Though she could not give the children the laughter and love and joy of a family that was *complete*, it was at least right that they should be able to enjoy little things like apple tarts.

He feels safe here. The thought warmed her more than the scent of cinnamon and apples rising from the pan. Adina was aware of a greater danger beyond these stone-and-wood walls, but at least Hirschel felt secure. She set the tart down on the table and produced a butter knife. "An extra big piece for my special helper, ja? And also for you, Adina, because you helped me peel the apples."

"When can we go outside, Tante Eva?" Adina was watching her curiously. "At first you said because it was snowing we could not go outside, even though we like the snow. And now it is raining and the snow is all gone and we are still inside. Is it because of the bad men? Because Herr Ramond said we are safe here. He said—" Adina bit her lip and frowned seriously as she tried to remember the words exactly. "He said we would be hiding ... in a re-fuge." She pronounced the last word carefully, not entirely sure of what it meant.

As Eva searched for a response, Hirschel laid down his fork and nodded solemnly. "He said we are hiding with the man who made me not sick. And Herr Ramond is going to go with him too."

Now it was Eva's turn to stare. "He told you *what?*" She dropped the knife with a *clank* and slowly sat down, facing the children.

"That we would be in a refuge with the man who made Hirschel better, and Herr Ramond would be going somewhere else to see him," Adina replied confidently for her little brother.

"I—I don't understand," Eva began.

"Herr Ramond said his name is Jesus." Adina frowned slightly. "He said that you know him too. Do you?"

Eva nodded mutely, looking from Hirschel to Adina and back again. Fragments of the children's sentences flashed through her mind, trembling now with a new and magnificent meaning. *I was sick too! Miracles ... Ask the children.*

At last she nodded again and repeated her yes. "And I think ... you should start at the beginning."

Karl tapped his foot impatiently against the timber wall of the bakery. *Trusted Since 1893*, the sign above him proclaimed. He tucked his chin further into the collar of his jacket and permitted himself another glance at the window. Inside the display cases, elaborate strudels and danishes tempted his meager salary. And, predictably near the center, a tray full of swastika-shaped cookies proclaimed just *who* this bakery was trusted by now.

Silently he wondered about the possibility of a free cookie. If he showed them his identification, he could probably take the whole tray home tonight. Karl turned away from the display case and back to the rain-lashed street. He had tasted a swastika cookie only once, when he had purchased one solely for the pleasure of biting off the crooked arms of the pinwheel—a petty protest against being rejected by the army. Within two weeks he had been employed by the Gestapo, still useful as a spy while his deaf ear made him unfit to be a soldier. He shook his head ruefully. The cookie had tasted like sawdust anyway.

A cold fog had descended and dissolved the mountains, leaving the city soaked and decidedly gray beyond his little lighted post. Few pedestrians were out this evening, though a handful of autos braved the rain and the river that ran where the Hauptplatz should be. *Krimmel should be here by now.* Karl scowled, checked his watch, and returned his gaze to the street. The electric streetlamps were winking to life now, their orange lights illuminated just how much of Main Street was underwater.

Karl glared out at the gloomy downpour a moment longer, his frustration finally dissolving into a snort of humorless laughter. There, just rounding the corner where St. Jakob towered, was Krimmel. Without hat or umbrella—an attempt at subterfuge? Karl wondered—the wiry informant was in the process of dashing from one storefront awning to the next in an attempt to stay dry. The technique was failing miserably, from what Karl could see of the man. Water darkened the gray of his thin overcoat to black, and he ran with quick, jerky motions. The image only confirmed Karl's assessment of him. *Foolish traitor. Pathetic backstabber.* Geoff Krimmel was so eager to comply with and support the Gestapo that he was seldom of any real use.

But Karl forced such thoughts aside as the man completed his final sprint to join Karl in front of the bakery. He and Krimmel served the same master, after all. The only difference was that Krimmel had once belonged to the One Reinhardt called Truth. He had belonged, and somehow, incredibly, he had forsaken Him and turned to render obeisance to the new Nazi party. Karl did not understand.

But he needed Krimmel tonight, so he raised his hand briefly in the *heil* as the informant approached.

"Heil Hitler, Agent Zehr," Krimmel panted as he attempted to brush the water from his soaked overcoat.

"Terrible night, isn't it?" Karl inclined his head toward the downpour and then nodded at Krimmel. Water streamed from his short, gray-blond hair and glistened like sweat on his sallow cheeks.

"Terrible," the informant agreed wholeheartedly. He glanced hopefully to the lighted window of the bakery. "May we go inside?"

"No. Safer out here." Karl adjusted his cap and halfway-savored the disappointment that radiated from Krimmel's shivering frame. "But I appreciate your coming, Herr Krimmel. I will not take much of your night."

Krimmel nodded and tried to smile, but the temperature reduced the expression to something of a grimace. "The church is plotting nothing right now, Herr Zehr. Christmas coming … nothing. They are feeding some of the Jews who were not arrested, but that is all."

Karl considered the shivering man again, suddenly conscious of how little the traitor knew of the Gestapo's policies. Even the newest agent was aware it was as dangerous to give as to receive when criminals of the Reich were concerned. But Krimmel's ignorance was not a bad thing tonight. Not at all.

"Are you in possession of a Bible, Herr Krimmel?" he asked sharply.

Unsure of how to answer, Krimmel glanced first at the darkening sky and then at the golden light that streamed from the window of the bakery. At last he nodded. "Yes. Why? They trust me, you see, when they see I take the same risks as them—"

"So they will understand that it was confiscated by the Gestapo."

Krimmel blinked twice and then shook his head in feeble protest.

Karl feigned confusion. "You do not *read* it, do you? A loyal Party member like yourself? Surely you don't believe in the things of these foolish dissenters!"

"No, but—you see … it helps them trust me," he finished lamely.

Relieved, Karl nodded and smiled at the scrawny man in front of him. "I am *helping* you, Herr Krimmel. When you go to church and no longer have the book, they will ask and you can tell them the Gestapo confiscated it. There was nothing you could do." Karl shrugged broadly and smiled. "Perhaps someone will feel sorry for you and lend you one of their Bibles. Then you can come and tell me about that, ja?"

The last sentence won Krimmel over. The sacrifice of old friends and acquaintances was his specialty, after all. "I will destroy the Jewish book of lies myself!" he proclaimed, a trifle too loud for Karl's liking.

"I would not put you to the trouble, Herr Krimmel," Karl replied hastily. "I will take it off your hands tomorrow."

"At the headquarters?"

"Yes. Or here, if you prefer," he added, noting the worry on Krimmel's face. The informant nodded in relief. "But be on time," Karl finished pointedly.

"Yes, of course," he babbled. "And there are others at the church who carry Bibles. Why, Eva Gottlieb and Klaus Pieters have *whole* Bibles like mine! Outrageous! No attempt to remove even the obvious Jewish Scriptures! And—"

"And so you will set an example with no Bible at all. I will see you *tomorrow*, Herr Krimmel," Karl finished firmly. "Thank you for your information." With that he turned and walked quickly into the rain.

But not even the icy downpour could wash away the unease that clung to him. Certainly it was merely the effect of working with Krimmel, he told himself. He could not look at the man without feeling like he had just stepped over a snake. *Reluctant to give up a book he cares nothing about but delighted to report on anyone from the church!* He sighed his disgust to the wind as he neared his apartment. There was more than Geoff Krimmel's obeisance weighing on his mind tonight.

If Krimmel comes through, tomorrow I will own a Bible. The thought was almost frightening. Not an edited Nazi Bible but—unless Krimmel was lying—a whole, unaltered book. Though owning a Bible was not specifically illegal, Karl knew of people who had been deported for such a thing. This was 1938, after all. Laws were not strictly necessary. More depended on the outlook and disposition of the heads of the Gestapo and SS—and Karl knew where he stood with that. If the book was discovered with him, Fredrik could have him arrested. *Could? He would order it on the spot.*

Karl had reached his apartment building now. Already soaked to the skin, he stopped at the foot of the metal staircase for a moment, lost in the tumble of his conflicting thoughts. *I hope Krimmel is as foolish as I think he is.* If he was, tomorrow would go smoothly enough. The informant would hand the book over to him and disappear, no questions asked. And Karl would take the Bible home and do ... what? Read it? That would be like looking through the bakery window at the deserts he could not afford to buy. Last Sunday's service had showed him that much. Hungry though he might be, Karl knew there was nothing good left in him with which to purchase the peace he craved.

But still he would read. Perhaps this self-inflicted torment would mask his disquiet over his newest assignment. *The churches.* As of yesterday, the German Evangelical Church had made it illegal to display the name *Jehovah*. Churches that did not comply could be considered as synagogues—and destroyed. Karl shook his head. St. Jakob had removed the Name on its own months ago. The handful of other cathedrals in Villach would likely follow suit. All, that it, except Christ Church. Karl was almost certain they would fight this new law. *And then Fredrik will crush them. Or he will sign papers and send agents like me to arrest them, so that Mauthausen can do the actual crushing.*

One thing was certain: this would not be an easy week. Perhaps having the Bible on hand would not be such a bad idea after all.

Eva lay on her back staring up at the dark ceiling. The bed beneath her felt wonderfully soft after more than a week of alternating between the chair and the floor. Katrina would not be pleased, she thought ruefully—but then again, Katrina had not heard the story Hirschel and Adina had told her tonight.

"We thought Hirschel would die one night, except then he woke up and told us about a dream where a man with hurt hands and feet carried him. And after that he was not sick anymore!"

Hirschel had smiled happily and confirmed Adina's words and then added his own speculation that Herr Ramond might be an angel.

It was almost too much to absorb in one night. Eva had asked them question after question, trying to take it in. "His hands and His feet, you said? And what did He look like?"

"I don't exactly remember, except His face was nice. Kind of like Papa and Mama and Herr Ramond and everybody else who's nice, but more."

Eva remembered reading somewhere that children's angels saw the face of God, but the children themselves? *Only Hirschel actually saw Him,* she reminded herself. *But Adina believes so easily, because He made her brother well.*

So. That was what Ramond had in mind when he spoke of miracles. *But why—*she shook her head gently as her joy flickered beneath a fresh assault of doubt. *Why not Ramond as well? Or why not Reinhardt, for that matter?*

So many questions. But in the children's eyes, there was only one, and one answer to go with it.

"Herr Ramond said that Jesus made Hirschel well. Who is He? Do you know Him?"

She had said yes. Yes, she knew Jesus. She had known Him since she was four, younger than Hirschel, and these past four years she had been a pastor's wife. *And yet ...*

In the months since Reinhardt's death, had she run to Him? Had He been as close to her as He was to these children who had only once heard His name?

"Please, Lord," she whispered into the dark room. "Make me like a child again."

Showdown

Eva slowly scanned the faces in the church basement. The five men gathered here were deacons, old and trusted friends of Reinhardt's. The dim light of the cluttered storage room let shadows play across their visages, perfectly echoing the solemnity of this meeting.

Eva hung back as the men gathered around the church's old altar. Water stains marred the dark patina of the wood in several places, the result of a flood some thirty years prior. By that time, Christ Church had been nearing its seventieth year and was completely unwilling to part with its first altar. A woman in the congregation embroidered a delicate lace cloth to cover the stains, and nothing more was said.

Not until two years ago had Reinhardt convinced the congregation to replace it. A new, more ornate altar had taken its place beneath the picture of Jesus, and this battered Communion table had been retired to the basement.

Now the five weary deacons of Christ Church clustered around it. Klaus Pieters, a dignified man in his late forties, motioned Eva closer. "There is room, Frau Gottlieb. Please join us."

Eva obeyed, feeling suddenly young and shy in the company of these grave teachers who had overseen the church in the recent months.

Klaus nodded gently at her before he cleared his throat to speak. "I will tell you why we are here," he began without pretense. "Two days ago a law was issued from the chancellery in Berlin, though it may have come from the mouth of hell itself."

"Are they not one and the same?" muttered a short, balding man. Eva recognized him as Ari Fischhof.

The men murmured in agreement as Klaus held up a hand for silence. Eva thought she glimpsed a hint of sorrow written on his craggy features. "Yesterday the false church declared—and Herr Hitler has given them his support—declared that we are forbidden to display the Name of the LORD our God. He has ordered the Name Jehovah removed from every church in the Reich."

Eva gripped the smooth edge of the altar tighter. No, she had not heard of this new decree. And judging from the stunned silence that fell in the room, the deacons had not heard it either. A moment passed before anyone spoke.

"At least Herr Hitler cannot take the Lord's name from our hearts," offered a stout man named Dietmar.

"Nor shall he take it from our church!" Ari countered angrily.

"Peace, men." Again Klaus raised his hands. "That is what we have gathered to discuss tonight. Are we to continue as we have since the Anschluss, disregarding every law that contradicts our worship? Or will we obey this edict for the sake of preserving those who worship here?"

"We are being baited." Stefan Happ spoke in measured tones. All eyes turned to regard the youngest deacon. With jet-black hair and boyish features, the man could have easily passed as Reinhardt's younger brother. "They have tired of waiting for us to break their rules, so they have made a law that we have broken already." He shrugged slightly, as if to say that nothing less could be expected from Hitler and his henchmen.

This time there was no pause before the room erupted.

"The Gestapo has never needed an excuse before—"

"Why should we listen now? We—"

"For the sake of the congregation, we should—"

"Do you doubt what they are capable of? We saw—"

Klaus raised his voice to be heard above the tumult. "Gentlemen! Peace! Are you trying to be heard all the way in Berlin?"

Heads dropped at Klaus's rebuke, and the angry roar subsided. Klaus nodded in satisfaction. "Good. Now we will discuss this as civilized men. And women," he added apologetically, glancing at Eva.

Again Ari was the first to speak. "Perhaps we are being baited"—he nodded toward Stefan—"but why should we back down now? The Gestapo is above—no, the Gestapo is *below* any law whatsoever. As far as we know, they did not even charge the pastor with any crime before they killed him. They …" Ari faltered and stopped as he remembered Eva's presence.

"I am well," Eva murmured. "Please, continue."

"They will do what they will, regardless of what action we take," Ari finished heavily.

"I say we should comply." Dietmar crossed his arms over his barrel chest, daring anyone to argue.

"Why?" Klaus asked quietly, and Dietmar exploded.

"It is not such a large thing! The Name Jehovah is only written once in our sanctuary. It is a foolish decision to sacrifice the entire congregation over that single stained-glass window!" He thumped the altar in front of him. "Many were angry two years ago when Pastor Gottlieb purchased a new altar. But they survived. And so we will survive this too!"

Ari's dark-blue eyes flashed fire. "This is not a matter of decoration, Dietmar. If we obey them when they tell us to take God's name from our churches, why should we not obey them when they demand His name erased from our hearts as well?"

Klaus nodded slowly. "A good argument, Ari."

"But what do we hope to gain?" The tall and pensive Roland Eder spoke up for the first time. "We defy their laws time and time again and hope the knocking on our doors is not the Gestapo coming to cart us off to Mauthausen. We dare to show mercy to the Jews, all the while praying *they* do not catch us in the act." He rubbed a hand across his thin face, and Eva noticed the dark circles beneath his eyes. "We are simply enduring. But for how long? For what purpose?"

Eva sighed softly at the weariness in his voice. She knew the feeling well, that voice of quiet defeat that whispered in her darkest moments. *But let us not become weary in doing good, for at the proper time we will reap a harvest if we do not give up.* She managed a faint smile at the verse that came unbidden to her mind.

"…should be put to the congregation for a vote." Stefan was just finishing as Eva turned her attention back the little group. "It is their lives that are endangered along with ours."

Klaus nodded again, somehow looking older and more spent than he had when the meeting began. "We have heard from everyone, then. Is that the consensus? To have the congregation vote?"

The four other deacons murmured assent. Eva looked from one face to another, seeing the same weariness etched on each one. *No! Do not become weary. Not like this. Not like this.*

"Unless anyone objects ..."

Say something! Say something, Eva! Her heart pounded in her throat as she gathered the courage to speak. Suddenly dizzy, she leaned against the altar and focused on the sad and gentle face of Klaus. *Speak to him. Just to him ...*

"Please," she managed after a moment's hesitation. She blushed as she felt the rest of the men turn to her in surprise.

"What is it, Eva?" Klaus asked kindly.

"I—I do not think the congregation should decide this. I think we—I think it should be settled tonight."

"Oh?" Klaus was surprised but not critical. "And why is that?"

Eva drew a deep breath as she tried to organize her thoughts. "This law ... they are daring us to blaspheme. To no longer worship or pray in the name of our God." She looked steadily at Dietmar. "It *is* much more than a question of decoration or display." Nodding to Stefan, she added, "Perhaps they have set a trap for us. But if we are to be faithful to our Lord, then we must walk into it."

"Eva—" Dietmar's voice was almost patronizing, as if he were reasoning with a child. "Eva, that was Reinhardt's cross to bear. It is not yours." He sensed Klaus's disapproval from across the room and hurried to finish. "Perhaps ten days ago we would have chosen that course. But the pogrom— can we still afford to assume that these men are not just as eager to smash our lives as well? Now that we have seen what they are capable of, should we not exercise some prudence?"

"Perhaps it is time for us to be fools for Christ," Klaus admonished. "Listen to Eva."

Eva swallowed hard. "When Reinhardt lived, I was afraid," she began softly. "I was afraid—so frightened that I might lose him." She closed her eyes, bracing herself against the memories that came rushing at her. *Waiting. The empty house. Katrina … and then Ramond. The children.* For a moment she considered mentioning Hirschel and Adina to the deacons, but she thought better of it. They would know in a few days anyway.

"The thing I most feared … it came upon me." Eva let the pain show in her eyes. "I thought I could not bear it, couldn't live alone. But …" she stopped again, wondering how to explain the miracle that had been born in her heart in the past ten days. "The LORD has been enough. What I couldn't do, He has done. And I will trust in Him. Not in our obedience to an evil law. Not in my ability to hide." Her voice had been gaining strength with each sentence, and now she lifted her head and met the eyes of the men who gathered here. "I will trust the LORD and do good. And perhaps He will let us enjoy safe pasture."

Absolute silence followed her declaration. Eva dropped her gaze, shaking inside from the intensity of her words.

At last Dietmar spoke. "You are right, Eva Gottlieb. It is as Reinhardt would have said. Please forgive me."

She nodded quickly at him, suddenly uncomfortable in the spotlight.

"The LORD has used Eva to remind us of the truth tonight, gentlemen," Klaus rumbled. "The Name of God will not be removed from our sanctuary. May He forgive us for even considering it. Now go in peace, and may the LORD keep you."

Karl filtered into the church in the midst of the Sunday morning worshippers. The issue of the name weighed heavy on his mind. Slipping into a pew near the back, he craned his neck to see around a portly churchgoer who stood between him and the stained-glass window in question. It was no use. Sinking back into his seat to wait, he fingered the paper he feared would be the death warrant of this little church. *If they do not comply, they leave us no choice.*

The rotund gentleman abruptly sat, and Karl's heart sank. Yes. Still there. Beneath the picture of an old, robed man with his arms spread toward fire that seemed to be falling from the sky, the inscription proclaimed: *Jehovah, He is God!* Karl glanced away from the portal, crumpled the paper in his pocket into a little ball, and forced himself to *wait*. Perhaps someone would announce a plan to remove the name. Maybe after they finished their endless rounds of singing and prayer, one of the deacons would get up and declare that the offending proclamation would be erased.

But even that slim hope wavered and dimmed as he stood and sat in time with the congregation. Today's songs seemed to have been chosen for their defiance.

> My soul, be on thy guard,
> Ten thousand foes arise …

He did not bother to mouth the words today. What did it matter? He was one of the ten thousand foes, and the destruction that was coming on this church would not be held off by any stretch of pious soul-guarding.

> Oh, watch and fight and pray,
> The battle ne'er give o'er,
> Renew it boldly ev'ry day
> And help divine implore.

His answer was there, in the lyrics the congregation so confidently sang around him. Even before Pieters ascended the steps of the pulpit and began his solemn announcement, Karl knew what the outcome would be.

Yes, the church elders had been made aware of the decree ordering the removal of the Name Jehovah from their church. And no, they would most certainly not comply.

"How can we expect any help from our Lord," Pieters boomed, "if we are too frightened to call on His name?"

Karl sat up straighter in his pew, studied the scuff marks on his leather boots, nervously scratched his deaf ear, and wished to be somewhere very far away from these churchgoers and their lost and noble causes.

It was all too similar to the night Reinhardt was arrested. He remembered standing in the dim prison corridor, talking to the doomed pastor, presenting him with a picture of this day and accusing him for making it come to pass.

"Is you God worth that? Worth the suffering, not only of yourself, but of all those you hold dear?"

A pause. Terrible in its silence. He saw the anguish of that impossible question play out across the pastor's face, and then—"Yes."

His own stunned silence replied to Reinhardt's assertion. At last he managed to croak, "I hope you are right. But ..."

That had been his only reply then. Now he spoke it in silent response to the thundering voice of Klaus Pieters. *You say your God will protect you. Though I cannot see how, I hope for your sake you are right.*

Two days had passed since Klaus Pieter's announcement at the church. They been two tense days, comprised of forty-eight interminable hours, but still nothing happened. No ominous notice appeared nailed to the towering oak doors of the church. No midnight visit shattered the darkness with pounding fists and furious Gestapo agents. As the second day drew to a reluctant end, Eva allowed herself to believe everything was going to be all right.

All right. She halfway-smiled at the irony of the word. *My husband is dead and I am hiding two miracle refugee children in my house while the threat of destruction hangs over all of Christ Church, and today I am all right.* It was odd how quickly a situation, *any* situation, could seem normal. Today she had not been surprised at all when she came downstairs to find Hirschel and Adina already at the table. In fact *under* was the more specific preposition, as the children had been hiding in a fort constructed of a drooping tablecloth and a forest of chair legs. Adina had automatically looked up when she entered the room, and Eva had caught her eye almost immediately. Then she had proceeded to search every cupboard and crevice of the kitchen for her missing children before sitting down at the table, much to Hirschel's delight. They had laughed together as she made breakfast, lighthearted despite the worry that tugged at Eva's thoughts.

If the Gestapo came here, searched this house ... where would Adina and Hirschel hide? Triggered by the memory of the innocent game of hide-and seek, the thought froze Eva midmotion as she bent to run water for a bath. Suddenly the bathroom seemed a sinister place in spite of the pale, green-tiled walls and the elegant ivory-hued bathtub. *What if they came when one of the children was in the bath? There would be no time—and no way to hide a dripping wet child or disguise a bathtub full of water! What if—* Eva gripped the edge of the tub and tried to bring order to her frantic thoughts. *The attic. Attic would be the best place to hide. But we won't need it. I have not been bothered once by them since Reinhardt. No. Safe here. Adina said ... refuge.*

It was that last thought that evened her breathing and dispelled her terrible imaginings. Eva reached to turn the tap, grimacing at the feel of the ice-cold metal. Strange that she should be so comforted by the words of a child, but then again—she wondered as she held her hand beneath the stream of water and waited for it to warm—was it not these children who had come to her carrying a story about the power of a God who was still greater than all the machinations of evil?

Satisfied that the water was warm enough now, she maneuvered the stopper into place and called for Hirschel to come in and take his bath.

And then the knocking erupted at the door.

Deliverance

IN A MATTER OF seconds Eva thrust her head under the stream of water, yanked the stopper out and flung a towel around her shoulders. Scarcely breathing, she opened the bathroom door just enough to slip out.

"Hirschel! Adina!" Her voice was a hoarse whisper as the pounding continued. A moment later she spotted the children in the gloom, huddled together at the foot of the staircase.

"Upstairs," she mouthed, and Adina jumped to her feet. Tugging Hirschel behind her, the girl lunged up the stairs. Eva counted to fifteen before she replied to the noise outside.

"I'm coming! Just a moment, please—" She waited ten more seconds, hoping her voice had been steady, hoping the children had had time to hide. The insistent knocking continued, still unaccompanied by any voice. *Please, God—*

At last she advanced toward the door. Holding her breath in an attempt to steady herself, she parted the curtains to peer out ... and saw Katrina.

"You!" she hissed ferociously, sliding back the bolt and unlocking the door. Katrina opened it from the other side and stepped gratefully into the warmth. With more force than was strictly necessary, Eva slammed the door behind her and shoved the bolt into place before turning to face her friend.

"What in the name of all things good and *sensible* do you mean by coming here at nine thirty and pounding on my door like Herr Hitler himself, without even calling out to let me know who it is?" Eva demanded in a choked whisper. "I sent Hirschel and Adina to hide upstairs because I thought you were the Gestapo! You could have at least called my name! Would that have been so hard? 'Eva, Eva, it's me, Katrina,'" she mimicked. "Instead you try to knock down my door and give me a heart attack?"

Katrina stood meekly in front of the door, enduring Eva's tirade in silence. "I'm sorry," she murmured at last. A bundle stirred and meowed faintly in her arms.

"You brought Maestro?" Annoyance flared briefly and then deepened into genuine worry. "Trina? Is something wrong?"

"Yes. No. I'm sorry." Katrina sighed and leaned her head back against the door. "Can I sit down?"

Uncertainty replacing the anger of a moment before, Eva merely nodded. Katrina shoved herself away from the door and moved slowly through the short hallway to Eva's living room. A fire was burning brightly in the fireplace, and the orange light reflected off the chestnut patina of the baby grand piano and deepened the red fabric of the settee and chairs.

Pausing at the back of the settee, Katrina stared into the fire a moment and then inquired, "Eva? Who chopped wood for you this winter?"

"Men from the church," she responded distractedly, noting her friend's slowness of speech. "Tea?"

"With milk and honey."

"Yes. Like the Promised Land," Eva muttered. She turned back into the hallway on her way to the kitchen. "Adina? Hirschel? It's all right. You can come out. It was only Aunt Katrina," she called. *And Aunt Katrina is going to be explaining herself very shortly,* Eva added silently. Not waiting for a reply, she walked briskly to the kitchen to put the kettle on and search for the jar of honey she kept on hand for Katrina.

Something large and furry buzzed up against her leg as she poured the boiling water over the tea. The fragrant liquid sloshed in the cup and almost spilled over as she jumped to avoid stepping on Katrina's pet.

"Cat. There is something wrong here besides you, eh?" She poured cream into the mug, watching it swirl and cloud the tea. Lastly, she dipped a spoonful of honey in and carried the cup back to the living room.

"So. Trina, what's wrong?" Eva extended the question along with the tea. Katrina took the cup gratefully, and for the first time Eva noticed how cold she looked. "Did you walk?"

"Yes."

"Why—" Eva began and then checked herself. "Please start at the beginning."

Katrina sipped her tea and stared into the fire. "I'm sorry," she repeated softly. Then, "Why is your hair wet?"

"Because I thought you were the Gestapo. Please, go ahead."

"I was frightened," Katrina offered at last, with an embarrassed shrug.

"You walked more than two kilometers to my house in the dark with your cat and nearly beat the door down because you were frightened?" Eva turned to glare accusingly at Maestro as he sauntered into the living room, unwilling to be completely angry with Katrina.

"The hospital—they were talking about … our friend today. Gestapo came. They would have interrogated him, except he is rarely conscious long enough to say guten morgan. It seems his father is a prisoner of the Nazi state. Legally they could arrest him as well. Though they probably won't because even the Gestapo minions are intelligent enough to know tuberculosis is bad and they could catch it from him." Katrina offered Eva a half smile. "That did not stop the two of them from lurking like slugs in the corridor for the better part of an hour, pestering all of us and muttering things about *useless mouths*. And then tonight, there was an arrest down the street, and—I … I panicked. I wanted to be *here* and not *there*, I suppose." Katrina smiled wanly and ran a hand through her long chestnut hair.

Eva recognized the emotion in the gesture: anxiety and exhaustion and *aloneness*, all rolled into one. "Of course you are welcome, Trina." She nodded and flicked her foot warningly at Maestro. *I cannot say if here is any safer than your flat downtown, but you are welcome all the same.* She ignored the thought and plunged ahead. "Beds are a bit of a problem, but we'll make do. The children's baths can wait until tomorrow. You have work"—Katrina nodded—"but if you are here tomorrow night, we'll make a party. Music. Food. Games … pin the tail on the cat, perhaps."

Katrina ignored her friend's jibe and clicked her tongue for Maestro. The massive brown-black cat considered her with brooding amber eyes for a moment before launching himself into her lap. Purring loudly, he allowed himself to be petted for less than a minute before biting at her fingers and leaping back to the floor.

"I shouldn't have brought him, Eva, I know." Katrina followed Eva's bemused gaze to the cat and shrugged an apology. "Tomorrow night sounds wonderful. I will go back after that, I promise."

"You are always welcome, Trina." Irritation now completely vanished, Eva touched her friend's fingers and smiled. "You have done so much for me since …" The rest of the thought remained unspoken in the air between them.

Katrina nodded. "I still wish you could leave this place."

Eva simply glanced at the stairwell and shrugged, as if to say, *too late now.* "I made a promise. To myself and … to you. I didn't tell you then, but I promised I couldn't—that I wouldn't …" Eva paused, almost shy. "I wouldn't leave you alone here. If God opened a door and we could suddenly leave Austria—you and me and the children all together—I would not hesitate. Not for a moment. But if not, then … together. Yes?"

She raised her eyes to meet Katrina's and was surprised at the emotion shining there. Slowly, humbly, Katrina nodded and managed to say, "Thank you." For once she had no other words. She swallowed hard and nodded. *Yes. Together.*

"Frustrated" was not a good word, Karl decided, as he waited shoulder to shoulder with a dozen other agents in the corridor outside the Inspekteur's office. Such military precision was not required by the Gestapo as a general rule, but Fredrik had wished it to be so in Villach. And, like nearly everything else, the will of the evil little man had become the law.

But not today, Karl mused. That was why he and the others stood in such tense silence in the cold hallway. A telegram had come from the Old Castle in Klagenfurt today—from Dr. Weimann, addressed specifically to Fredrik Schmidt. That event was not terribly unusual in and of itself. Gestapo offices all over the Reich served merely as fixed points to hold the vast web of watchers together. Communication was frequent and essential.

But this telegram! The Inspekteur was indeed in a black mood today.

That, coupled with the fact that the message concerned the church issue, filled Karl with both hope and fear. Hope because Schmidt would only be furious if his designs against the church were somehow thwarted. And fear of what he would do if they were—

"Ten to one we're sent out to arrest the whole pathetic group." Fleicher, looking none too impressive himself with his oily complexion and soft face, murmured his bet from near the end of the line.

Nods of approval and excitement bobbed up and down the row of agents. Karl's reluctant but precise report of Christ Church's defiance had sparked a righteous anger in many minds. *Who do they think they are, embracing Jewish lies over the words of the Fuehrer himself? They are no better than the Jewish pigs! Weaklings and fools! Who do they think …?*

Karl shook his head in disagreement. "We would have been back already with the first group. Something is wrong." He cleared his throat impatiently and hoped his voice had not betrayed him and inflected *right* as he spoke *wrong*.

"Pieter saw him mouth *Christ Church*," Thomas asserted. No one commented on his remark. After all, it was this bit of knowledge that had sparked the first speculation. "We are all Gestapo—does he think we don't know?" the grim giant of a man finished sullenly.

"Hard to hide from a group of eavesdroppers and spies." Karl grinned with feigned lightness. Other words whispered in his mind as soft laughter echoed up and down the line. *Traitor. Coward. Fool.* He cleared his throat again, wondering if he was coming down with something. He made a mental note to stand outside somewhere in the rain today.

"But you, Karl—always at the church. The Inspekteur is making a religious man out of you!" Fleicher was laughing, but Karl saw the spark of interest in Thomas's beady eyes.

He shrugged as noncommittally as he could. "My faith is in a just cause. The Fuehrer and the good of Germany." He had barely finished the rote response when the sound of angry footsteps in the room beyond warned the entire group to silence. Karl arched his eyebrows as if to say, *I told you so,* and then the thin door flew open.

A dozen "Heil Hitlers" greeted Fredrik as he glared out at his assembled agents. The Inspekteur did not look well, Karl thought with a flash of foreboding. Pinched and irritated in the best of times, today the man's face was a contorted shadow of rage. Murder flashed in his eyes.

"We are not carrying out the order against the churches here." Anger trembled behind the clipped words, but Karl was somehow relieved. *Right, and not wrong!*

"Why, sir?" Pieter wondered aloud.

Fredrik whirled in the doorway to glare at the fresh-faced agent who had been foolish enough to pose such a question.

"Klagenfurt wishes that we show leniency to dissenting churches in the softhearted and misplaced hope they will join our cause. We are not to interfere."

This time not even the dark specter of Fredrik Schmidt's anger prevented the questions from rippling through the line.

And who would stop us if we did? Karl wondered. Another glance at the seething *Inspekteur* gave him a clue. *Perhaps not us, but him.* Strangely encouraged at the thought of Fredrik's vulnerability, he allowed the appropriate expression of anger at the quarry's escape to flicker on his face for a moment.

"You are dismissed. Go!" Fredrik barked, retreating back into his office and slamming the door. The flimsy wood trembled, and the walls did not prevent the steady stream of Fredrik's rage from pursuing the agents through the hallway and down a flight of stairs.

So their lost cause was perhaps not so lost after all, Karl mused as he stood at the edge of the stone bridge. Below him, frigid gray water seethed and foamed angrily at the first intrusions of ice. Locals said this river was almost always completely frozen over by Christmas. The waterway had been open to ice skaters for as long as anyone could remember, but this year there were rumors that the Nazis might not permit it. And why not? Nearly every other free spirited and innocent thing had already been denied.

Karl made a face somewhere between a smile and a grimace as the scene of the familiar SS holiday dances suddenly interposed itself onto the pewter water. *Two dozen men in heavy boots would only be the beginning.* Karl pictured a tribe of SS goons careening wildly across the imaginary ice, and for some reason the image delighted him. He mentally added a few faces from the Gestapo headquarters and nominated Fredrik to light the bonfire. *Oh yes. On the ice. He might do it, too, if he could put the match to books or Bibles.*

The amusement of the game evaporated as quickly as it had come. He blinked and stared out at the opposite bank. Lights coming on across the river reflected orange and yellow in the turbulent foam. Water was still water, and Fredrik Schmidt was just as likely to burn heretics to the Nazi Party and his own thirst for power. *Or have them thrown in prison and executed, and then tried and found guilty.*

Bad memories seemed to linger at this bridge. Karl sighed and then sneezed twice. At least that scene was not being played out again tonight, with every other member of Gottlieb's congregation. The relief in that simple fact was enough to keep Karl from feeling the cold wind that whipped about him on the bridge, laden with the promise of more snow. *But what stopped him? Disapproval from Klagenfurt, I'm sure, but why? Mercy has never been the preferred tactic of the Nazis.*

Both his good ear and his deaf one were numb with cold. Karl turned reluctantly from the water and back toward East Villach. The streetlamps of the downtown glowed orange off the low white sky, reminding Karl of fire. He grimaced. For no reason at all, the voice of Klaus Pieters resounded in his mind. "How can we expect any help from our Lord if we are too frightened to call on His name?"

Was this their answer? Karl wondered. He had fully expected a dozen arrests, at the very least. Probably the closing of the church as well, and perhaps the razing of the building. Such actions had been implied in the orders from the German Church. *But Christ Church is allowed to continue as if the law did not exist. As if Fredrik did not want anything more than to see them all in prison or worse.*

Such a turn of events had been unlikely, unforeseeable ... but a direct answer to Pieters's prayer? Karl could not quite believe it. He was not willing to forget how heaven had been silent on Kristallnacht, the night of the broken glass. *Or when we arrested and executed Pastor Gottlieb. Certainly he must have been a favorite up there.*

Why this now? Why silence then? Perhaps this church business was nothing, a chance favorable outcome from the aggravating of tensions between two men who deeply mistrusted each other. Still, Karl decided he would read the Bible tonight. And as he started toward the city and sneezed yet again, he entertained the hope that he might stay home and read the book tomorrow as well.

Of Christmases Past

THE LAST FEEBLE GLOW of sunset flared red as a malevolent wind rattled through the winter-stripped trees. Eva held tighter to the children's hands and tried to walk only in the puddles of light that spilled from the windows of shops and cafés and restaurants. The streetlamps were flickering to life beside them, but tonight their artificial light only seemed to highlight the shadows. She had hated this night even as a child—*Krampusnacht*, the night before St. Nicholas Day, when men dressed as demons and came out to haunt the streets. *And we are walking along this road for—bread? I should have remembered! It was not so important to have bread tonight.* But the auto was parked a block behind them, the bakery two streets ahead.

"Look only at me," she murmured as a shadow flitted from tree to tree across the street.

"What's wrong, Tante Eva?" Adina's grip tightened, reciprocating the tension in Eva's voice.

They were not far from the bakery now. "Tonight is a night when … men act like bad little boys and put on masks to scare people." Images of the hideous horned masks and bared fangs of "Krampus" made an unwelcome entrance in Eva's thoughts.

"But we are not scared of them. Are we?" Hirschel asked anxiously when Eva did not respond.

Another shadow. Half a block from the bakery. Movement and faint laughter from among the dead trees in the park across the street.

It was not the enactment of the mythical devil sent to punish children that urged her feet to keep time with her racing heart, Eva reminded herself. When she was eight she had yelled at one of the ugly impostors to *go away!* and he had run. Her father had laughed and swung her up on his shoulders and called her his brave girl, and until tonight that had been the end of her Krampus fears.

Chains rattled somewhere in the breathless darkness, and Eva was certain she saw a figure moving behind the line of parked autos. *Do not frighten these children,* she warned the apparition fiercely. *If you dare jump out at us I will tear your evil mask off and tell you to go home!* The thought made her defiant for a moment, until she imagined the unmasked Devil saluting and then dragging Hirschel and Adina away from her forever.

"Jewish children!" the creature cackled. "Forbidden! They are MINE—"

She gasped and forced the vision away. "Jesus," she whispered weakly, as the sound of unseen footsteps quickened to match their pace. She squeezed the children's hands more tightly and moved instinctively away from the street. *Apartments!* A mile of locked doors until the bakery! The rattle of unseen chains increased beside them, and—

"Go away."

Eva whirled but saw no one on the deserted street. The footfalls that had been so menacing a moment earlier now sounded almost contrite as they scurried away. Eva closed her eyes and sighed in relief.

"Tante Eva? Who was that?" Hirschel's voice shattered the tense darkness like a wrecking ball.

"I—"

"It was a friend." A tall, blond stranger stepped from behind the last car and bowed slightly.

Startled at his sudden appearance, Eva simply stared for a moment before terrifying recognition flooded through her. "You—the church ..."

"Yes." Still nodding, denying nothing, the man continued to smile faintly at her in his odd, remorseful way. "It is unwise to be out tonight, Frau Gottlieb," he said softly. "Too many troublemakers about."

Regaining some control over her shaking limbs, Eva jerked her head down in a quick nod of acknowledgement. "Danke," she offered curtly, and then stepped around Karl to hurry into the bakery.

The last chime of midnight mellowed into silent darkness as Eva slipped out of bed. Groggily she wondered if she had slept at all. Grinning monsters had paraded through her mind for the past two hours, finally transforming into the hard, shadowed features of the Gestapo agent on the street tonight.

And yet he seemed … sad. Worried—she shook her head, not willing to let her tired thoughts spin any further in the blackness. She reached for the throw at the end of the bed and wrapped herself in it. *The shoes. Fill them with candy and then try again to sleep.* Eva gingerly opened her door and shuffled toward the kitchen. There was a bag of chocolate pralines on the highest shelf in the cupboard, behind a half-used canister of salt and a container of rye seeds. She had saved them especially for tonight.

You think *the finest chocolate comes from Switzerland and Belgium*—she smiled softly at the reminder of the longstanding dispute between her and Reinhardt. *But really, the finest chocolatiers come from Vienna! There was a shop near my house, where some of the best chocolate makers in Europe came to learn! There they could put a café into a single praline …*

The memory faded into the lonely blackness of the kitchen. Eva pulled the blanket tighter, forcing her fingers between the knitted stitches. Had those words truly been spoken a year ago? Were those sacred moments once ordinary days, now made precious by their absence? *Gone … is a hard word to understand.*

Chocolate in hand, she padded out of the kitchen and up the stairs to the master bedroom. Hirschel and Adina shared it now. It was just as well, she reasoned as she felt along the floor for the little shoes. At least she no longer started awake in the middle of the large featherbed, reaching for *him.* Methodically she counted the chocolates into Adina's slipper. Five for her, five for Hirschel, and one for Eva, to eat and remember …

Would I have believed it if someone had warned me? she wondered as she cupped her hands around the foil-wrapped candy. *Could I have imagined this—standing alone in the dark, filling the shoes of two Jewish children with the last of the Viennese chocolate for St. Nicholas Day?*

Suddenly Eva did not want to taste the last chocolate. She slipped it into Adina's shoe and returned to the kitchen for two oranges to complete the gift. *Hirschel and Adina are children of a friend of mine*, she rehearsed as she retrieved the fruit. Yes. That was good. Much easier to review the past she and Katrina had written for the children than to face the story she lived. Mentally she rehearsed the "facts" they had established: *Their mother became ill suddenly. They lived abroad until now, when the father sent them to me to keep them out from underfoot. Identification papers are tangled somewhere in the Gestapo bureaucracy of Vienna.*

It was all a game of bluff, she knew. One persistent Gestapo agent could easily discover that—the thought made her tread more quietly on the stairs, as if her footfalls might somehow bring the wrath of the Nazis into the sleeping house. But this game of lies had seemed more certain than the alternative of keeping two lively children concealed for months on end. *Hide them outdoors*, Katrina had advised. *In the city. At church. In the park. And we will pray no one asks questions.*

"But what does a Christmas market *look* like, Tante Eva?" Adina's voice was insistent from the backseat.

Eva smiled as she scanned the curb in search of a place to park. "It looks like a little village in the middle of the *Hauptplatz*. No cars will drive there today, and there will be lots of little yellow houses with wreaths and decorations on them. And that is where you must help me look for a present for Aunt Katrina."

There was silence in the back as the children considered their mission. Eva parked more than a block away from the beginning of Main Street. She suddenly wanted to share in the children's surprise: to gape at the festive pine booths and sip hot chocolate and follow the magic strains of "Silent Night" in and out of the maze of sellers until the musician was found.

"Ready?"

"Ready!"

Eva delayed opening the door a moment longer, unaccountably frightened of the instant Adina and Hirschel would be out of her sight. *There is nothing to fear in daylight*, she reminded herself, choosing not to look at the brooding sky. She smoothed an imaginary crease from her black felt coat and pretended not to see Hirschel's impatient frown.

"We're going," she declared, opening the door and stepping out before she could change her mind. The cold air that stung her face seemed oddly quiet, devoid of the cheerful clamor that had marked this market in past years. In a moment Hirschel and Adina were beside her. Two small hands held tightly to hers as they began their march up toward the market.

Smaller and more subdued than Eva remembered it, the Christmas market was nonetheless festive and mysterious in the children's eyes. Just as Tante Eva had promised, little pinewood houses stretched in two rows up the Hauptplatz—a town inside the town! Dark-green garlands and satin ribbons decorated booths that sold everything from hot chocolate to Christmas ornaments to fresh-baked pastries.

"How come there's oranges in the snow?" Hirschel was already drifting toward a pyramid of the bright fruit heaped in a carton dangerously within reach. Eva tugged him back.

"Maybe they need the oranges to be cold, like snowballs, so they can make a snowman out of them!" Adina suggested brightly. "But how do they get oranges in the winter?"

"They grow somewhere far away, where it's still warm. Then people pick them and put them in a ship and sail them to us."

"From Palestine?" Adina's question was loud, audible above the murmuring crowd. Conversations hushed abruptly. The white-bearded orange seller squinted in their direction.

"No, not there," Eva answered hurriedly. "Somewhere else warm. Maybe from Africa." She pulled the children forward, away from the curious eyes of the orange vendor and the whispers of the people who had overheard Adina's question. The market seemed to stretch on forever, reaching up the length of the street and overflowing into Kirche Platz in front of St. Jakob. Eva spotted the towering Christmas tree at its center, just in front of the marble column of the Trinity. She moved toward it as if there was some safety to be found near the rich green branches.

"What do we get for Aunt Katrina? Can we get her some cake?"

She stopped and followed the little boy's gesture to the array of breads and strudels supplied by a bakery behind the little Christmas houses. Studying them for a moment, she shook her head in feigned displeasure. "When Aunt Katrina comes for Christmas Eve, I will make something much better than that."

"Really?"

"Truly." Eva nodded solemnly, grateful for the distraction that kept her from scanning every passing face and trying to discern friends from foes. "We need to find a present that *isn't* food. Then we'll have lunch."

"What about those?" Adina pointed to a tray of bright jewelry on the other side of booths. Eva let herself be led toward the collection of rings and necklaces. She remembered that jewelry was always a poor second to books where Katrina was concerned. But then again, booksellers offered a considerably more limited selection these days.

"What's Aunt Katrina's favorite color?"

"'Blue and silver and a flash of purple, like the clouds at dusk on the first day of autumn.'" Eva laughed. "So I think we are looking for something silver. Or blue or purple. She also likes light green, so I'm glad you're here to help me!"

Now they were at the jewelry booth. "Guten tag, Frau." The wizened old vendor nodded slowly at Eva and Adina and the top of Hirschel's head. "And Heil Hitler, I suppose." His off-white mustache seemed to droop with the words.

"Guten tag." Ignoring the last part of the greeting, Eva nudged Adina to explain their mission.

"We are looking for a present for our Aunt Katrina. She likes silver and blue and purple, and green, I think. And Tante Eva says we cannot get lunch before we find something she will like," Adina finished seriously.

"So many colors." The vendor smiled and tugged the corner of his mustache. "I believe I have the perfect thing." He bent stiffly to rummage beneath the shelf. When he emerged, he cradled a black velvet board hung with a dazzling array of pendants. "Venetian glass." He smiled again, revealing a row of lonely and uneven teeth. "From across the border. Nothing else has so many colors, you see."

Adina seemed transfixed by the sparkling drops of rainbow on the velvet sky. Even Eva had to admit the joyful swirls of color would make Katrina smile.

"I want to see!" Eva boosted Hirschel up to the level of the satin-draped shelf and watched his eyes widen at the blaze of color.

"Which one do you think, Tante Eva?" Adina's fingers drifted between a shimmering green rectangle and a silver-lavender heart.

"It can be difficult to choose, Frau. What is your friend like?"

The question put Eva instantly ill at ease. Pretending to have heard differently, she stammered out Katrina's description of clouds and fall skies and lowered Hirschel to the ground.

"Ah. Then *this* is the one." The old man gently guided Adina's hand to a teardrop-shaped pendant smaller than the others. Silver rippled with blue, and—yes! in the heart a barely perceptible trace of purple.

"It is perfect," she admitted. Adina nodded happily. "How much?"

"Twenty reichsmarks."

"Twenty? Impossible. Ten."

"For such fine glass! I cannot go lower than fifteen."

Eva nodded in agreement and fished through her handbag for the money. Was it her imagination, or was the vendor studying Adina? She did not meet his eyes again as she paid and took the pendant. "Danke," she murmured.

"Heil Hitler, Frau Gottlieb."

The coldness of the unexpected recognition clung to Eva as she hurried the children away from the booth. Perhaps he had simply remembered her name at the end of the purchase, she reasoned. But then why had he sent her on her way with a *heil*? Or asked about Katrina?

The rest of the Christmas market experience was concluded at lightning speed. Pretzels were hastily purchased from a vendor across the street, the giant town Christmas tree briefly inspected on the way out of the market. A web of little spider-swastikas matted the green boughs. *And the sparrow tree—where is it?* The second, smaller evergreen, decorated each year in strands of breadcrumbs, was nowhere to be seen. The absence was not surprising, in a land where men were considered of less worth than a sparrow by virtue of race. Besides, this new Nazi Christmas was a strong holiday. It had no use for weak and frivolous creatures. No place for them but the labor camps.

This realization made Eva squeeze the children's hands more tightly as they left the murmuring Christmas village behind.

Silence of the Soul

WOULD THE CONGREGATION OF Christ Church carol in the square this
year?

The simple question had been discussed and dissected and argued from
every possible angle by the deacons, and only then had the unsatisfying
answer been reached. Eva shifted position in the pew as Klaus Pieters
announced that, contrary to tradition, the church would not assemble to
lead townspeople to the service this Christmas Eve.

It was a gesture certain to provoke the Gestapo, an unnecessary show
of defiance. Or was it faithfulness? Loyalty and trust to the Christ whose
birth they celebrated? Pieters continued to defend the decision while Eva
considered the question yet again. It was not terribly different from their
choice to keep the Name and the pictures of the prophets in the sanctuary,
was it? *We stood there; here we fall back. We fight for truth, and we dance with
disaster. Is this bravery or foolishness?* The two were becoming increasingly
blurred.

Hirschel poked her arm, urging her to her feet as the congregation
stood to sing. She rose, smiled into his gap-toothed grin, and then found
the words to the hymn frozen in her throat. *Here! These children are the
line I cannot cross!* she realized suddenly, clearly, as the song rose and fell
around her. She looked down to see Adina proudly following the words in
the hymnal. Hirschel could not read, but he hummed loudly beside her.
*Precious! Did I realize it before? God, You must help me protect them! Take
them away from here! Please, show me …*

⁜

During the autumn that followed the pastor's execution, Karl had begun to distance himself from the three other agents who had come with him from Berlin and the rabble of watchers from Villach. His sullen, brooding presence had been acknowledged and tolerated at the edge of the group of men. But now, as the days flowed toward Christmas, his behavior could only be classified as "solitary." He accomplished everything required from him with mechanical precision—met with every eager informant, meticulously updated the files of the watched, reported on the activity in Christ Church. Twice in the past weeks he had seen innocent men pass through the prison on their way to Mauthausen. They had been neither political dissenters nor Jews nor troublesome Christians. Simply ordinary men who had appeared on the wrong side of a slanted report. All this had been clear at their arrest, but Karl had done nothing. What was there to be done, after all?

After work each night Karl would vanish, avoiding the invitation to the drinks and laughter of the others. Soon the invitations stopped coming, but he was somehow too far removed to care. He paced the streets and alleys of Villach until exhaustion and cold brought him back to his apartment. And then ... then, with numb fingers and chapped hands, he would turn the pages of the forbidden book, read the black and white words until the searing longing became too great within him. Until he could not bear another word of truth or justice or mercy when his own life was so full of withered lies.

Krimmel had left the crisp black ribbon bookmark at the book of Matthew, a barrier marking the distinction between the Jewish writings and what they called the New Testament. It was a distinction Karl understood less and less. These stories of Jesus were centered around Jerusalem, grounded in continual references to the promises given by the God of Israel.

Yes, this would certainly get him into trouble.

Karl sighed and gently laid the heavy book on his desk. Rising slowly, he swept a stack of bills and brochures and information and half-finished drawings over the Bible out of habit. Even another Gestapo agent would be hard-pressed to find anything in the mild natural disaster that passed for a desk. The words he had just read echoed as he shuffled to the window that looked out at nothing. *And you shall love the LORD your God with all your heart, with all your soul, with all your mind, and with all your strength.* Matthew 22:37

But the LORD was not his God. Did that exempt him? *And the second, like it, is this: You shall love your neighbor as yourself.* Matthew 22:39 Karl snorted at that. Love? Love your neighbor? He was paid to spy on his neighbor and everyone else's. He sighed and watched the sound of his confusion make a foggy circle on the window pane. It was an accurate symbol, he decided. Cold clouds and banks of unanswered questions. The silence of an ear that would never hear and the piercing words that he could not comprehend. He might as well have been trying to read the Bible in Portuguese or Greek. *If anyone desires to be first, he shall be last of all and servant of all.* Mark 9:35

Absent here was the grappling, merciless struggle for survival. In these pages, at least, the weakest were valued, loved. Even the sparrows were fed by the hand of God, the children taken and blessed, the cripples made whole—the world was upside down. Or perhaps right side up?

It was just this, the "meekness and flabbiness of Christianity" that so disgusted the Nazis, from the Fuehrer himself down to Fredrik Schmidt. In their eyes it was a rebellion against natural law. A celebration of human failure! And yet—and yet, Karl remembered Reinhardt Gottlieb, kneeling on the cobbles, waiting for the gunshot that would end his life. Face turned into the light. Serene. Unafraid.

"Is your God worth that?"

The pastor had said yes. And then, more incredibly, he had lived it. Walked out of the prison and up into the cold darkness as calmly as if he were strolling home. Done nothing to defend himself as Fredrik clubbed him to the ground. Waited perfectly still … died, leaving that "yes!" ringing in the courtyard behind him.

So that left Karl … where? He had seen these words were true. They were true, but they could never be spoken over him.

Replacing the Bible beneath the assorted catastrophes and trinkets of his life, Karl switched off the light and went to bed.

Karl woke later than usual, almost late for work. Through the hurried business of finding clean clothes and tugging the familiar gray cap over his wiry blond hair he almost forgot what he had read the night before. It was not until nearly an hour later, while regretting the absence of breakfast over a stack of tip-offs and other assorted betrayals, that the words tugged at the edge of his memory.

"I believe the children in the care of Eva Gottlieb are of Jewish descent." Karl blinked and reread the scrap of paper. Then he closed his eyes, trying to remember the night a few weeks prior. *Gottlieb's wife and two children. A girl and a little boy. She was more frightened than them, because she recognized me*—Karl frowned and thought harder. Eva's face had been illuminated by the light of the bakery, but he had not gotten a good look at the children. *But the church! They were with her last Sunday and several Sundays before that.*

He returned his gaze to the slip of paper, slowly nodding. Yes, he remembered the faces of the siblings now. Hirschel and Adina. Their dark brown hair was not unlike Eva's, but the eyes—yes. It was quite possible this unknown informant was correct. He sighed softly. No evidence was presented in the spidery handwriting, nothing but suspicion. *But suspicion is weightier than life these days.* The morose thought surprised him. This was his job, after all, but—children? Innocent. *Fragile, like the sparrows. And, they say, loved by Him.*

He drummed his cold fingers on the paper, unsure of what to do. Across the room, Pieter coughed loudly and then sniffled. Winter colds had ravaged the ranks of the Gestapo in the past weeks. Few were immune. Karl smiled at his own pun and then, slowly, covered the paper with his hand. It did not immediately burn through his skin, flash blue and red and announce its presence with sirens. That was a step in the right direction.

"Karl?" Pieter croaked. "Trade me seats? The sun ..." He nodded to the small square of light that fell on Karl's desk and tugged miserably at the collar of his coat.

Karl glanced at the high window and shook his head quickly. Too quickly. "You cough on that chair for an hour and then ask if I want it?" A good save. That paper was at least as warm as the sunlight now. "I'd rather not be sick again. Sorry." Karl hoped Pieter was too ill to notice the guilty falseness of his smile. In any case, the agent's next words were lost beneath a gigantic sneeze.

Eva Gottlieb—the paper. Karl ignored Pieter's mumblings about drafty apartments and long outdoor watches and the general accursedness of Villach in the winter—not that Berlin was any better, mind you—and tried desperately to concentrate. *I promised the pastor—but what is a promise made to a doomed man, now dead? Not worth the punishment, if I am caught …*

The cold laughter of the SS guards on the train platform suddenly returned to underscore the endless possibility of terrors. It could be judged as treason. For that, the penalty was death. Always. The form that death took was left to the discretion of the executioner, but Karl did not doubt Fredrik's creativity. *Only a fool would risk his life for fourteen little words,* he assured himself. He spread his fingers and stared at the words through the gaps. *Children … Eva Gottlieb … Jewish.* He remembered Reinhardt, pleading for Eva's life. *Four words. If it takes a fool to risk his life for fourteen, how foolish is the person who is put in danger by four?* A widow. Two children who might or might not be Jewish. What could he do with that?

Love your neighbor as yourself. Matthew 22: 39

Impossible command. Whether the charge was true or not, Karl would be guilty of hiding it. If he took the paper home and burned it, Gottlieb's wife might pass another day in safety, but he would have practically signed his own warrant for arrest.

Love your neighbor as yourself. Matthew 22: 39

Why, despite that, did he find himself *wanting* to obey?

Love your neighbor … Matthew 22: 39

He was only guilty if caught, Karl reminded himself as he slipped the paper into his pocket.

Christmas Eve at the Gottlieb house was a bittersweet affair. Eva had been in the kitchen since noon, preparing the traditional supper of fried carp and the wonderful chocolate cake known as *sachertorte.* Difficult to make, sachertorte was generally purchased from any number of bakeries at Christmastime. Eva was perhaps the only woman in Villach who made it at home. But she *had* promised Hirschel a surprise for Christmas, and Katrina was joining them for supper tonight.

Now she set aside the apricot jam and pointed her two hopeful taste-testers toward the cookies on the table. For the sachertorte they must wait. Eva quickly washed her hands and glanced at the cuckoo clock above the stove. It was half past five—Katrina would be here any minute. She instructed Adina to help her wipe down the counter while she jammed candles onto two painted wooden candlesticks and placed them on the table.

The doorbell rang. *Why is she on time now, of all days?* Eva wondered as she ran to answer it.

"Fröhliche Weihnachton! Happy Christmas!" Katrina declared, perhaps a bit too brightly.

Eva gave her friend a half smile as she ushered her in. "Happy Christmas, Trina. We were almost ready for you."

"I can see." Katrina laughed, dusting flour from Eva's sleeve. "Go and clean up. I'll keep Hirschel and Adina out of the food for you."

Katrina was already answering the questions that came from all directions at once as Eva made her way to the bathroom in the dark hallway. Suddenly the memories she had managed to fend off all day came crowding back. *Christmas last year. Reinhardt smug and secretive, refusing to say a word about his gift for me. Not even the slightest hint—what a surprise it was!*

A smile stole over Eva's gentle face. The stillness in the dark bathroom filled her with quiet remembering. She saw again Reinhardt's genuine delight as she opened the box to find a delicate necklace of pearls.

"It's beautiful! But how—"

"Shhh." He had laid a finger across her lips. "Don't worry. Just wear it."

Gingerly, halfway afraid the pearls might melt like snowflakes, Eva lifted the necklace up and slipped it over her head. She turned toward Reinhardt, only to see his frown.

"I'm sorry, Eva," he said in mock disapproval. "You're too beautiful for the pearls."

She giggled and shook her head. Reinhardt kissed her gently. "Happy Christmas, Eva."

Happy Christmas ... Happy Christmas ... Happy Christmas. The echoes receded, and Eva reluctantly returned to the present. Last year, Christmas *had* been happy. So close to Italy, Hitler's designs for Austria had been nothing more than a shadow on the horizon. *Did anyone realize how quickly the eclipse would come?*

Eva sighed as she turned on the light. Ghosts of memories hovered in every room of the house. She had only to close her eyes to glimpse them. *Reinhardt calling for me to hurry up, it's past time to leave for church! Firelight reflecting off silver tinsel until the Christmas tree itself seems encased in light. Simple joy at the beauty of it. Quiet conversations carried on long into the night on Christmas Eve.*

The images were clear yet irretrievably beyond reach. It seemed cruelly unfair that time moved so completely on! Not even the tiniest scrap of a life remembered could be relived. Eva could only gaze at them, cradle them like a jewel in the palm of her hand. There was sharp sorrow in their vividness but also comfort.

Oh, Reinhardt, I know you're waiting for me. I know I'll see you again. But sometimes … sometimes a lifetime is so long.

The cloud of remembrances clung to Eva, somehow shielding her from the cold aloneness of this night. Not until she rejoined the little group in the kitchen was the spell broken.

"Eva, I hardly recognize you without the flour—" Katrina started to tease but faltered as she saw the necklace.

Her eyes flitted from Eva's face to the pearls and back again. Yes, Katrina remembered. *Are you certain you can do this?* the probing gaze enquired. Eva replied with a firm nod. Tonight there would be tears, but for now they would continue for the sake of Adina and Hirschel.

The night before Christmas in Villach had always been greeted by the sound of carols in the square. Songs of joy and peace would rise in the frosty night, swirl toward the glittering stars, and then the stars themselves would come and join the song. From the villages and hamlets scattered across the slopes that hemmed Villach, men and women would gather in little groups around torches that bobbed and winked down to the half dozen churches of the city. From the valley floor, the dancing lights could be seen in almost every direction: merry pinpoints of fire marking the way of worshippers seeking the newborn King.

That was the memory Eva carried with her, at least. This year no carols were sung in the street. The stars remained cold and aloof above the silent hills, and churchgoers filed meekly past the rowdy SS bonfires and dances into the dim sanctuary. Here, within the red-brick walls that could not quite keep out the noise of the unholy Nazi celebration in the park beyond, they sang the quiet words of "Silent Night."

As Klaus Pieters ascended the stairs to read the Christmas story, the thought occurred to Eva that heaven was the only thing silent tonight. The demons across the street shouted loudly. She had seen the blond-haired Gestapo agent slip away from the light of their fires to invade the sanctity of even this small celebration. *But Reinhardt would have smiled at him all the same. Asked someone to pass a Bible to our Gestapo friend, because he certainly needed one.* She slowly shook her head. He really had done that once, about a month after the Anschluss. The watcher had stormed out of the church, and for a week there had been peace.

"Now it came to pass in those days that a decree went out from Caesar Augustus." Luke 2:1

Hirschel and Adina were hearing the story for the first time, but Eva let her mind wander through the familiar words. Tonight only candles lit the sanctuary. The glow of a hundred tiny flames reflected off the dark, narrow windows. Pieters's face looked solemn and ancient in the flickering shadows. It was easy for Eva to imagine him as one of the shepherds in that cold field, keeping watch over the flock by night. Along with Reinhardt.

"And behold, an angel of the Lord stood before them, and the glory of the Lord shone around them, and they were greatly afraid." Luke 2:9

There was no glory tonight, though they were still afraid. Just as there had been no stars on the mountains, no angel came down to announce good news of great joy. The crèche that stood in front of the pulpit was the only testimony to their ancient, magnificent message. Eva halfway listened as she studied the features of the kneeling figures. For the first time, she recognized the hint of sadness on Mary's wooden face. Joseph gazed down at the baby King in undisguised wonder, but in Mary's eyes she seemed to read the whisper of coming sorrow. What would the good lady have done, Eva wondered, if she had been allowed to glimpse the destiny of her holy child?

Hirschel laid his head against her shoulder, tugging Eva back to holy hush of candlelight and shadow in the sanctuary. She wrapped her arm around the sleepy five-year-old and pulled him close.

"Glory to God in the highest, and on earth peace, goodwill to men!" Luke 2:14

Eva wondered what she would have done in Mary's place. What she would do now, in her own dark night?

"Then the shepherds returned, glorifying and praising God for all the things that they had heard and seen, as it was told them." Luke 2:20

The story ended abruptly. Eva remained seated a moment after the rest of the congregation stood and began to sing. Why did they not read Matthew's account tonight as well? The massacre of the innocents would have been a more fitting end for the Christmas story here beneath the shadow of the swastika. Katrina glanced sharply at her and took Adina's hand as if she had overheard the dark thoughts. Then she looked at Hirschel and nodded once. *There are still miracles,* her eyes seemed to say.

Eva smiled weakly. *Yes. You are right, of course.* But peace—on earth, or simply in her heart—was still terribly far away tonight.

After the service, churchgoers milled about the nave in pockets of intense conversation. Missing in the crowd were the twice-a-year pious. Nominal attendees had scattered with the first wave of persecution, and now only the faithful and the traitors remained.

"Frau Gottlieb?"

Eva flinched at the sound of her name—even here, in the relative safety of the church. She turned to face the stocky, russet-haired speaker and tried to smile politely. "Herr … Werberg. Good evening."

"Yes. I—good evening." Werberg fumbled, casting a sideways glance at the back of the lean Gestapo agent framed in the doorway. He was not watching—not for the moment, at least. "Frau Gottlieb, I deal in … rare books."

Eva greeted this declaration with a smile and a blank nod.

Werberg stammered wildly. "I—I—your husband. He appreciated my work. 'Eternal treasures,' he said …"

Pain flickered in Eva's eyes, followed by sudden comprehension as she recognized Reinhardt's words. "You—"

"Yes. Something I would like to show you ... Thursday, perhaps? Thursday evening? Are you free?"

"Of course. What—"

"Seven thirty then." Werberg handed her a twice-folded slip of paper and nodded once more. Then, abruptly, he spun around and hurried out into the cold.

The cold of the snowy night easily penetrated Karl's worn double-breasted overcoat as he made his way home from the Christmas Eve service. The noise from the celebration in Stadt Park pursued him on the wind, easily extinguishing the feeble glow of peace he had sensed within the walls of Christ Church. They worshipped the Fuehrer tonight by the light of their bonfires, he knew. The SS and civilians gathered beneath the dead trees tonight were the true servants of the Reich, the ones who had given to Adolph Hitler not only their support and enthusiasm but their minds and hearts!

Karl stomped snow from his shoes and clattered up the metal staircase. He unlocked the door and slammed it, somehow fearful that tonight his thoughts would be overheard and the shadows in the park would *know* he was not one with them!

In the dark of his apartment other noises replaced the singing. A chair scraped back on the floor above him; muffled laughter and a child's delighted squeal filtered through the thin walls. He stumbled into his bedroom and pulled the blue blanket-turned-curtain across his window. Only then did he turn on the light and grope for the old Bible beneath the chaos on his desk.

Karl groaned softly as he pulled his chair directly under the bare lightbulb and began to read. The Crucifixion! On this one night the Christians had dedicated to hope, he found himself trapped in the account of the cruel death of their Christ. *Not even one night? One night to hope in something that could win against the dark?*

It was not to be. The story in Luke followed a brutal pattern, one Karl knew far too well. *Betrayal. Arrest. Beating. Interrogation. Accusation. Torture. Death.* How many times had he thrust others onto this path? How many times had he facilitated betrayals and arranged arrests in the name of the Reich? How many times had simply watched the suffering of the innocent?

Condoned it? Rocked back on his heels in self-righteous satisfaction as a gunshot ended the life of another traitor to the Reich?

Now he walked the path beside the One who was more innocent than all of these. Karl read the words and cried out in anguish because there he saw himself! He was one of the guards, raising a rubber truncheon to strike the face of the Savior! His voice was one with the chorus of lies that condemned the righteous One to death. He was Pilate, turning Jesus over to the mob, turning away the one chance he had to embrace Truth!

Yes. In the shouts and fury of that terrible day, he saw Karl Zehr, heard the final confirmation of the sentence he had already passed upon himself.

Guilty!

In the weeping of the women along the road, he heard the accusation.

Guilty!

The clang of iron on iron, the hammer, driving a nail through the hand of the One who could have—who might have—

Guilty!

"And then Jesus said—" Karl suddenly stopped. He marked the place with a trembling finger and tried to understand the unbelievable words. "And then Jesus said, 'Father, forgive them, for they know not what they do!'" Luke 23:34

Time stood still in the dingy apartment. The lightbulb hummed loudly in the silence.

Forgive them, Father! The prayer was somewhere between a cry and a groan. *Forgive them!* Impossible words. Impossible request, Karl thought as he read and reread the plea.

Forgiveness offered to the guards, the executioners, the spies? Forgiveness for the most guilty? For him?

And so it was on this, the darkest night of the year, that Karl finally turned away from the false light of the bonfires. He closed his eyes and ears completely to the shouting, chanting crowds, and in the silence of his soul he heard the Voice, still speaking.

Forgiven.

Strength to Love

The day after Christmas was usually a letdown. Excitement and anticipation swelled all through December, bursting to a climax on Christmas Day—and then, just like that, it was gone. This year, Eva welcomed it with relief. Christmas's passing meant the end of coaching Adina and Hirschel in unfamiliar holiday traditions, the end of forced festive greetings from neighbors, and a tapering of the unrelenting stream of memories that had haunted her day and night. Down came the wreath; a little bit of feeling was tucked away inside the box. Out went the candles; searing remembrances were darkened, though not extinguished, with the flames.

Eva was on her hands and knees picking tinsel and evergreen from the carpet when a pair of red stockings skipped past. "Tante Eva?"

Adina's face bounced into view as she plopped down on the floor beside Eva. "We have a present for you!"

Eva sat back on her heels and pushed her thick hair away from her eyes. "Really?"

Hirschel, who had been lurking at the kitchen door, came running as Adina nodded. Brother and sister shared a quick glance and then Adina began to sing in a clear, high voice.

"*Baruch atah, Adonai ...*"

Hirschel joined in with a wavering soprano. "*Eloheinu melehk ha'olam ...*"

They continued their song, confidently forming words in a language completely foreign to Eva. She listened, entranced both by the beauty of the music and the mystery of the sounds. When at last the children concluded, she applauded enthusiastically.

"Very good! Very good! But—what does it mean?"

"It's the blessing we sing on the first night of Hanukah," Adina explained. Haltingly, she began to translate.

"Blessed are you … Lord God … King of the … universe?" The child paused, grappling with the next phrase of Hebrew.

"It's all right, Adina." Eva held up her hand to stop her.

"Did you like it?" Hirschel asked imploringly.

"I liked it very much. It was beautiful." Eva declared. "Such a wonderful present. Thank you!"

She stood to enfold both children in an embrace, silently grateful that her house was a short distance from town. If anyone in Villach had heard …

Today such a song would call down the wrath of the Nazis. The little birds who sang it would be crushed, and "Deutschland Über Alles" would play at the funeral.

Eva shook her head, struggling to banish such dismal thoughts. *Can I not enjoy even a few moments with these children unhindered by dread?* Yet her fears were grounded in terrible fact. The evil that swallowed up Adina and Hirschel's parents would now gladly destroy their small lives as well. *Why?*

Reinhardt had asked the same questions. When rumors of the brutality in Vienna reached them, when construction on the prison camps in Austria began, when "Juden Verboten" suddenly appeared on shops all throughout Villach, together they had wondered what reasons lay behind such caustic hatred. But calling for answers was akin to demanding rationale from an avalanche. Unhindered by logic, it barreled on in gleeful destruction.

"There is no reason for it, only deluded self-justification," Reinhardt had concluded. "But our job is not to make sense of the darkness. It is to fight it. To stand by truth, when the rest of the world would cast it into the flames. So we must stand. No matter what the cost, Eva, we must stand."

Her skin prickled slightly at the remembered intensity of his words. Had he somehow foreseen that he would fulfill his own charge so completely? That for him, living for truth would mean dying for it as well? *Oh, Reinhardt ...*

"What's wrong, Tante Eva? Did our song make you sad?"

Eva tried to smile as she shook her head, startled by Adina's perception. "Come sit with me," she offered, swallowing hard against the bitter taste of grief.

Hirschel had wandered off to raid the fast-dwindling supply of Christmas cookies, but Adina climbed up beside Eva and watched her seriously.

"Are you sad, Tante Eva? Sometimes I am sad. When I miss Mama and Papa."

Eva stroked Adina's hair, conscious of the *knowing* in the girl's brown, almond-shaped eyes. They held a wisdom that came from grief, the burden of a child forced to grow up in a single terrible day.

Eva sighed and then smiled sadly. "I miss my husband." Nothing else needed to be said. A thousand sorrows could be summed up in a sentence like that: "I miss ..."

Adina slowly nodded. "Herr Ramond said Herr Reinhardt was very brave. And kind, because he would not turn us away even though we are small. That is why he brought us here." She turned her searching eyes to Eva's face. "I would miss him too."

"Herr Ramond is very wise," Eva managed at last. Tears came again, washing away the illusion of self-possessed control.

Adina scooted closer to lay her head on Eva's shoulder. "Don't be too sad, Tante Eva." The little girl's words were muffled. "He's all right now. Herr Ramond said. 'Cause he gets to be with Jesus."

"Karl Zehr? Yes, he is here. Second desk on the left."

Karl looked up quickly at the sound of his name. A short, blond delivery boy stood at the end of the room, watching the Gestapo agents with undisguised fascination. Karl raised his hand halfway, and the boy nearly ran toward his desk.

"A telegraph for you, sir. From Berlin, you see ..." The boy's voice was hushed, as if he were talking in a holy place. Pale blue eyes wandered across the papers strewn across the desk while Karl frowned and fished for change to tip the boy.

He is, Karl thought, *probably the first civilian since the parade to be happy to see a Gestapo agent.*

The delivery boy did not seem to notice the smallness of the coin Karl pressed into his hand. He pocketed it proudly and then snapped off the salute.

"Heil Hitler!" The gesture was completed with the same mechanical precision Karl recognized from his own years in the *Hitler Jugend.*

He simply nodded and smiled slightly at the delivery boy, who now looked confused.

"Danke," Karl said, dismissing the messenger and returning to what he had been reading. When he looked up again, the boy was gone. Only then did he tear open the envelope.

HELMUT ZEHR DECEASED. STOP. BURIED YESTERDAY. STOP.

The address of a particular graveyard was given, and nothing more. Karl stared at the curt words for more than a minute before slowly folding the paper and replacing it in the envelope. *My father is dead.* Still, the recognition of that fact did not come. Father—the man who had sulked and bellowed and drank and cursed God and the Bolshevik Jews and the Weimar Republic and forced Karl to take that first job as a Gestapo agent in Berlin—was dead.

Karl tugged at his deaf ear, the result of a beating too long ago to remember, and continued to stare at the envelope. A dull ache churned in his stomach. Was it regret? he wondered. They had parted on peaceful terms, at least. His father had even managed a smile as Karl boarded the train for newly annexed Austria—probably more proud of the uniform than of the son who wore it. Karl added this commentary with only a trace of bitterness. It had always been that way, after all.

He tore his eyes from the little envelope to stare out at the gray winter wasteland beyond the window. Long minutes passed before he jerked upright with a sudden, startling certainty. His father was dead. Gone was the force that had kept him at the Gestapo long after he had come to loathe it. Karl was free to go.

"I'm sure you'll have a good evening. But mind, Katrina—they can be quite a handful!" Squeals of protest followed her out into the biting wind.

Eva jumped as Katrina laid a hand on her shoulder. "Why are you going to meet with Herr Werberg, Eva?"

She twisted to face her friend's questioning gaze, suddenly embarrassed that she hadn't told Katrina sooner. They could have talked it over and worried about it together, but now—

"He said he worked with Reinhardt. With the refugees. And I hope ..."

"That he will help us now?"

Eva nodded and then smiled at how naturally Katrina had included herself. "Yes. We have waited for more than a month now, Trina. I didn't know who to look for—but why would *he* wait so long?"

Katrina shook her head, framed by the doorway's glow. "Perhaps he is afraid?"

Eva smiled weakly. "He would not be the only one. But I should go—I'll be late."

"Greet God!" Katrina called in farewell. But her words were lost on the wind.

Eva was not sure exactly what she had expected to find at Hans Werberg's house. A candlelight dinner, however, was certainly not it. She was instantly uncomfortable as he escorted her into the dimly lit dining room. *For the sake of Adina and Hirschel I must be strong*, she reminded herself. Offering a silent prayer, she allowed him to seat her.

"Eva, I'm sorry for bringing you here like this." He gestured toward the ornate place settings. "A show, you see? For whoever happens to be watching."

He must not be terribly concerned about the watchers, or he would not have said that. Eva frowned and shook her head no to the wine he offered. "You worked with my husband," she stated at last.

Hans took refuge behind his chair and nodded. "Yes. I worked with Reinhardt."

"So you can help me."

Hans sat down slowly, the expression on his face wavering somewhere between feigned unconcern and nervousness. "Perhaps."

Eva bristled at his hesitancy. "Perhaps? Herr Werberg, *were* you involved in my husband's work with refugees?"

"Yes, but I—"

"Good. So if I tell you I have two children in my house without passports or papers of any kind, two Jewish children who would like very much to leave the Third Reich and never come back, then perhaps you could offer a better answer than *perhaps.*"

Hans ran a hand over his red beard and then drummed his thick fingers on the table. "Reinhardt never said … never told me you were involved in all this. In fact, he said that you were not. You see?" He shrugged and finished lamely.

"I was not. And then Hirschel and Adina appeared at my door the day before the pogrom with—asking for help." Eva sighed, frustrated that the long weeks that had passed since she first welcomed the children seemed to be ending without an answer. "I know nothing about your smuggling of refugees. I did not even know who from the church was involved, until you told me you were. What can I do?"

Hans abruptly excused himself to get the soup. For long minutes the silence was broken only by the clanking of dishes, and then he reappeared with a pot in hand. He kept it in front of him like a shield as he sat down.

"Herr Werberg, I came to your house because you said you worked with Reinhardt. My husband was gone every other week helping families and children like Hirschel and Adina to cross the border. If you are not willing to do the same, I will find someone at the church who can."

Hans shook his large head slowly. "There is no one else at the church, Frau Gottlieb. That is not to say that you could not try to drive them into Italy yourself—but you will most certainly be stopped and searched. I promise you. The trains would be another option—but you say they have no papers? Without the proper documents, it is impossible to purchase a ticket."

"What about the river? That is where Reinhardt went, is it not?"

"You would need my help for that, Frau Gottlieb."

Tears of angry frustration stung Eva's eyes. She spread her hands helplessly. "So *will* you help us? Help them? Or did you invite me to dinner to tell me it is impossible?"

"I did not say I would not help you, Frau Gottlieb. But we must be careful." He nodded sagely and sipped a spoonful of the pumpkin soup. "As I said, the river is the least-regulated way across the border. In the spring there is always a small crowd of fishing boats, and the border guards pay little attention—"

"In the *spring?*" Eva's voice rose in disbelief. "Herr Werberg, it is not yet January! You guessed on your own that the children were not who I said they were! How long until the Gestapo does the same?"

For the first time, Hans's stout face softened with genuine sympathy. "I'm sorry, Frau Gottlieb. I can't ask the contact to come for the children any sooner. The Drau is frozen in some places. Nothing sails in the winter—it would only endanger him and your two children."

Eva closed her eyes and pressed her fingers to her head. "No other way?" she asked at last, in a small voice.

"I'm afraid not." Hans stuck his lower lip out and shook his head. "But I think—I'm sure you can do it. Keep the children safe, that is to say." He spoke faster, as if he were embarrassed by his own clumsiness. "I only guessed the children were refugees because I knew Reinhardt. That is to say, if I didn't know Reinhardt, I wouldn't have had any reason to wonder."

"And what grounds did they execute my husband on, Herr Werberg?" Eva demanded. "*They* also have a reason to wonder. I am watched and followed—"

"Here?" Hans blanched.

Eva shrugged as if it did not matter anymore. She glanced over the soup and crystal and narrowed her eyes cynically. "To the *show?* Perhaps."

There was an uncomfortable pause before Hans nodded. "I will do what

I can, Frau Gottlieb," he said at last. "But I think you should be prepared to wait until spring."

Eva left Hans Werberg's house with equal parts of hope and dread. Finally she knew who would help Hirschel and Adina escape! But not until spring? The weeks since November had ground past in constant tension. How could she possibly keep the children safe for another two, maybe three months?

I will do my best, but there are no guarantees, Frau Gottlieb. Hans's parting words were a sobering reminder that, even if spring came without incident, there was no promise of safety until Hirschel and Adina were on the other side of the border. Eva glared at the river as she drove over it. The faint gleam of her headlights flashed across gray, angry water. *Not frozen.* She could not see the purpose in this dangerous, seemingly senseless delay. So why would Werberg insist on it?

Reinhardt trusted him, she reminded herself. He had never spoken of Werberg to Eva, yet he had trusted him to play some important part in this dangerous game of mercy and treason.

Eva parked the auto and rapped lightly on the door. "Trina! Open up, it's me!" she called softly. She knocked twice more before the door opened.

"Sorry, Eva," Katrina whispered as she ushered her friend inside. "I was putting the children to bed, just as you knocked, and …"

Eva nodded slowly, suddenly exhausted from the contemplation of possibilities and dangers. "That's good. Good."

"We only had sandwiches for supper because I didn't want to burn your kitchen to the ground. You know what happens when I try to cook." Katrina was rambling now, calming her friend with stories and remarks about trivial things.

Eva found it strangely comforting. She let Katrina talk for a full five minutes before interrupting. "He will help the children."

Katrina stopped her recitation of the fantastic story involving talking kittens and airplanes that she and the children had made up and closed her eyes in gratitude. "Thank God."

"But he says not until the spring."

"*Spring?*" Katrina's reaction was much the same as Eva's. It was no wonder—they had worried together, talked and planned endlessly around the thousands of terrible uncertainties. Katrina herself had written the story Eva and the children now recited. But she had not imagined it would have to hold for—how long? Three more months? Four?

"We will simply have to wait for him." Eva grimaced and closed her eyes.

"So we will." Katrina's voice was steady again, taking control. "But we know now. Someone who can help ... in a matter of weeks."

"Twelve or fourteen weeks, Trina." Eva smiled, though there was no humor in the words. She seemed to shrink where she leaned against the wall. "And *then*, if by some wild streak of luck the Gestapo have not already found out—"

"The children wanted you to kiss them good night," Katrina interrupted. "Hirschel made me promise I would send you up. We will live one day at a time. Go tell them good night, Eva. It will be all right." The last sentence was added as an afterthought, the prayer of both hearts. *It must be all right, in the end ...* But there had already been too many unhappy endings for either woman to believe such a thing.

Hirschel and Adina's breath formed an even cadence as Eva entered the dark room—a sure sign both children were asleep. She stooped to brush her lips across Adina's forehead. The girl did not stir. Circling the bed, Eva did the same to Hirschel. "Good night," she whispered.

Hirschel blinked up at her sleepily. "Mama?" His eyes found her face as he gave a little sigh of recognition. "Good night, Mama," he murmured.

For a long moment Eva simply stood, frozen by the little boy's words. Then, slowly, she backed out of the room, feeling like she was falling. *He saw me. He knew who I was. And he called me Mama!* She didn't know what to make of the emotion that throbbed in her chest. Amid her hope and despair of the children's escape, the fact they were leaving her had somehow eluded her grasp. Now it came crashing down on her with terrible clarity.

Spring may never come for them—for us. But even if it does, then I must take these children that I have grown to love and leave them in the hands of strangers. Eva wanted to weep. How could she turn and leave them to their fate? Trust that someone she had never met would care for the two precious souls? *But if I truly love them, I can do nothing else.* The bleak truth of it brought her to the ground. If, *if,* everything went perfectly, then Hirschel and Adina would leave her in a few months and never come back. And if it did not—if someone asked, if just one person found out—then the result would simply be the end. *Do they send children to Mauthausen?* Eva tried not to consider the question. *Or do they simply ... end ... things—oh, God! They must survive! Must go!*

But the certainty of the declaration made it no easier to bear. How would she leave them, drive into the night without ever knowing if they made it to safety? She did not have the strength for such love! Yet was that not what Ramond had done? He had loved them as she did now. She had seen it in his eyes, the wrenching loss on his pale face as Katrina took him away. But he had not protested. After nearly giving his life to see them to Villach, he had surrendered the children to Eva.

Selfless. The word echoed hollowly in Eva's grief-numbed mind. She rested her face on her knees, hardly surprised to find it wet with tears. *Oh God! What will I do? I love them as if they were my own children! How can I leave them to the mercy of a stranger? Who will sing to them and give them baths and tell them stories and dry their tears?* Eva huddled against the smooth paneling of the doorframe, cringing from the weight of the questions. *Who? What? How, O God?*

I AM. The assurance of the words at first took Eva by surprise. Slowly she willed her heart to silence until only that phrase echoed there. *I AM.* Not *I was,* or *I might be. I AM.* Here, now, watching Eva cry as Adina and Hirschel slept. *I AM.* Unbroken presence, from before the beginning to long after the end of time. *I AM.* With the children and Ramond while they struggled through the mountains. Hearing their cry as Hirschel came close to death, and reaching down to make the little boy whole. *I AM.* At the moment of the impossible good-bye, still distant as of yet, with all three hearts as they were wrenched apart. *I AM.*

Cautiously, but with increasing confidence, Eva felt her heart reply to this resounding promise. *Where can I go from Your Spirit? Or where can I flee from Your Presence? If I take the wings of the morning and dwell in the uttermost parts of the sea, even there Your hand shall lead me, and Your right hand shall hold me.* Psalm 139: 7, 9-10 The song of trust did not dull her sorrow at the coming parting—her grief burned hot against her heart. But among the embers lay a resolution newly forged.

Hirschel and Adina would live! They would be free! Eva would love them until the day they left, even though the love might break her to pieces. And on the night they fled, she would entrust their lives not to strangers but to the great *I AM*.

Sacrifice

COLORLESS LIGHT SEEPED THROUGH the window and cast pallid shadows across the wooden floor. Half a dozen Gestapo agents conversed in morbid anticipation from two rows of straight-backed chairs. Karl had not left after all, though today the image of the three ticket counters of Villach's West Station glowed in his mind like a vision of a door into paradise. It would be so easy, he knew, to walk out of here, to turn in his resignation and leave Villach a free man.

He kept his eyes riveted on the door that gaped behind him, as if to keep away by sheer force of will those who were bound to emerge. This dismal room was well suited to what would soon commence. Once-white walls were a sooty gray from the dust of years gone by. A single window boasted a view of the windswept courtyard where executions were accomplished, and a large picture of Adolph Hitler brooded over the gathering.

Karl knew full well why he was here. He, along with the other agents of the secret police, was to preside over the "trial" of a man who had crossed the Nazis one time too many. It was all a spectacle, he knew. The trial would be a charade, acted out for the benefit of … who? The Inspekteur, perhaps? A reminder to Villach that the Gestapo could do what they wanted, when they wanted, to whomever they chose, that every whim of the Inspekteur's mind could be acted out with capricious cruelty? Never mind that the man accused had probably lived a most unassuming life until today. By the time the trial was finished, he would be proven a dangerous criminal to the Reich!

If evidence to the contrary later happened to emerge ... well, who really cared about the truth anyway, these days?

A hushed expectancy fell over the room at the sound of footsteps in the hallway. A middle-aged man with salt-and pepper hair and spectacles appeared, flanked by two guards. Fredrik led the grim little procession.

"Mauthausen." It was breathed from lips throughout the room with a mixture of horror and excitement. The effect was a rippling tide of misery that rose to engulf the unfortunate man who now stood handcuffed in their midst. The prisoner trembled visibly, and Karl tugged his ear in disgust. Mauthausen was bleakness and despair and death. In the seven long months since the Anschluss, it had gained its well-deserved reputation as the most notorious of Austria's prison camps. And this man was slated to go there.

Fredrik skimmed past the formalities of a court hearing. What did it matter? The prisoner's guilt had been decreed with his arrest.

"By order of the Gestapo, you are charged with attempting to publish lies of malicious intent in the newspaper of Villach, and with blatant disregard for the distinction between the Aryan race and those of lower breeding," Fredrik intoned.

The man seemed to find within himself a hidden reserve of courage. He squared his shoulders and mustered an indignant reply to the Gestapo's charge. "I—I offered food to a hungry boy! Would you arrest me for a kindness?"

"Silence!" Fredrik raged. "You were not granted permission to speak!" He nodded to the guard on the prisoner's right, and a blow to the stomach brought the defendant to his knees.

The unexpected brutality dissolved the man's courageous facade. He cowered on the ground, not daring to raise his head for fear of being struck again.

Karl grimaced at the unholy scene. The prisoner knelt almost directly in line with Hitler's menacing portrait. His guards stood ramrod-straight, glaring down at him with concentrated scorn. In Karl's mind it evoked the image of some ancient pagan ceremony. Here, in this room, an innocent life would be sacrificed to please the god of Germany!

Confident in his role as the priest of this darkness, Fredrik continued: "His crimes are as stated. Does anyone object to this man's guilt?"

Karl swallowed hard against his rising nausea. There were indeed other ways out of Villach. The instant of decision lingered impossibly long. He saw the newsman out of the corner of his eye. *One word. One word is all it would take.* Stunned silence would be broken by shouted accusations, angry fists, and finally arrest. He would join the current prisoner in Mauthausen. *But it would be right.*

Karl almost stood. Almost proclaimed the man's innocence at the top of his voice. But then a thought came over him that paralyzed him completely. *Eva Gottlieb.* She was the reason he had stayed this long, and his deportation would put her in immediate danger. Karl tried desperately to pray. *Innocent One—Truth—what can I do? How do I choose?* He held his breath, hoping urgently for an answer. *What can I do?* The dreadful cry echoed until his temples pounded with it. But no answer came.

"Guilty!"

The prisoner's sentence sounded strangely like Karl's own.

Karl stumbled through the rest of the day in a haze of disbelief. *I could still do something. Still help him. Get the man out of prison before the train comes.* But in his heart he knew the decision had been made.

"That was interesting." Pieter, fully recovered from his winter cold, strolled past Karl's desk with a laugh. "Did you hear him? 'I didn't mean it! I didn't know the child was Jewish!'" Pieter snorted with disdain. "Groveling, lying coward!"

"Men will say many things when faced with death," Karl countered, voice shaking slightly with controlled loathing.

"Sure. He'll talk rocks out of the quarry at Mauthausen." Smirking at the prisoner's fate, Pieter left Karl alone.

When at last it was time to leave, Karl wandered aimlessly through the streets of Villach. In the back of his mind was the perverse hope that Fredrik had sent someone to follow him on this pointless trek. The thought of one of the proud guards shivering in the frigid winter night lifted his spirits somewhat.

Flickering images of the day's horror haunted him as he walked. *The man's innocence. Kindness brought to its knees by cruelty. Fredrik's gloating victory. My silence.* Was that silence justified by the lives on the other end of the scale? Karl didn't know. Sharper than his grief at the prisoner's fate was the accusation that he had been too frightened to act. That if Eva Gottlieb had not been concerned, the outcome of the terrible play would have been the same. *What could I have done?* Karl was drained, too numb even to pray. Perhaps he truly would leave Villach tonight. Catch a train into Italy and not come back. He would gladly forsake his position, this nightmare, if not for the promise that had kept him silent today. If not for the sake of Reinhardt Gottlieb's widow. If only …

Shaking now in the icy air, he lurched homeward. Shoppers regarded him curiously as he staggered up the street toward St. Jakob. Head lowered, he refused to acknowledge their open stares. So lost was he in his guilt and helplessness that he never saw the street gleaming dangerously slick before him.

Karl slammed into the cobbles with such force that for a moment he couldn't breathe. Blinking stupidly at the sheen of ice, he willed his lungs to inhale. Air returned gradually, and the pain came with it. He felt blood oozing from an abrasion on his forehead, warm against cold wind.

He was almost grateful for the sting as the shriek of the train pierced the air above him. What he had done was now sealed—completely, irretrievably decided.

Betrayal

Winter stretched on interminably in Villach, yet at the same time each day flew by too rapidly to hold. Eva and the children continued to act out their elaborate charade until they themselves were almost fooled. It was a dreadful game, Eva knew. The love that knit them together was genuine, but it was founded on a lie. Someday Tante Eva would again be only Eva Gottlieb. Soon Hirschel and Adina would be alone. The joy, the family—it was all a temporary role, a careful show for whomever might be watching.

Sometime in January, Adina grasped the falseness of the play. Though she never spoke of it, Eva saw it on her face. Silent tension hovered over the group whenever they ventured into public. They had become performers for a deadly audience that observed from the shadows. Only Hirschel remained oblivious. For him, the joy was real, and Eva was glad of that. By unspoken agreement neither she nor Adina let on the awful truth of the act. They simply continued in their parts: loving aunt and unconcerned child.

So the weeks passed in a mixture of joy and regret, longing and fear. As spring drew nearer, Eva began to wonder again how she would say good-bye. She tried to burn each detail into her memory: Hirschel's adoring smile, the dark brown shine of Adina's hair, the siblings laughing together before bedtime. On an impulse, she looked into getting travel papers for herself, but her request was denied by the police. It was clear: once the Drau stirred from its icy winter sleep, it would sweep Hirschel and Adina away. Eva would be left to continue a more painful charade on her own.

As the snow banks began to recede and the icicles splintered and fell, Eva waited with anxious dread. Each lengthening day cast the shadow further into her heart. What was planned would happen. The children would be free.

Two weeks before Easter the word came from Hans Werberg. From here to Italy, the river was passable. Eva reread the message again in disbelief. *Eleven days from tonight, between ten p.m. and midnight.*

The entire message consisted of one sentence, scrawled along the edge of a newspaper article. Such small, careless words! As if two lives—Eva's world—did not depend on it.

Weary. That word seemed the most fitting as Karl trudged from the oppressive confines of the Gestapo headquarters. He was tired tonight—a fatigue that seemed to spring from the center of his soul.

"Karl! Join us for a drink?"

He did not even turn as Pieter's voice carried through the still air. The other agents could wonder. They could follow him, ask their questions … tonight he could not find the strength to care. The heavy gray sky pressed down on his shoulders, an echo of the darkness he dared stand against—

Karl scoffed aloud at the last thought. Perhaps if he could truly stand, he would not feel so helpless, so guilty. If he could only take off this mask, let them see the truth in his eyes … maybe then his heart would not be sick with the nearness of the evil around him.

But I cannot. For the sake of one I must play this part until … until when? How long, Lord? His thoughts became a prayer, whispered in such despair that he wondered if they could be heard in heaven.

Love the LORD your God … love your neighbor. Matthew 22:37, 39 He was still as far away from fulfilling that charge as he had been before Christmas. While what was once true of him had become a lie, it was a lie he acted out daily. *Karl Zehr, Gestapo agent. Still making arrests. Still meeting with informants, reporting to Fredrik.* He had stayed to protect Eva Gottlieb … how many had he harmed in the waiting? He was trapped, stained by this darkness that was blacker than the blackest night. *And so alone …*

He shivered as a stiff breeze cut through his thin jacket. He wandered through quiet residential streets toward the downtown, to the bright pools of light that seeped from cheery storefronts and restaurants. It seemed he alone stood in the shadows tonight.

The desire to step into the light came rushing in with a longing that left him trembling. *To leave behind this darkness and fear! To know for certain that the light does shine in my heart!* But he could not take off his mask. Not tonight. He knew he had to play the part until Eva was safe, but tonight he feared the role would destroy him.

Karl leaned his head against a tree in the gathering gloom and silently voiced his anguish. *What am I? Who am I? I do not know anymore! Once I thought I heard Your forgiveness, but tonight I am lost. Can … will You … forgive me? Please, forgive me and take away the shadows! Innocent One!* "I need you!" He whispered the last sentence aloud. The words were hollow in his ear, mocking the silence that replied to his plea.

And then peace came. In the stillness there was a promise of a love that would not fail. Here, in the shadow of evil, light flooded Karl's heart once more.

"You are feeling better today?"

Ramond nodded silently, his gaze never leaving the little square of blue sky in the corner of the room. The nurse who greeted him today was not Katrina.

"Is there anything you need?"

For a moment he considered asking her why hospital rooms were so blindingly white, or if he could have a book. Quickly he decided against it. The crooked cross she wore on her armband warned him to silence. Besides, Katrina had promised she would bring him something to read tomorrow.

The nurse left, shutting the door. He heard the lock click. *Is she worried I will escape?* Ramond wondered. That fear was certainly unfounded. Only yesterday Dr. Brandt had come in to congratulate him on surviving and then in the next breath announced that his left lung and part of his right had been too severely damaged to expect anything but a partial recovery. Ramond was effectively crippled.

The shadow of a sparrow flashed past the high window, and Ramond's thoughts returned to the children. They were still in Villach, he knew. Still with Eva Gottlieb. What was it Katrina had whispered yesterday as she had helped him shave? "A hard lesson Eva must learn again next week. The lesson of good-byes." So they would flee next week. He stared at the outline of the clipboard at the foot of his bed. Hirschel and Adina would be safe. He closed his eyes, fighting the dizziness that made the little white room spin and tilt wildly to one side.

"They will be safe," he whispered aloud, a prayer and the answer to a promise. In his heart he was glad, even as he opened his eyes again and glanced around the sterile confines of the hospital room. Those two children were the purpose in the broken pieces of his living. Now he would pray until they were safe—and then?

I will go home. Of that Ramond was sure. As soon as he was strong enough, he would return to Salzburg, to whatever was left of his family. To all the grief and hope and unanswered questions that remained …

He leaned back on the pillows and stared up at the white ceiling, wishing for even a water stain to fill the empty surface—anything but useless space or blank existence. He had not expected to live. During the last days of the journey he had felt his strength failing, and in the face of death prayed only the children would be safe. But that prayer had been answered, and still he lived. He remembered the words that had been spoken to his heart as they entered Villach. "Take courage, my son! You are nearly home."

The promise had seemed so real then, so near! He had been ready to go! Now, trapped within a broken body, Ramond was not certain he was ready to live. The farewell he had whispered to the children returned as a taunt.

"You will be somewhere good, Herr Ramond?" That was Adina, so full of worry and compassion.

"Somewhere … very good. With Jesus … I will … be … with Him."

Ramond remembered the joy, the longing, beneath the ragged pain in his own voice. How he had wanted that! How he wanted it still! To see *Him!*— and to be home, home, free from this land of shadow and grief! He had been close, he knew. Yet for some reason—for some *purpose?*—he had lived.

The sparrow returned abruptly to the window, rapping the glass twice with its beak in salutation.

"Hello, little friend." The bird considered him with a single bright eye before diving away from its perch. Ramond was sorry to see him go.

In the renewed silence a verse tugged at the edge of his memory. *Two sparrows—no, five sparrows, sold for two pennies, and none are forgotten by God.* Luke 12: 6-7 The words leapt to life, suddenly clear in his mind. "But the very hairs of your head ... are numbered. Do not fear, therefore, you ... are of more value than many sparrows." He whispered the last two sentences aloud, conscious of the sudden peace in the room.

"Are you not worth more, Ramond? Do not fear. For I AM with you ..."

The promise again, renewed after these long months of silence! Ramond laughed into the quiet of the blank white walls. They were only unfilled, he realized. Stretched canvas-tight around the promise of a good plan to paint them. And in the waiting he was no longer afraid.

Hirschel and Adina will say their good-byes at the church on Palm Sunday. In a way it was fitting, Eva thought. By next Sunday—Easter—they would have started a new life. *Thursday they will leave.* Thursday night, when the bells fell silent, Eva would drive them to the river, say good-bye ...

There are still four days, she reminded herself. Four days to love and hope. On the way to church she rolled the windows down, laughing as the children stuck hands and faces out the window into the rush of warm spring air.

She gave them last-minute instructions as they approached the church. "Today they will give us willow branches when we go inside. They are to hold"—she twisted back to look at Hirschel—"and not to fight with. We are celebrating Jesus coming to Jerusalem today. Do you understand?"

Hirschel nodded and smiled sweetly, and Eva resolved to keep him close through service today.

Four days more ...

Karl slowed his steps as he approached the castle-like tower of the red-and-yellow-brick church. Slipping off the path, he leaned against one of the ancient pines in the park. He watched as wary churchgoers crossed the parking lot and disappeared inside. Many came from cars parked at least a block away, heads down, determined steps striding toward that door. Karl had never determined if the people were defiant in spite of fear or merely fearful in their defiance. One thing was certain, though: they were afraid of him.

He straightened and resumed his walk to the front of the church. He had hoped they would see the change. Had it been too much to ask: a small miracle, the acceptance of these people he had once hunted? Someone at the door stood handing out slender willow branches. He glared in stony silence as Karl passed. Yes, it was too much.

He spotted Eva and her children by the wild blur of yellow and green from across the room before settling in to the pew farthest from the front. No one would be forced to sit near him, at least. He sang the opening hymn loudly with the congregation, drinking in the words. Did they notice? He had never requested baptism—Fredrik Schmidt would surely find out, and who would believe him here, anyway?

Two rows forward, Krimmel's neck twitched as the informant fought the urge to look back at Karl. Tomorrow they would meet and compare notes on the church's behavior—notes Karl would burn before he made his report to Fredrik.

"Come to Me." Karl stared into the face of Christ as he waited for the prayer to end and the next hymn to begin. It was those words that had first called him here, to this impossible place. He had only hoped he would not be so alone.

After service, most of the congregation drifted from the nave to the park outside. Danger notwithstanding, it was a beautiful day. Karl yawned and positioned himself in a puddle of sunlight against the wall. He wondered if they noticed he did not prowl and skulk and listen for any whisper of treason. That he simply tried to keep out of the way—a sheep in wolf's clothing. Karl yawned again and then straightened as Eva swept past with the two children. Was it his imagination, or was there a deeper shade of sorrow in her gentle eyes?

She stopped to talk with a group of women just inside the entrance. Karl only overheard snatches of their conversation.

"Children ... good-bye ... back to Vienna ..."

Karl leaned back against the wall and closed his eyes, willing himself not to show surprise—or hope. If Hirschel and Adina were leaving, would Eva go with them? For a moment, he almost smiled. Almost. Before he remembered the children could not possibly be going to Vienna because they had not come from the city in the first place. *So ... where?* He had known for some time that they were not who Eva said they were—a quick call to the Vienna Gestapo headquarters had told him that. And there were rumors from the hospital about the mysterious hiker who was being treated for tuberculosis. In his delirium, they said, he repeated two names again and again. *Hirschel and Adina.*

Karl watched their retreating forms as Eva led the children from the church. Suddenly she stopped, turned, and scanned the near-empty nave. A stout, red-haired man returned her look and nodded slightly. Satisfied, Eva hurried out. Karl continued to watch the shorter man from across the room. *Werberg, isn't it? Hans Werberg?*

Werberg glanced quickly at Karl and then tried to assume an air of nonchalance. It didn't work. Karl could sense the man's edginess from where he stood. Werberg spun on his heel and made a beeline for the door. Without stopping to think, Karl followed him.

Werberg hurried along the sleepy streets at a speed surprising for his short stature. Karl strolled far behind him, careful to keep the red-haired man just in sight. It was not difficult. Werberg was too nervous to blend in with those out for a Sunday walk, and he did not even attempt to lose his pursuer among the sunny, still-bare trees that lined the roads. Karl watched him scurry up the stairs and disappear into a tall ivy-mantled apartment building. A few moments later he picked out movement at a window on the second story. The silhouette seemed to be pacing.

Karl wondered at the man's fear. His presence at the church had become an accepted danger. People fell silent and glared when he passed, but no one actually ran. Werberg's terrified face appeared suddenly at the window. Karl grinned and saluted, reminded of a boy with a pocket full of stolen sweets. The face disappeared as abruptly as if had come, and a heavy curtain slid across the window. Karl lazily kicked a tree trunk. When ten minutes passed without any movement from inside the house, he shrugged and turned to wander home.

"No!" Hirschel cried, small hands pounding Eva's legs in protest. "Not going! I'm not going except … if you come with us!" He dropped to the ground and looked up at Eva with pleading eyes. "Can you come with us?"

Eva closed her eyes and slowly sat beside him. *If only. If only.* The reasons she must stay ran through her mind once more. There was Katrina, of course. And what remained of Reinhardt's congregation. Her disappearance would bring the wrath of the Nazis down on all of them. Of that she was sure.

"Can you, Tante Eva?" Hirschel tugged at her arm.

Eva pulled him onto her lap. Yes, she knew why she could not go. But right now nothing seemed more important than rocking Hirschel, telling him not to cry.

"I wish you could be my mama," he sniffed.

"I wish you were my little boy." She hummed the first two bars of a wordless song, wondering how to explain why good-bye *must* be said, though neither side could bear it. "There are bad men here, Hirschel."

Just then Adina entered the room, her wide brown eyes reflecting the same sad certainty as Eva's.

Eva sighed and motioned her to sit. "I promised Ra—Herr Ramond I would send you out of Germany. So you must go, you see?"

"We have said good-bye a lot, Tante Eva," Adina offered quietly, scooting closer to whisper something in her brother's ear. Eva nodded mutely. Katrina had told her what little of the children's story Ramond knew. *First their parents. Then Ramond. Now me as well …*

It was too much, too many good-byes in the space of a single terrible year. *And when they make it to Italy? How many more farewells will they face, even in freedom?*

"Adina, Hirschel, I can't go with you to Italy. I can't go with you, but you will not be alone." Gently she untangled herself from Hirschel's arms and turned him to face her. "God holds you in His hands."

"Hurt hands?" Hirschel quavered.

Eva nodded, smiling now through tears of her own. "Yes. Hands scarred by love." She paused, searching for words. "He knows you by name. Adina. Hirschel. And He loves you! Remember, whenever you look up at the stars. When you see a flower open or a snowflake fall. He loves you! Wherever you go, whatever happens, never forget that."

Karl knew he was late for his meeting with Krimmel, but the knowledge did not hurry his steps. Today was simply too nice to be spent running from one appointment to another. He slowed farther as he rounded a corner and the brown stained-glass windows of St. Jakob came into view. If Krimmel was on time, he would be waiting for Karl in the café of the old hotel just beyond the church. That alone was enough to bring him to a halt. The sight of Werberg hurrying from an alley on the other side of the cathedral was only another excuse.

The stocky man seemed to recognize Karl a moment later. He stopped, hesitated, and then ran toward him. Karl barely had time to react before the man was in front of him.

"Watch the river!"

Karl frowned and stepped backward. "Watch the river?" He repeated Werberg's words with measured deliberateness, immediately connecting them to Eva Gottlieb. "When?"

Werberg gulped and tried to slip past him to the safety of the alley behind him—not knowing or not willing to tell.

"Tonight?" Karl pressed urgently.

Eyes wide, Werberg at last found a voice to deny the question. "No. No. Not—no. Next week. Not tonight."

Karl smiled coldly, certain the man was lying. "Heil Hitler, Herr Werberg." He stepped sideways and snapped off the salute in dismissal.

Werberg paled, and without another word, bolted past Karl. Karl viewed his retreat with a mixture of disgust and relief. Werberg would not go to anyone else with his information, of that he was sure. *But ... the river. Almost certainly tonight ...*

Karl changed his mind and turned back from the café. Krimmel and the church report would keep for another day. The irony of the tip-off was not lost on him. That a friend of Eva's would betray her into the hands of an enemy who was really an ally ... he shook his head, the ghost of a smile on his hard face. It would have been amusing were it not so serious.

✳

Karl strolled back into the Gestapo headquarters as if he had all the time in the world. As if he were not suddenly hopeful about the end of his duty here or troubled by an elusive sense of impending disaster. Necessity forced all emotions into the background, and he slipped easily into the role he had played so many times before. He nodded to Pieter, who hovered only inches above the paper before him.

"There is a microscope under the files on my desk. Sometimes they write their own confessions in atoms in the bottom left-hand corner." Karl grinned and feigned surprise in response to Pieter's glare. "I don't want you to ruin your eyes. You are on the river patrol tonight, aren't you?"

"Ja," Pieter snapped. "And I blame you."

"Me?"

"You gave Fredrik the idea of fishing for subversives out there. And since your pastor was captured there, we haven't seen a single person! Like Villach. Nothing happens. I should have applied in Vienna. Jews and pastors and journalists—at least there is work for us there! But yes, I am scheduled to be out tonight."

Karl forced a sympathetic smile in reply to Pieter's litany of boredom. Phrasing his question carefully, he said, "I seem to have better luck at the river than you, ja? If you are so bored, I will take your place there tonight."

Pieter arched a pale eyebrow suspiciously, but the expression was ruined by an enormous yawn. "And what do you want?"

"For you to take my place in the morning. So I can sleep."

"Until noon? That's hardly fair." Pieter protested. "It will only take two hours or so to sweep the river!"

"Fine. You do it then." Karl sounded fed up.

"No, I'll take your shift in the morning."

"Agreed." Karl nodded, and then paused. "What time do I leave?"

Pieter gave him a triumphant grin. "Whenever Fredrik says you can leave. He may send you out more than once. Seems like he's expecting a whole army of Bolsheviks to materialize there where the communist pastor was arrested."

Karl glared at the man, but his mind was racing. "You are a swindler. Probably a good trait to have, now. Will the Inspekteur be coming?"

"No. I think Thomas will go with you."

Nodding again, Karl wondered if there was any way to convince the brawny agent to stay home as well. It seemed unlikely. He could make him the same offer he had Pieter, but if either found the other out ... Such maneuvering was sure to be noticed. This arrangement would have to work. He saluted Pieter and turned to leave.

"Where are you going?"

"Home. If I'm going to be up all night, then I'm taking a nap."

Outside, Karl jogged the half-block to Christ Church. The clock on the bell tower read three-fifty. He waited for the bells to begin their inevitable early tolling. Broken clouds sent light and shadow dancing over the silent steeple for a full two minutes before he remembered they had flown to Rome for Easter. *Or something like that.* The flighty timekeepers would be within the Reich again on Saturday night. Karl turned and struck out for the edge of town. If his warning was heeded, Eva and her two children would not.

I Lift My Eyes unto the Hills

HEAVY SILENCE PERVADED THE kitchen as Eva peeled potatoes for the soup. *The same meal that was "hello,"* she remembered. Adina was drawing something at the table, and Hirschel simply sat beside her. They had already said good-bye, and these last few hours were strained. Eva felt somehow guilty, as if she could have stopped this impossible parting. If only she had held on to each moment more tenuously, lived every second more fully ... but now the time was truly gone.

Sudden knocking exploded into the thick silence, making Eva jump and spill milk into the flame beneath the pot. It sizzled loudly as she hurried to the window. Had Katrina come to say good-bye again? Eva had told her not to come. Tonight it would be better if no one was seen with her ...

Eva drew back the curtain and froze. It was the man—the watcher from church! *Now? So close to escape? God, help us!*

He pounded harder as the curtain swished back into place.

The children were both watching her now, frightened by the sound and whatever they glimpsed in her face. Suddenly dizzy, Eva decided he must not come in. She would not bring this Gestapo creature under the same roof as Hirschel and Adina! The anger of that thought lent her a reckless courage. She opened the door, stepped out, and slammed it behind her.

Karl edged backward, clearly startled by Eva's sudden appearance. "Frau Gottlieb ..." he began uncertainly. "May we step inside?"

"No."

Karl glanced at the quiet road behind him, praying no one from the

Gestapo saw him here. "Very well. I need you to listen to me. Listen closely. The river is patrolled at random." He saw her pale at his words and then check her terror. "There will be no one there until an hour after twilight, but after that I can guarantee nothing."

He watched her expression move from confusion to fear to anger. No doubt she was remembering another time in the same place. *Reinhardt's execution and the questions and anger that followed. My foolish promise to protect Eva and deliver his letter. The storm ...* Back then Karl had been the messenger of doom, as he was now. Eva's alarm confirmed was he had already guessed: the river was her only hope of safety for the children and—hopefully—herself as well. Discovery there by the Gestapo would mean the end for all of them. *But they can escape. Tonight will not end in tragedy!*

Eva's fright hardened into angry bravado. "I don't know who you are, or why you would concern me with your schedule for guarding the river. I will be sure to pass the information along so the Drau does not escape." She narrowed her eyes.

Karl stared past her to the stone fronting of the house. "I am a friend," he said simply. "If you value your life, or the lives of the Hirschel or Adina, heed my advice."

His utterance of the children's names had a shattering effect on Eva. She opened and closed her mouth, but no sound came out.

"An hour after twilight," he repeated in an urgent voice.

The wind blew stronger, sending clouds scudding across the sky like giant, ragged mice. Casting another anxious glance in the direction of the city, Karl backed away from Eva.

"*Grüss Gott*—greet God."

There was no reply as he jogged back toward Villach.

Eva leaned weakly against the wall, ignoring the pressure of the uneven stones against her back. The brief spring sunshine had passed, and winter winds reawakened in the lengthening shadows. From the house the river was barely visible. The distant glint of water was clutched so tightly within the bare tree-branch claws that it might have been a mirage. *Skeleton*

sentinels. She shuddered. In a few hours she would leave two pieces of her heart in the shadow of those grasping branches. *But is it a trap?* She stared until her eyes watered at the cluster of pine trees where the Gestapo agent had disappeared. How could she know if his "hour after twilight" was a guarantee of safety or a prearranged meeting with the secret police?

The cold air did nothing to slow the tumble of her frantic thoughts. Why would this Gestapo agent—the same man who had come with Reinhardt's letter that terrible day in August—suddenly call himself a friend and play the part of a concerned protector? Did he think she would be foolish enough to believe him? But the realization that came on the heels of that memory was more bitter than the wind in the dead trees. *Hirschel and Adina—he knows!*

"The river is patrolled at random. If you value Hirschel or Adina ... the hour after twilight." Fragments of his warning hung like an executioner's sentence in the darkening sky. The wind licked the tears on Eva's cheeks, mocking her as she realized that this long hoped-for escape was nothing more than a cruel game of cat and mouse.

"Help us!" Eva cried aloud, but her plea bounced off the valley walls and returned unanswered. She looked toward the highest peak. *I will lift my eyes unto the hills ...* Psalm 121:1 A few rays of the sunset's golden-pink light had broken through the gathering clouds to shimmer on the snow, and the effect was dazzling.

She gazed desperately at the light, begging it to stay. When the dark came she would leave and *they* would be there, waiting ...

No! There must be some way! Her heart rebelled at what she knew was inevitable. But to keep Adina and Hirschel here another day would be suicide—the Gestapo *knew!* Somehow they had peered around the careful acting and glimpsed the truth about the children.

"Hirschel. Adina." She whispered the names aloud. What threat were they that they should be hunted like this? *Children! Dear God! My children.* The clouds shifted to reclaim the wayward light, and the mountains' radiance paled to gray. Eva closed her eyes against the terror of the shadows and bit her lip. They had to at least attempt to run. *God, help us!* The fear of the chase echoed in the gusting wind.

We will not be easy prey, though, Eva willed. She would not give the arrogant Gestapo agent that much pleasure. The hour after sunset would find unbroken silence by the river bank.

"Tante Eva! Is the bad man gone? What's wrong?"

Adina and Hirschel ran to her as she opened the door. Suddenly weary, she nodded as she stooped to embrace them. "He's gone," she said thickly. Without thinking, she added the futile assurance: "He won't come back." *He will not need to,* she thought grimly as she shuffled back to the kitchen. *We are going to him.* She apologized for burning the soup. It had seemed so important that this good-bye meal be perfect ... perhaps it didn't matter now.

Quietly she instructed Adina to set the bread on the table as she ladled out the potato soup, careful not to scrape the bottom of the pot. Outside it was now entirely dark. With careful control she poured three glasses of milk and carried them to the table.

"Dear God, thank you for this food. And please keep us safe from the bad men and bless Tante Eva and maybe make it so we could stay with her. Amen."

Eva smiled sadly at Adina's prayer, hoping God was especially listening to children tonight.

"Tonight is called the night of the Last Supper," she said softly, wondering why on earth Werberg had chosen this date.

"'Cause it's our last supper with you?" Hirschel looked worried.

"No. The name is much older than tonight. It was the last supper Jesus had with His disciples." In a singsong voice, Eva recited the words she had learned long ago. "'This is My commandment, that you love one another as I have loved you. Greater love has no one than this, than to lay down one's life for his friends.' John 15: 12-13 She stopped, smiling at the new light in the children's eyes. "Remember that love," Eva whispered. A gust of wind crashed against the house like a wave, and her voice broke. "Whatever happens tonight ... remember."

The hour of promised safety came and went, and Karl prayed Eva and the children had left. Had she believed him? There was no way to know, nothing that could be done now. The mountains had trapped the front rolling in from the north, stifling the valley beneath layers of cold cloud. A sullen roll of thunder rumbled in warning as the two men stepped into the garish light of the parking lot in front the headquarters.

"Storm tonight," Thomas muttered.

Karl nodded his assent.

"Hurry up! I don't want to be out all night in this!"

Karl swung himself into the car, cheerful at the nearness of the storm. His long vigil here was nearly over! Suddenly he was certain Eva Gottlieb had listened. This coming rain would cover the tracks of the fugitives well, and tomorrow he would be free.

Adina's gaze drifted slowly across the room. She was memorizing it, Eva knew—fixing in her mind the place that held so much happiness for her and Hirschel. *The gilt frame of Eva and Reinhardt's wedding picture. The piano keys glowing softly in the dim light. The pink settee and stone fireplace reflected in miniature on the face of the grandfather clock.* Slowly her eyes met Eva's.

"Are you ready?"

Adina held on to Hirschel with one hand and fingered her thick braid with the other. Traveling hair, Eva had said, as she brushed and braided it this morning.

The two children stood together for a moment, seeming very alone once more. "Ja," Adina murmured at last.

"Then we must go."

Holding tightly to one another, Hirschel and Adina followed her out of the warm safety of the house and into the keening wind.

Where Does My Help Come From?

Eva was strangely in control as she pulled the car onto the road and headed away from the city. The noise of the night was somehow comforting, masking the rumble of the engine and muffling the fear in her heart.

Hirschel and Adina were silent in the backseat. *Perhaps they are invisible that way,* Eva thought. Did they sense the dark like she did? The night, as taut and breathless as the moment the conductor raises his baton before a waiting orchestra? Eva downshifted carefully as she navigated a curve in the road. The river was already in sight. Somewhere along the shadowy shore would be the silhouette of a massive, weather-ravaged pine and an overflow of scrub where the auto could be reasonably well-concealed. From there they would walk about a hundred meters farther and make their way to the water.

Her thoughts were oddly disconnected as the dark road unfurled in front of the car. She remembered Reinhardt joking about the danger of this route. "In the auto we sheep are at least safe from German shepherds!" He had been right. Only human hunters prowled this road at night—

Eva started to hum the bedtime prayer she had sung so many times with the children. "I am small, my heart is pure ..."

"That none may live within but Jesus alone." Hirschel and Adina finished the little song and lapsed into silence again.

"Tante Eva, I see the tree!" Hirschel's voice seemed like a shout in the quiet car.

A moment later Eva located the towering landmark. She had already begun to ease into the grass when the light appeared. Without thinking she swerved right, jerking the car back onto the road. *Driving! Just driving! Not stopped, not suspicious!* For a wild instant Eva was grateful this terrible game ended in the blaze of headlights and not the dark of the riverbank. The car slowed.

"Get down!" she hissed, and then, "Help us, God!"

Hirschel and Adina instantly obeyed, squeezing themselves into the cramped space between the seats. Eva grasped the steering wheel desperately, trying to still her trembling hands. *Maybe—maybe it isn't the Gestapo.* She tasted metal. *Please—God … not Gestapo.*

An arm protruded suddenly from the window of the approaching vehicle—the conductor's baton at last, falling, falling. Eva braked raggedly on the edge of the road.

"I'm sorry," she whispered in farewell as a huge shadow emerged from the vehicle. "I love you." It devoured the distance with a strutting march. "So sorry …"

"You will now get out of the car." Though it wasn't necessary, the shadow bent until his leering face filled Eva's window. *German shepherds.* His voice was harsh with self-assurance. Eva remembered the children, and, slowly, she opened the door and stood.

The man laughed as he recognized her—a terrifying sound in the crazy half light. "Eva Gottlieb! The pastor's wife! Come crawling back to find where we killed your coward of a husband?" She slammed the door in reply, an action that seemed to infuriate her captor. "I think I will show you." He grabbed her arms and twisted them cruelly back. Eva cried out and fought against him. *Hirschel! Adina! Oh, God!*

"We aren't very fond of Bolshevik cowards in the Third Reich." His voice shook with unreasonable hatred.

"I—I—" Eva's throat constricted in fear. In her mind she heard only Hirschel's laughter, and she struggled harder in her captor's iron grip. *God! Where are you?* Only silence responded to her plea—silence and the murmur of the river that could have carried the children to freedom. *Could have … God, so close!*

"You are the Bolshevik! Let me go!"

The shadow laughed at her obvious panic. "Karl!" he cried, dragging her toward the Gestapo car. "Look what I've caught!"

Her breath came in rapid gasps as the man name Karl emerged from the vehicle. "What is it this time, Thomas? A Jewish assassin? An Austrian conspirator?"

Thomas was not put off by the sarcasm in Karl's voice. "Gottlieb's wife! Up to the same tricks he was, no doubt. Dirty little Bolshevik!"

Karl froze for a moment and then stepped into the light.

"Eva Gottlieb?" For a split second his face registered shock, and then he mastered his surprise. Eva gasped in recognition. *The watcher from church!* He shook his head almost imperceptibly, warning her to silence. Eva bit her lip and looked away. He had been telling the truth! *We would have been safe, if only ...* But now it was too late. She had failed.

"It is an hour to curfew. Do we now arrest people for driving at night?" With an effort, Karl recovered the same bored tone, almost humoring Thomas.

"She is the wife of Gottlieb!" Thomas announced, shoving Eva forward until she was pinned against the grill of the auto. He shook his ponderous head as if her crime should be completely obvious. "By our law she is guilty of his treachery." It was a clear challenge—Karl had watched Christ Church, and therefore Eva, for months. He should have acted against her then, now he should allow the arrest to proceed unquestioned.

Eva shook her head, desperately searching Karl's face for some sign of mercy.

Karl shrugged. "Very well. You take her away, and I'll search the car. But Thomas—" Karl waited until the man turned back to face him. "You will not lay so much as a *finger* on her until I come back."

Thomas looked at him quizzically.

"She's mine," was Karl's only explanation. Thomas grunted something in reply as he fastened Eva's handcuffs and jerked her toward the gaping door of the Gestapo car.

Karl watched the taillights fade into blackness. Tonight was suddenly far too much like the night of the pastor's arrest. *It is even his car.* The dark was suddenly alive with memories.

"You are hiding something, and I will have the truth!"

"The truth has been with you for a long, long time. The light shines in the darkness, and the darkness did not comprehend it."

"Treason!"

"But men loved darkness rather than light, because their deeds were evil—" John 3:19

Karl inhaled sharply, not wanting to relive any further the night that had started him on this crazy path. *Children. The children must be in the car.* The darkness on the road was complete. Karl couldn't see his own hand, much less the car parked several meters away. Kicking himself for not having so much as a lighter in his pocket, he shuffled forward.

A burst of lightning split the sky with the intensity of a prison searchlight, illuminating the auto and the shoreline in negative. Karl angled to the left until he could feel the smooth metal of the hood.

"Hirschel? Adina?" His voice sounded small in the night. A rain-laden gust of wind was the only reply. Karl opened the door and called again. This time he heard a tiny whimper from between the seats.

"I know you don't know me, but I need you to listen," he said gently. "The man who would hurt you is gone. It is safe to come out." He waited in the silence of the car for a few moments, feeling remarkably like a lost child himself. "We don't have very much time. You know why you're at the river. Where do you need to go?"

At last a tousled head peeked out from beneath the seat. "Where is Tante Eva?" the girl asked defiantly.

"At … the Gestapo headquarters. She was arrested," Karl said slowly, careful to keep his voice even.

"Will you arrest us too?" Adina was suddenly joined by another silhouette.

"No."

A thoughtful silence followed his promise. At last the two children clambered out of the car, and Karl sighed with relief.

"It's very dark. Are you a bad man?"

It was the girl's voice again, still shaky. Karl almost smiled at the question. *Yes? No? Both, perhaps?* "Don't be afraid," he said softly in reply. "Where do you need to go?"

"We passed the big tree and now we are going to the river. There is a man with a boat—" Adina nudged her brother, and he stopped abruptly.

Karl nodded briskly. He didn't want to hear more. Taking both children by the hand, he started toward the tangled shadows of the tree line. Thunder exploded almost directly overhead, scattering the first fat raindrops like shrapnel. Hirschel squeaked and clung more tightly to Karl.

"Don't be afraid," Karl repeated, surprised at the smallness of the hand in his own. "A storm is a good thing for you tonight."

"Why?"

"Because it will make you hard to find." Karl winced as he struck his shin against a fallen log. Carefully, he lifted first Hirschel and then Adina over.

"But you found us."

"And now I am hiding you again." Karl stopped short as the sound of the river filled his ear.

Halting a few meters from the bank, he instructed Adina to announce their arrival. Someone replied after a long pause.

"Come forward. Careful now, the river is cold. Can you see the boat?" The voice was coaxing. He struck a match, and the tiny flame flared up like a beacon and then faded. "Follow the light."

Karl hung back as the two children made their way to the boat. Not until he heard the hollow echo of footsteps on wood did he venture to speak.

"Bitte—you must stay here for a bit longer."

"Reinhardt?" The voice was puzzled, hopeful. Karl felt suddenly ill. *Reinhardt! Of course. So this is who he was protecting.* The pastor's defiance now made perfect sense.

"Reinhardt Gottlieb is dead," Karl replied flatly. "I am a friend."

"What kind of friend?" The demand was punctuated by an ominous clicking. Karl's fingers brushed the Luger at his side, and then he dropped his hand and stepped into the open.

"I am unarmed. Shoot me if you wish." He held his breath. Several seconds passed in charged silence. At last the voice, not bullets, broke through the darkness. "We heard the Gestapo and feared the worst."

Karl nodded, though he knew the speaker could not see him through the blackness. "They took Eva. That's why I need you to wait here. I—"

"You are not the one who brought the children here?"

"No, that was Reinhardt's widow. Who is by now at the Gestapo headquarters in Villach." Karl's Berliner accent grew sharper with the words. He was suddenly tired of arguing with the disembodied voice on the boat. "I can get her out, but she'll need to leave the Reich. Is there room for one more?"

"In this business it is best not to ask too many questions. So I will not inquire as to how you plan to rescue anyone from the Gestapo. But how do I know you will not return with a legion of Nazi forces to capture this small boat?"

"Because I am—was—Gestapo. I was in the car when Eva was pulled over. I knew someone would be at the river for the children as soon as I saw her here. If I wanted to arrest you, you would already be on your way to Mauthausen."

He waited to see what affect this revelation would have on the speaker. There was a long silence, followed by a resigned reply.

"Then we have nothing to lose. If you are as good as your word, I will take on one more passenger tonight. If not, it is already too late. I give you two hours. Now go, and may God go with you!"

Karl wasted no time clawing his way back up to the road. He slipped into Eva's car and raced toward Villach. *Two hours!* It would have to be enough.

The storm broke in earnest as Thomas screeched to a stop in front of the towering pink building that was the Gestapo headquarters. Eva could see Christ Church through the broken branches of the park. Had she ever realized how close the two buildings were? For a year they had worshiped on the edge of the shadow—but now it was truly night.

She heard a door slam, and then the Gestapo agent yanked her from the car and herded her through the freezing rain. She was shivering uncontrollably by the time she stumbled into the sparse lobby.

"Look what I caught! The pastor's mate!" Her captor, still as much a part of the night in the harsh white light as he had been on the road, bellowed the words like a conjurer. Two scrawny agents materialized almost instantly.

"Where's Karl?"

"Coming." The paw at her back shoved her into the center of the lobby.

"Little thing, isn't she?" They circled Eva like birds of prey.

"Soft, too."

Eva jerked away from the clammy touch. *God, please! Don't let them—*

The rough voice behind her laughed. "Dark hair, though. You sure she's not a Jewess?"

"Wouldn't put it past that communist of a pastor."

The shorter of the two agents leaned forward until Eva could smell the onions and beer on his breath. "Pretty lady. You'd tell us if you were a Jewess, now, wouldn't you?"

Eva shook her head frantically, searching in vain for a safe place between the two long desks of the lobby. A massive picture of the Fuehrer glared at her from one wall, granting his evil benediction to the scene. The bloody banner of the broken cross menaced from the opposite corner. "God!" she whispered. "Help ..."

Her captor seemed to find her little prayer uproarious. He guffawed again, propelling her toward a corridor that yawned open beside the flag. "God will not help you here!" He laughed. "Though perhaps Karl will!"

"Karl?" The short agent was incredulous.

The big man shrugged. "He claimed her. Been watching her for a long time, he has."

Eva blanched and twisted in his grip.

"She fights!" The short one raised his hands in mocking surrender. "Leave her for Karl, then."

Still laughing, the brawny Gestapo agent hurried her along until they reached a nondescript door at the end of the hallway. He flung it open with a hollow *clang* and forced Eva down the stairs two at a time. She stumbled at the bottom, landing on her hands and knees in the filth of the prison floor. Her captor dragged her upright and pressed her against the wall. He bent down until his face was only inches from hers, until Eva could see nothing but his cold black eyes and leering smile.

"Karl has you first, woman. But he will certainly share."

With that, he grabbed her shoulders and propelled her forward into the seemingly endless corridor of bare lightbulbs and windowless doors. Eva squeezed her eyes shut, as if in opening them again she could wake up from this nightmare. *Buried alive! Adina! Hirschel! Karl?* She was still shivering, still soaked and trembling in the cold of this underground maze. She swayed slightly as the Gestapo agent stopped in front of a cell with bars instead of a solid door.

He made a great show of reading out the number. "Cell twenty-seven, Eva Gottlieb. The same cell where we held that husband of yours! Quite a privilege!"

Eva couldn't move. The agent shoved her into the tiny cubicle and slammed the door. She listened as the slap of his feet faded into the humming, groaning quiet of the prison.

"Reinhardt," she whispered, aching. She desperately scanned the graffiti that covered the dirty walls. *His name, a Scripture, something ...* There was nothing. Broken, she sank to the floor in the dimmest corner of the cell.

"Reinhardt ..." How she missed him tonight! She buried her face in her knees, tasting the salt of her tears. *Here! They took him here while I waited ... waited up for the husband I would never see again. I never said good-bye. Not to Reinhardt. Not to the children—dear God! Are they safe? Are they waiting, while I am here?*

The pain of her grief was a physical force, bearing down on her until she could not breathe. *Reinhardt! Were you as scared as I am? What did they do to you here? And why, why did you have to go?*

Unanswered questions and prayers ran together into one final requiem. Could God see her as she sobbed in this tiny cell? The three walls seemed to lean inward in a suffocating embrace. *Buried alive! God! Where—where were You? Where are You?* Wherever He was, it was not here, in this place where evil reigned. Exhausted with grief, Eva slept.

The Giving

"Where is she?" Karl demanded breathlessly.

Thomas eyed him with amusement. "I wouldn't have guessed it of you, Karl!" His large face split with an uneven grin. "But if you're in such a hurry ..." He lent extra stress to the word *hurry*. "Then she is in cell twenty-seven."

Karl nodded curtly and hastened down the corridor. He ignored the obscene snickers that echoed after him. Thomas and Rolf knew nothing, really. It mattered little what they thought he had in mind. *But Eva! If they have hurt her ...* He swallowed hard and resisted the urge to jog up the stairs. *Quietly. Slowly. Fredrik may be in tonight.* The vile little man had the night off, from what Karl knew. But his *dedication* brought him into the Gestapo headquarters at all hours. Karl held his breath as he opened the door at the top of the stairwell and then let it out with a sigh. In the dark corridor no light leaked from the crack beneath the door.

And unlocked, too! Karl hesitated for only a moment outside the Inspekteur's office.

Love the LORD your God with all your heart, and with all your soul, and with all your strength ... Matthew 22:37

He nodded once in decision and stepped into the cluttered room. *Transfer papers—on the desk? In it?* He removed a stack from the drawer and thumbed hurriedly through it. *Yes. Here.*

It was easy, remarkably easy, to take a pen and sign the name of Fredrik Schmidt to the paper for Eva's transfer. Karl slid the form into the puddle of light on the desk to scrutinize the scowling signature. It would do, he decided. Voices echoed faintly in the corridor, urging him to hurry. He folded the slip twice and shoved it into his pocket.

And love your neighbor as yourself. Matthew 22:39

Karl shuddered in spite of himself as he strode through the prison's twisting corridors. The dampness, the relentless light, the monotony of walls of unrelieved cages—a man could quickly go mad down here. He ran a hand over his aching eyes, not certain he was entirely sane.

"Why, Pastor?" Confusion edged with anger tinged the echo. He remembered his demand. *Why did you throw your life away?*

"My Savior has always been faithful to me. I cannot turn away from Him."

For months Karl had wondered at the pastor's response. Church had little enough to do with dying at the barrel of a Gestapo gun. But tonight he had seen the reason in the little hands of Eva's children. And he thought perhaps, in the Voice that had forgiven him, he had heard the answer.

He stopped suddenly in front of cell twenty-seven. It was a bit of an oddity, with open bars that put the prisoner on display instead of a heavy door to close him in. Karl closed his eyes as the details of that night came flooding back. *I grabbed the bars as I talked to Gottlieb.* Whatever the oafish Thomas lacked in intelligence, he more than made up for in cruelty.

He fumbled with the keys as he let himself in. For a moment he simply stood, trying to connect the child-sized figure in the corner with Eva Gottlieb. He recognized her, and yet—how small she looked, asleep on the floor of the cell! How fragile!

"Frau Gottlieb?"

There was no response.

"Frau Gottlieb, bitte!" He edged closer, not quite daring to touch her. "It is important!" Something in his tone must have awakened her, for she sat up with a start and immediately pressed herself closer to the wall.

"Frau Gottlieb, your children are safe," he soothed, as if he were talking to the children and not about them. "I took them to the boat, and they are waiting for you."

Eva did not seem to grasp the importance of his information. In a small voice she asked, "Was this really ... where Reinhardt ... was?"

Karl grimaced at the pain in her eyes. Wishing he could change the answer, he confirmed what Thomas must have told her. "Yes. Here—for a few hours before ..."

Eva turned to face the wall. "How?" she breathed in a barely audible voice. It was a question that must be asked, regardless of whether she could bear the answer.

"They shot him," Karl replied quietly, witnessing the scene again. "At dawn, and the first light ..." His voice trailed off. "I—I have never seen anyone die so bravely, so unafraid." He closed his eyes, and when he opened them again they seemed somehow clearer. "You must have known he was protecting refugees. Like the children. He died protecting them. We stopped him near the river, and ... I suppose he guessed that we would search. When the Inspekteur questioned him, he preached a little sermon to us. Talked about truth and light ... Fredrik accused him of treason. And so we never searched the river."

Eva nodded through silent tears.

"But he ... he saved one more in dying. Someone who he could have never reached in life. His bravery—love for a God that I thought was silent ... it changed me." Karl concluded his account with a note of wonder in his voice.

Eva nodded again, slowly. Her voice was a whisper. "I never knew. Thank you ... for telling me." She bit her lip as the meaning of Karl's last sentence sank in. "And I'm so sorry ... I didn't believe you—"

Karl brushed aside her apology. "He made me promise to protect you. So please, listen now. Your children are safe. You must join them, leave Villach immediately."

Eva wiped her eyes and nodded once. "What"—she cleared her throat and tried again—"what do I need to do?"

"Stand up, please. You are being transferred to Mauthausen." He produced the document, and Eva frowned in confusion. Karl rushed to explain. "You cannot simply disappear, Frau Gottlieb. You are here now—the only place to go is Mauthausen. So the records are in order."

Understanding dawned on Eva's pale features. "Thank you," she whispered, hardly daring to believe it.

Karl smiled and nodded, but his blue eyes held a shade of sorrow. "They did not hurt you, did they?"

Eva shook her head, and Karl sighed with relief. "Good. Thomas—good. But … I'm sure you know what they think I am here for?"

Eva blushed. "That—"

"Exactly. And for your sake as well as mine, you must act like it. Can you do that?"

She nodded uncertainly.

"Good." Karl closed his eyes and inhaled deeply, regaining for the last time the control that would enable him to scoff and curse and bluff his way to the edge of madness.

"Follow me."

The corridor between the lobby and jail was unnaturally silent. Karl set the pace at a near-jog, dragging Eva behind him. "Don't look up," were his only instructions as they entered the bright lobby.

Thomas, lounging by the door like a sleeping bulldog, snapped upright at their approach. "Heil Hitler, Herr Zehr!" He saluted Karl with exaggerated enthusiasm.

Karl returned the greeting, grinning, still moving toward the door.

Thomas stood to block the exit. "Are you planning on taking her on a date?"

Karl shrugged. "It was cold down there."

Thomas remained rooted in place. With a sigh, Karl produced the folded paper. "She's being transferred, Thomas." He enunciated each word carefully. "Fredrik wants her in Mauthausen. Efficiency, you see."

"The Inspekteur?" Now Thomas looked truly confused. "He wasn't even here tonight!"

"The man has an uncanny sense of what goes on here. He dropped in," Karl replied coolly. To Eva's surprise, Thomas moved aside.

"May her train be very late." He laughed.

Karl slammed the door of the building, cutting off the noise of Thomas's bellowing mirth. He stood for a moment with his head bowed, letting the strain of deception run out of him. A light rain misted the air with cold droplets. Eva regarded Karl with a mixture of concern and fear.

"You act very well." Her breath puffed out in frosty clouds.

Karl nodded slowly, seeming suddenly much older. His face was drawn in the orange glow of the streetlamps. "Yes. I … I suppose I do. We should go."

They climbed into the Gestapo car in uneasy silence. Eva sensed she was missing something as they pulled away, but what exactly that could be eluded her.

"Where are we going?" she demanded, suddenly frightened that Karl would demand some price from her in exchange for freedom.

"Your house. You are not coming back, Frau Gottlieb. Unless all this someday changes … I thought you might wish to take some things with you."

Never come back? Eva paled at the thought. "Please," she began hesitantly. "I have friends here. Katrina Donsky. Do you know her, at the church? Is there any way—"

"No." Karl was suddenly brusque. "There is not time tonight. I cannot do more."

Eva had no time to ponder his words as he pulled up to the stone cottage.

"Five minutes."

She didn't move. Belatedly, Karl remembered the handcuffs around her wrists. He hurried to unlock them and then sat back as she scrambled out of the car and ran inside. He let the engine idle, unaccountably worried that Eva would not come back out. No light appeared in the windows. He imagined her moving through the familiar darkness, gathering whatever was precious, saying good-bye …

One minute. He tapped a finger against his deaf ear nervously. He had nothing to say good-bye to. No one who would miss him. It should not be this hard …

Eva suddenly reappeared, clutching a small valise and a bundle to her chest. She turned her back to the car and studied the cottage one last time. Her lips moved silently in farewell. *To Reinhardt, who I loved here. To Katrina, who I swore I would never leave. To the other dear ones who must stay behind ...*

She lingered a moment more and then rejoined him in the car.

Eva watched Karl with confusion as he turned and accelerated toward the river. His face was pale in the glow of the dashboard, locked in a grim determination that frightened her. *What is he not telling me?* Surely, after all the pretending and terror and waiting of this night, there would not be any further danger! The drive seemed to confirm her hopes. The road was entirely deserted—empty of all life but them. Karl studied the tree line intently, searching for the place Eva had been arrested.

"Here! This is it." Eva declared abruptly, recognizing the gnarled pine Hirschel had first spotted. Wordlessly, Karl braked in the grass, and she sighed with relief. *Safe!*

Only then did she realize that her protector was shaking. "Karl?" she asked in a small voice, the name a question. "Karl?"

"Pray," Karl said hoarsely. He closed his eyes and rested his head against the steering wheel. "For me—pray."

Eva gasped in sudden, terrible understanding. "Is my life to be your ... death?"

Karl did not speak, and in the silence was her answer.

"No!" Eva cried fiercely. "There must be another way. Come with us! You have done all you can, now live!"

He lifted his head, tired. "I cannot," he said softly, almost gently. "They will not search long for you. But I ... I was one of them. They would never stop hunting me."

Eva shook her head in horror, denying the truth in his words. "They will kill you when they realize what you did for me! You don't have to go back. It is your choice. Please, choose life!" She was pleading now, desperate that this man who had saved her should live.

"I—I did. Some time ago."

In the dim light Eva glimpsed the impossible peace on his face. "Your life."

Eva sank back, stunned. "Why?" she choked.

Karl did not hesitate. "Because it is what Christ would do … did." His voice was firm now. "Because it is right. Because … because I want … I want you to live." In his eyes something flickered for an instant and then vanished. Was it longing? Regret? Love?

The silence that fell on the car felt almost holy. Karl drew a deep breath and steeled himself—yes, to say good-bye. His words sounded foreign to his own ears.

"You must go, Frau Gottlieb."

Eva followed Karl mutely through the darkness to the river bank. The danger seemed unreal here, so close to the murmuring waters.

"Are you certain?" It was a closing, hopeless plea.

Karl grasped at a rough tree trunk as if to steady his resolve with its firmness. "Go, Eva. I am certain—go! Live. Free. With your children …"

"I will," she whispered brokenly. "Karl, I'm so sorry! I—"

"Don't." Karl's voice was sharp. "There is no need. I made that choice. Now go!"

He did not watch as Eva made her way to the edge of the liquid darkness. Did not listen as she called out and was answered by the voice on the boat. Not until the craft had pulled away from the shore did he raise his hand in farewell.

"Remember us!" he cried, hearing his voice echo hollowly in the rain-washed air. "Remember!"

Tracings of Eternal Light

EVA HAD NO MORE tears left to weep as the shadows of Villach's winter-stripped forests faded into the night. Somewhere among the lifeless trees, she knew, stood a man whose death sentence had already sounded. Did he stand there still, watching the unbroken blackness for some sign of those he had rescued? A crisp breeze rushed over the stern, and for a moment she thought she heard words in the empty air. *Re ... Remember ...*

"Did you know him well?" the boatman asked softly, coming up behind her.

"Karl?" Eva shook her head. "He was Gestapo."

"He said the same when he brought the two children down to me. 'I was Gestapo,' he said, and asked me to stay." The mellow voice trailed off into the blackness.

"He was there when my husband was killed," Eva offered quietly. "He brought me the letter ... Reinhardt's letter. And then he was at the church, all those months. But we never knew. He told me when to leave tonight, and I thought it was a trap. So he set me free and he stayed." She turned toward the shadowy outline of the boatman, hands spread in a struggle to understand. "I am safe, but I can never go back. Never say good-bye. And he will die because of me."

"*Nein*, child. You will live because of him. He chose his way. A reflection, we see this Mourning Thursday."

Eva shook her head, too drained to comprehend the stranger's words. What was it Reinhardt had said about the nameless men he worked with?

Pastor and professor turned smuggler and sailor, and good friends in low places?

"Look at the river," the boatman instructed, at the same time gesturing to where the clouds had torn back from the stars. "Do you see the darkness behind us? The mud we leave in our wake?"

She nodded tiredly.

"But now see the rest of the river. Where the water is clearest ... can you see the stars, Frau Gottlieb? The shadows and reflections of heaven?" He waited for her assent, weighing his next words carefully. "I have seen that river in the hearts of men. Many are so gorged with blackness that even true light is dark to them. But by God's grace, a few are mirrors. Purified by Him until it is His reflection that shines there. Like the water. Like tonight. Do you see, Frau Gottlieb?" Again he swept his arm skyward, greeting the stars. "It is so much larger than us. Deeper. Purer."

Eva wondered if he was talking about the night sky or what Karl had done.

"And on the eve of Good Friday, too ... I often think God's heart must break when He looks down on all we do to each other. I ask why He stops evil men with our frail obedience instead of an earthquake or fire from heaven. And why He often does not stop them at all. But, Frau Gottlieb ... how His heart must sing when He sees someone willing to love with all the vulnerable strength He gives!"

"Vulnerable strength?" Eva repeated, slowly understanding. Remembering the light of the love of Calvary, and recognizing the bright reflection of it in what Karl had done. "Perhaps you are right. Maybe in some hearts truth is engraved in eternal light. But what of the others? The darkness?" Bitterness tinged her voice at the memory of the prowling men in the Gestapo office. They did not only reflect the night, they were consumed by it. "They killed my husband. They will destroy Karl. When all the mirrors have been shattered, what then?"

When the man replied, his words were sorrow mingled with hope. "Even ... even if every flame is extinguished, and every light bearer crushed, God will remain. If the entire river were dried up in an instant, the heavens would still be ablaze. They are foolish men—foolish to think that by destroying the reflections they will annihilate the One from who light comes. Still ..." He sighed quietly as he remembered how many, many candles had already been snuffed out. "We grieve for them. Our hearts break, but they must keep beating. Because the light still shines in the darkness ... so we will keep living and reflecting His glory."

It was too dark to see, but Eva was certain she heard a smile in the man's voice. "Two children—your children—are asleep below deck. They will be happy to see you."

"Thank you. For waiting ... thank you."

Eva lingered at the railing a moment more as the quiet footsteps retreated from the stern. Starlight sparkled between the silent hills that hemmed their path. She smiled softly at the memory of Adina's prayer— was it only hours ago? *Please keep us safe from the bad men and bless Tante Eva and maybe make it so we could stay with her.*

"Amen," Eva whispered, and turned to feel her way to the room where the children slept.

Karl strained his eyes upward, hoping for some glimpse of the sky. Intersecting strands of darkness wove a canopy above him that obscured all but the tiniest glimmer of light. The single star that shined seemed impossibly far away tonight. He took a shuddering breath and stared unseeingly out at the river. Eva was gone, safe. That was right. He had also been right, in what he had told her—a Gestapo agent was too valuable to simply disappear. He would be hunted wherever he went, unless he went directly to them.

Karl lowered himself carefully to the ground and pulled his knees to his chest. There was no other way, he knew. Maybe he had always known. He closed his eyes, listening with one ear to the splashing of the river. Somewhere in the storm-quieted night a bird sang. He smiled at the sound. It was from another river, a day with sunshine so very long ago. A picnic beside the Spree in Berlin, and a five-year-old boy tearing across the bright grass beside the bank ... "Catch me, Mama! Try and catch me!"

He blinked, surprised to find the world still black around him. Other memories crowded out the picnic. The long winter. His mother's death. The oath he had sworn the day he entered the Hitler Youth. Suddenly he wished for the confirmation class he had never taken. He broke off a twig and rolled it almost reverently between his fingers, amazed at its firmness. It would be here in the morning, though he would not.

In a whisper he repeated the words that had brought him to the terrible waiting of this last and lonely vigil. "Love the LORD your God with all your heart and with all your soul and with all your mind and with all your strength. Love your neighbor as yourself ..." Matthew 22: 37, 39

The cold hours slid past unmarked in the silence of the night of mourning. At some point his gaze returned to the river. It had changed from black to deep purple, rich like wine with the coming dawn. Suddenly he remembered the impossible words he had read on Christmas Eve beneath the bare lightbulb in his room. *Father, forgive them!* He had traveled the path of suffering alongside Him and found forgiveness. Now, beneath the lightening sky, he prayed for the strength to walk it alone.

Fear not them which kill the body but are not able to kill the soul. Matthew 10:28

Karl rose stiffly, summoned and strangely comforted by the command. Was it his imagination, or did the darkness recede at the words? He brushed himself off and began the climb back to the auto. He had been right last night, after all. Today he would be free.

"Look who showed up!"

"A good night, was it?"

"Sorry to see her go?"

These and a dozen other taunts greeted Karl as he entered the Gestapo headquarters for the final time. *They didn't know!* It was all he could do to play the part without letting his surprise and hope show. He managed a tired grin in response to their jests.

Pieter came up and slapped him on the back. "You look ready to drop!"

"I did not get much sleep last night," Karl replied truthfully, eliciting a roar of laughter from the sordid group. But Pieter's observation was correct. Karl was ashen in the warm light of late morning.

"I would bet the pastor's wife got even less!" More laughter followed as Karl closed his eyes and shook his head slightly. He had been right to free Eva from this place, and right to ensure that these men would never find her.

"One of the benefits of the job, eh?" another agent quipped. "First choice of prisoners! We should arrest more beautiful women!"

"If only the Inspekteur were not in such a hurry to get rid of them ..."

Karl's eyes wandered to the window. Such a bright day. The old tree outside the office hadn't budded yet, though the tips of the branches were already swollen with the promise of new life. *Life!* How important those blossoms suddenly seemed! With an effort, he dragged himself back to this last charade.

"So Villach is rid of the Gottliebs!" Pieter trumpeted the words just as the door opened.

The celebratory mood evaporated instantly as Fredrik entered. "What about Gottlieb?" he inquired mildly.

"Rein-Reinhardt is dead ... His wife is gone now too. They are b-both gone." Pieter bobbed his head in confirmation of his own words, grinning foolishly and edging out of the Inspekteur's reach.

Karl looked back at the tree as Fredrik pinned Pieter with a frustrated glare. The Inspekteur's words were clipped as he asked, "And where, exactly, did Eva Gottlieb go? She was denied travel papers, wasn't she?"

"She did not need them to go to Mauthausen," Pieter blurted, baffled by Fredrik's incomprehension. "After she was arrested last night, she was transferred." His voice remained coaxing, as if he were trying to jog Fredrik's memory.

"Arrested? Transferred?" A black eyebrow wiggled on the narrow face. "Without my authorization?"

"With your authorization," Thomas offered, almost apologetic. "I saw the papers. They were signed."

"I was not here last night!" Fredrik shouted.

"But the papers—Karl ..." The big man's voice faltered as he drew the inevitable conclusion.

Absolute silence fell in the room, and all eyes turned to Karl. *Do not fear those who can kill the body but cannot kill the soul ...* Swallowing hard, he turned to face Fredrik's furious stare.

"Where is Eva Gottlieb, Karl?" The Inspekteur's voice was almost a whisper.

"I don't know," Karl replied evenly.

"Idiot! Where is she?"

Karl took two steps backward, looked out the window once more, and shrugged.

"What did you do with her?"

The sky was such a clear blue. Like water, or cerulean. Karl wondered why he had not noticed before.

"You are a traitor to the Fuehrer and to Germany!"

"I stand with a clear conscience before myself and my God. That is enough." Karl's voice rang with a holy intensity in the startled room. The mask had been dropped at last, and he stood before them now with steady courage.

Fredrik was wholly unprepared for such a transformation. "You are a fool!" he accused.

"No." Karl smiled slightly, certain now. The sun was bright at his back. "No. I am no fool."

"Treason!" Fredrik sputtered. "Betrayal—sold out the Fatherland for a woman! You choose death!"

"I have chosen life."

"Arrest him!"

For an instant no one moved. Fredrik shrieked the demand again, and then, with automatic precision, a blow from a rifle butt sent Karl to his knees. He did not resist as his arms were wrenched backward, or as handcuffs were tightened painfully around his wrists. Instead he looked upward, searching each stunned face in turn. None could hold his gaze. All eyes glanced sideways, away, unwilling to meet the pure fire that burned in his stare.

Abruptly Thomas dragged him to his feet, and Karl took his first halting steps toward freedom.

The Beginning

It had been four edgy days since Karl's unexpected defiance and arrest. Four days since his refusal to reveal anything to Fredrik. Four days since the doors to the prison had slammed shut with all the finality of the gates of hell.

Easter weekend had come and gone, mostly unnoticed by those in the Gestapo office. And though none spoke of it, there was not an agent in the Villach Gestapo that did not privately wonder what had become of Karl. The morbid curiosity was most acute for those who had witnessed his fateful confrontation with Fredrik. They could not quite forget the piercing assurance that had shined in his eyes, or the joyful hope he had seemed to carry with him into the dank confines of the prison. It was misplaced hope, they knew. No one withstood the Inspekteur's interrogations for long. Karl would break, and then he would die. There was no life to be found in that. But still, the echo of his bravery could not be dimmed. Furtive glances and half-asked questions replied to it now.

"Would you have guessed he would …?"

"Four days now …"

"Always a bit strange, but I never thought …"

"Is he still …?"

Fredrik appeared aboveground only occasionally now. He was constantly furious and sullen, and from that the agents concluded Karl must be holding his silence. *Four days!* It was unheard of. Four days of brutal questioning, and Karl remained unbroken! He could not be dead, they surmised. The body would have been brought out. No, Karl Zehr must be living—if such a tormented existence in the bowels of the Villach prison was to be considered life.

No one dared enquire after him. No one uttered a syllable in his favor. But four days had passed since Karl entered the land of the living dead, and he still clung to life.

The cottage roof sloped sharply upward, losing its pinnacle in shadow. Pale pink light bathed the room below in a gentle glow. Permeating the walls was a sense of peace, relief from the desperate journey four days prior.

Eva stirred and slowly sat up. Beside her, Hirschel sighed in his sleep and reached out to pat her pillow. Smiling, Eva kissed the little hand. Then she slid softly out of bed, careful not to disturb the mountain of colorful quilts that heaped the mattress. The wood was cool beneath her feet as she padded to the window to watch the sunrise.

Dawn was blossoming quickly above the hazy mountains, expanding to engulf the sky in a rosy blush. Gold and purple clouds streaked across the morning canvas like paint spilled in the east. Almost instinctively, Eva found her gaze drawn from the river to the jagged hills that marked the Austrian border.

The first rays of warmth would be brushing Villach as well. She thought of Katrina, who by now must have heard of her arrest. Would she find the note Eva had left for her?

If only you could have come with us, Trina. She could suddenly see her friend, hazel eyes and copper hair flashing as she urged Eva once again to leave Villach. *I finally listened, Trina. But how I wish we could have said good-bye.* She shook her head slowly, the image of Karl filling her thoughts. While spring sunshine flooded into the city, another candle guttered and died. A single tear coursed down Eva's cheek as she continued to watch the east. The darkness that had descended on her beloved home was nearly complete, broken only by … a reflection. *Reinhardt. Katrina. Karl. Ramond.* She sighed softly as she remembered.

"We must stand by truth, even when the rest of the world would cast it into the flames. We must stand." That was Reinhardt, steadfast and decided.

"When light and dark collide, does the darkness ever overcome the light? The first star, the hint of dawn ... a candle flame." Katrina's soft and fervent voice sounded through Eva's thoughts. "As long as even a single light glimmers, the darkness cannot claim victory."

And so not one light but many blazed out against the encroaching night.

"Pray. For me—pray." The haunting echo of Karl's plea played clearly in her mind. What had he endured for her sake? "It is what Christ would do ... did." Had he spoken those words, or had she imagined them? It made no difference. He had lived them.

She turned away from the window, away from the memories that lurked in the shadows of the frontier, to watch the sleeping children. Quiet joy filled her at the sight of them. They were safe now, a family. Was this what God had planned all along? Through the bleak and hopeless days after Reinhardt's death, the long, anxious months of acting, the fear and grief and terror of the escape—had this ending always been written in the mind of God?

And we know that all things work together for good to them that love God, to them who are the called according to His purpose. Romans 8:28 She had grappled with that verse months ago while the summer blazed to autumn and left her heart buried in the ashes. As she learned to love the children and then prepared to tell them good-bye she had clung to the words, praying that they were true. The verse had mocked her even as she fled Villach with the knowledge that a man would die in her place.

But now, in the space of a single heartbeat, she found that she believed it. *All things work together ...* Looking back, she could see clearly the chain of miracles that had brought them together, to this day. From the account of Hirschel's healing in the Alps all the way up to Karl's readiness to give everything to free her ...

"Thank you." She whispered the simple prayer in awed gratitude. "Thank you."

The words were not enough after all that had happened! *Hirschel and*

Adina … they are my children now. Her home and friends and possessions were lost to her, but in that moment Eva did not lack anything.

She glanced back toward the window in time to see the sun burst over the mountains with blinding radiance. The glassy surface of the river glowed for a moment like a street of molten gold. Colors filled the sky with such intensity that the very air seemed to sing—and then the instant passed. Heaven receded and earth was simply earth again, but Eva was content.

Karl lay prostrate on the sticky floor, his body shattered by the Gestapo's fury. He had no idea how long he had held his costly silence—time had no meaning in this pitiless underworld. There was only the distant tolling of the bells in the darkness and shouting and agony and somewhere … light. He gasped against the crushing pain in his chest and groaned. He was so cold …

The faint rhythm of footsteps penetrated his haze. *He* was coming back.

"God … the beginning … Eva's life … help me!" He fought to form the words around chattering teeth. Did his broken prayer even reach beyond the blackness of this cell? "Help … me," he groaned again as the door slammed open.

Fredrik glared down at him with a combination of loathing and triumph. This was the end, and both men knew it.

"Where did you take Gottlieb's wife?" he demanded, certain of his victory.

Karl's ragged breathing was the only reply.

"Where?!" Fredrik shrieked, kicking his captive in the side with brutal force.

Karl could not stay the scream that rose in his throat. *Fear not … them … that kill …* His breath quickened as Fredrik struck again and again.

"Tell me!"

Was the demand softer? Karl gasped and tried to turn, tried to shield himself from the blows that seemed oddly distant. Then the bellowed questions dimmed, quieted by the echo of music too sweet for words.

Light—radiant, glorious light—swelled to fill the filthy cell with a golden brilliance, driving away the shadows before it.

"Come home." A Voice called clearly with such love and richness that all fear vanished.

And Karl obeyed.

About the Author

PASTOR'S KID LEAH MCMICHAEL has grown up overseas, living in the United States, South Africa, Zambia, France, and now Morocco. At the time of this writing she is seventeen and a high school senior at George Washington Academy in Casablanca. American by birth, she in most at home among the colors and organized chaos of Africa. In her spare time she makes jewelry, reads voraciously, boogey boards, hangs out with her parents, friends and cat, and goes to school. She plans to major in English at college.